Terry Pratchett

THE AMAZING MAURICE *AND HIS* EDUCATED RODENTS

HarperTrophy®
An Imprint of HarperCollins Publishers

Harper Trophy® is a registered trademark of HarperCollins Publishers Inc.

The Amazing Maurice and his Educated Rodents
Text copyright © 2001 by Terry and Lyn Pratchett
Illustrations copyright © 2001 by David Wyatt
Printed in the United States of America.
For information address HarperCollins Children's Books,
a division of HarperCollins Publishers,
1350 Avenue of the Americas, New York, NY 10019.

Library of Congress Cataloging-in-Publication Data
Pratchett, Terry.
    The amazing Maurice and his educated rodents / Terry Pratchett.
        p.   cm.
    Summary: A talking cat, intelligent rats, and a strange boy cooperate in a
Pied Piper scam until they try to con the wrong town and are confronted
by a deadly evil rat king.
    ISBN 0-06-001233-1 — ISBN 0-06-001234-X (lib. bdg.)
    ISBN 0-06-001235-8 (pbk.)
    [1. Rats—Fiction. 2. Cats—Fiction. 3. Musicians—Fiction.
4. Swindlers and swindling—Fiction. 5. Human-animal relationships—
Fiction. 6. Humorous stories.] I. Title.
PZ7.P8865 Am 2002   2001042411
[Fic]—dc21   CIP
                                                                    AC

Typography by Larissa Lawrynenko
❖
First Harper Trophy edition, 2003
Visit us on the World Wide Web!
www.harperteen.com

CHAPTER 1

❧

One day, when he was naughty, Mr. Bunnsy looked over the hedge into Farmer Fred's field and saw it was full of fresh green lettuces. Mr. Bunnsy, however, was not full of lettuces. This did not seem fair.

—From *Mr. Bunnsy Has an Adventure*

Rats!

They fought the dogs and killed the cats, and—

But there was more to it than that. As the Amazing Maurice said, it was just a story about people and rats. And the difficult part of it was deciding who the people were, and who were the rats.

But Malicia Grim said it was a story about stories.

It began—*part* of it began—on the mail coach that came over the mountains from the distant cities of the plain.

1

This was the part of the journey that the driver didn't like. The road wound through forests and around mountains on crumbling roads. There were deep shadows between the trees. Sometimes he thought things were following the coach, keeping just out of sight. It gave him the willies.

And on *this* journey the really big willy was that he could hear voices. He was sure of it. They were coming from behind him, from the top of the coach, and there was nothing there but the big oilcloth mail sacks and the boy's luggage. There was certainly nothing big enough for a person to hide inside. But occasionally he was sure he heard squeaky voices, whispering.

There was only one passenger at this point. He was a fair-haired young man, sitting all by himself inside the rocking coach and reading a book. He was reading slowly, and aloud, and moving his finger over the words.

"Ubberwald," he read out.

"That's 'Überwald,'" said a small, squeaky, but very clear voice. "The dots make it a sort of long 'ooo' sound. But you're doing well."

"Ooooooberwald?"

"There's such a thing as *too much* pronunciation, kid," said another voice, which sounded half asleep. "But you know the best thing about

Überwald? It's a long, long way from Sto Lat. It's a long way from Pseudopolis. It's a long way from *anywhere* where the head of the Watch says he'll have us boiled alive if he ever catches us. And it's not very modern. Bad roads. Lots of mountains in the way. People don't move about much up here. So news doesn't travel very fast, see? And they probably don't have policemen. Kid, we can make a *fortune* here!"

"Maurice?" said the boy carefully.

"Yes, kid?"

"You don't think what we're doing is, you know . . . *dishonest*, do you?"

There was a pause before the voice said, "How do you mean, dishonest?"

"Well . . . we take their money, Maurice." The coach bounced over a pothole.

"All right," said the unseen Maurice. "But what you've got to ask yourself is: *Who* do we take the money from, actually?"

"Well . . . it's generally the mayor or the city council or someone like that."

"Right! And that means it's . . . what? I've told you this bit before."

"Er . . ."

"It is *gov-ern-ment money*, kid," said Maurice patiently. "Say it. Gov-ern-ment money."

"Gov-ern-ment money," said the boy obediently.

"Right! And what do governments do with money?"

"Er, they . . ."

"They pay soldiers," said Maurice. "They have wars. In fact we've prob'ly stopped a lot of wars, by taking the money and putting it where it can't do any harm. They'd put up stachoos to us, if they thought about it."

"Some of those towns looked pretty poor, Maurice," said the kid doubtfully.

"Hey, just the kind of places that don't need wars, then."

"Dangerous Beans says it's . . ." The boy concentrated, and his lips moved before he said the word, as if he was trying out the pronunciation to himself. "It's un-eth-ickle."

"That's right, Maurice," said the squeaky voice. "Dangerous Beans says we shouldn't live by trickery."

"Listen, Peaches, *trickery* is what humans are all about," said the voice of Maurice. "They're so keen on tricking one another all the time that they elect governments to do it for them. *We* give them value for money. They get a horrible plague of rats, they pay a rat piper, the rats all follow the kid out of town, hoppity-skip, end of

4

plague, everyone's happy that no one's widdling in the flour anymore, the government gets reelected by a grateful population, general celebration all around. Money *well* spent, in my opinion."

"But there's only a plague because we make them think there is," said the voice of Peaches.

"Well, my dear, another thing all those little governments spend their money on is rat catchers, see? I don't know why I bother with the lot of you, I really don't."

"Yes, but we—"

They realized that the coach had stopped. Outside, in the rain, there was the jingle of harness. Then the coach rocked a little, and there was the sound of running feet.

A voice from out of the darkness said, "Are there any *wizards* in there?"

The occupants looked at one another in puzzlement.

"No?" said the kid, the kind of "No" that means "Why are you asking?"

"How about any *witches*?" said the voice.

"No, no witches," said the kid.

"Right. Are there any heavily armed *trolls* employed by the mail coach company in there?"

"I doubt it," said Maurice.

There was a moment's pause, filled with the sound of the rain.

"Okay, how about werewolves?" said the voice eventually. The speaker sounded as though he was working through a list.

"What do they look like?" said the kid.

"Ah, well, they look perfectly normal right up to the point where they grow all, like, hair and teeth and giant paws and leap through the window at you," said the voice.

"We've all got hair and teeth," said the kid. "Is that any help?"

"So you *are* werewolves, then?"

"No."

"Fine, fine." There was another pause filled with rain.

"Okay, vampires," said the voice. "It's a wet night—you wouldn't want to be flying in weather like this. Any vampires in there?"

"No!" said the kid. "We're all perfectly harmless!"

"Oh boy," muttered Maurice, and crawled under the seat.

"That's a relief," said the voice. "You can't be too careful these days. There's a lot of funny people about."

A crossbow arrow was pushed through the

window, and the voice said, "Your money *and* your life. It's a two-for-one deal, see?"

"The money's in the case on the roof," said Maurice's voice from floor level.

The highwayman looked around the dark interior of the coach.

"Who said that?" he said.

"Er, me," said the boy.

"I didn't see your lips move, kid!"

"The money *is* on the roof. In the case. But if I was you, I wouldn't—"

"Hah, I just 'spect you wouldn't," said the highwayman. His masked face disappeared from the window.

The boy picked up the pipe that was lying on the seat beside him. It was the type still known as a pennywhistle, although no one could remember when they'd ever cost only a penny.

"Play 'Robbery with Violence,' kid," said Maurice quietly.

"Couldn't we just give him the money?" said the voice of Peaches. It was a little voice.

"Money is for people to give *us*," said Maurice sternly.

Above them there was the scrape of the case on the roof of the coach as the highwayman dragged it down.

7

The boy obediently picked up the flute and played a few notes.

Now there were a number of sounds. There was a creak, a thud, a sort of scuffling noise, and then a very short scream.

When there was silence, Maurice climbed back onto the seat and poked his head out of the coach, into the dark and rainy night. "Good man," he said. "Sensible. The more you struggle, the harder they bite. Prob'ly not broken skin yet? Good. Come forward a bit so I can see you. But carefully, eh? We don't want anyone to panic, do we?"

The highwayman reappeared in the light of the coach lamps. He was walking very slowly and carefully, with his legs spread wide apart. And he was quietly whimpering.

"Ah, there you are," said Maurice cheerfully. "Went straight up your trouser legs, did they? Typical rat trick. Just nod, 'cos we don't want to set 'em off. No tellin' where it might end."

The highwayman nodded very slowly. Then his eyes narrowed.

"You're a *cat*?" he mumbled. Then his eyes crossed and he gasped.

"Did I say talk?" said Maurice. "I don't *think* I said talk, did I? Did the coachman run away, or did you kill him?"

The man's face went blank.

"Ah, quick learner. I *like* that in a highway-man," said Maurice. "You can answer that question."

"Ran away," said the highwayman hoarsely.

Maurice stuck his head back inside the coach.

"Whadja think?" he said. "Coach, four horses, probably some valuables in the mailbags. Could be, oh, a thousand dollars or more. The kid could drive it. Worth a try?"

"That's *stealing*, Maurice," said Peaches. She was sitting on the seat beside the kid. She was a rat.

"Not *stealin'* as such," said Maurice. "More . . . *findin'*. The driver's run away, so it's like . . . salvage. Hey, that's right, we could turn it in for the reward. That's *much* better. Legal, too. Shall we?"

"People would ask too many questions," said Peaches.

"If we just leave it, someone *yawlp* will steal it," wailed Maurice. "Some thief will take it away! Much better if we take it, eh? *We're* not thieves."

"We will *leave* it, Maurice," said Peaches.

"In that case, let's steal the highwayman's horse," said Maurice, as if the night wouldn't be properly finished unless they stole *something*. "Stealing from a thief isn't stealing, 'cos it cancels out."

"We can't stay here all night," said the kid to Peaches. "He's got a point."

"That's right!" said the highwayman urgently. "You can't stay here all night!"

"That's right," said a chorus of voices from his trousers, "we can't stay here all night!"

Maurice sighed and stuck his head out the window again.

"O-*kay*," he said. "This is what we're going to do. You're going to stand very still looking straight in front of you, and you won't try any tricks, because if you do, I've only got to say the word—"

"Don't say the word!" said the highwayman urgently.

"Right," said Maurice. "And we'll take your horse as a punishment, and you can have the coach, because that'd be stealing and only thieves are allowed to steal. Fair enough?"

"Anything you say!" said the highwayman, and then he thought about this and added hurriedly, "But please don't say *anything*!"

He kept staring straight ahead. He saw the boy and the cat get out of the coach. He heard various sounds behind him as they took his horse. And he thought about his sword. All right, he was going to get a whole mail coach out of this

10

deal, but there was such a thing as professional pride.

"All right," said the voice of the cat after a while. "We're all going to leave now, and you've got to promise not to move until we're gone. Promise?"

"You have my word as a thief," said the highwayman, slowly lowering a hand to his sword.

"Right. We certainly trust you," said the voice of the cat.

The man felt his trousers lighten as the rats poured out and scampered away, and he heard the jingle of harness. He waited a moment, then spun around, drew his sword, and ran forward.

Slightly forward, in any case. He wouldn't have hit the ground so hard if someone hadn't tied his bootlaces together.

◆ ◆ ◆

They said he was amazing. The Amazing Maurice, they said. He'd never meant to be amazing. It had just happened.

He'd realized something was odd that day, just after lunch, when he'd looked into a reflection in a puddle and thought, *that's me*. He'd never been *aware* of himself before. Of course, it was hard to remember *how* he'd thought before becoming amazing. It seemed to him that his mind had

11

been just a kind of soup.

And then there had been the rats, who lived under the rubbish heap in one corner of his territory. He'd realized there was something educated about the rats when he'd jumped on one and it'd said, "Can we talk about this?" and part of his amazing new brain had told him you couldn't eat someone who could talk. At least, not until you'd heard what it'd got to say.

The rat had been Peaches. She wasn't like other rats. Nor were Dangerous Beans, Donut Enter, Darktan, Hamnpork, Big Savings, Toxie, and all the rest of them. But then, Maurice wasn't like other cats anymore.

Other cats were, suddenly, *stupid*. Maurice started to hang around with the rats instead. They were someone to talk to. He got on fine so long as he remembered not to eat anyone they knew.

The rats spent a lot of time worrying about why *they* were suddenly so clever. Maurice considered that this was a waste of time. Stuff happened. But the rats went on and on about whether it was something on the rubbish heap that they'd eaten, and even Maurice could see that wouldn't explain how *he'd* got changed, because he'd never eaten rubbish. And he certainly wouldn't eat any rubbish off *that* heap, seeing where it came from. . . .

He considered that the rats were, quite frankly, dumb. Clever, okay, but *dumb*. Maurice had lived on the streets for four years and barely had any ears left and had scars all over his nose, and he was *smart*. He swaggered so much when he walked that if he didn't slow down, he flipped himself over. When he fluffed out his tail, people had to step around it. He reckoned you had to be smart to live for four years on these streets, especially with all the dog gangs and freelance furriers. One wrong move and you were lunch and a pair of gloves. Yes, you *had* to be smart.

You also had to be rich. This took some explaining to the rats, but Maurice had roamed the city and learned how things worked. And money, he said, was the key to everything.

And then one day he'd seen the stupid-looking kid playing the flute with his cap in front of him for pennies, and he'd had an idea. An amazing idea. It just turned up, bang, all at once. Rats, flute, stupid-looking kid . . .

And he'd said, "Hey, stupid-looking kid! How would you like to make your fortu— Nah, kid, I'm down here. . . ."

◆ ◆ ◆

Dawn was breaking when the highwayman's horse came out of the forests, climbed over a pass, and was reined to a halt in a convenient wood.

The river valley stretched out below, with a town hunched up against the cliffs.

Maurice clambered out of the saddlebag and stretched. The stupid-looking kid helped the rats out of the other bag. They'd spent the journey hunched up on the money, although they were too polite to say that this was because no one wanted to sleep in the same bag as a cat.

"What's the name of the town, kid?" Maurice asked, sitting on a rock and looking down at the town. Behind the cat and the boy, the rats were counting the money again, stacking it in piles beside its leather bag. They did this every day. Even though he had no pockets, there was something about Maurice that made everyone want to check their change as often as possible.

"'S called Bad Blintz," said the kid, referring to the guidebook.

"Ahem . . . should we be going there, if it's bad?" said Peaches, looking up from the counting.

"Hah, it's not called Bad because it's *bad*," said Maurice. "That's foreign language for *bath*, see?"

"So it's really called Bath Blintz?" said Donut Enter. "It sounds like some kind of soap."

"Nah, nah, they call it *Bath* because"—the Amazing Maurice hesitated, but only for a moment—"because they got a bath, see? Very backward place, this. Not many baths around. But they've got one, and they're very proud of it, so they want everyone to know. You prob'ly have to buy tickets even to have a look at it."

"Is that *true*, Maurice?" asked Dangerous Beans.

He asked the question quite politely, but it was clear that what he was really saying was "I don't think that is true, Maurice."

Ah, yes . . . Dangerous Beans. Dangerous Beans was difficult to deal with. Really, he shouldn't be. Back in the old days, Maurice thought, he wouldn't even have eaten a rat so small and pale and generally ill looking.

Maurice stared down at the little albino rat, with his snow-white fur and pinky eyes. Dangerous Beans did not stare back, because he was too shortsighted. Of course, being nearly blind was not too much of a drawback to a species that spent most of its time in the darkness and had a sense of smell that was, as far as Maurice could understand it, almost as good as sight and sound and speech all put together. For example, the rat always turned to face Maurice and looked directly at him when he spoke. It was uncanny. Maurice had known a blind cat that had walked into doors a lot, but Dangerous Beans never did that.

Dangerous Beans wasn't the head rat. That was Hamnpork's job. Hamnpork was big and fierce and a bit scabby, and he didn't much like having a newfangled brain and he *certainly* didn't like talking to a cat. He'd been quite old when the rats had Changed, as they called it, and he said he was too old to Change. He left talking to Maurice to Dangerous Beans, who'd been born just after the Change. And that little rat was clever. Incredibly clever. Too clever. Maurice needed all his tricks when he was dealing with Dangerous Beans.

"It's amazing, the stuff I know," said Maurice, blinking slowly at him. "Anyway, it's a nice-looking town. Looks rich to me. Now, what we'll do is—"

"Ahem . . ."

Maurice *hated* that sound. If there was a sound worse than Dangerous Beans asking one of his odd little questions, it was Peaches clearing her throat. It meant she was going to say something, very quietly, that was going to upset him.

"Yes?" he said sharply.

"Do we *really* need to keep on doing this?" she said.

"Well, of course, *no*," said Maurice. "I don't have to be here *at all*. I'm a *cat*, right? A cat with my talents? Hah! I could've got myself a really cushy job with a conjurer. Or a ventriloskwist, maybe. There's no *end* to the things I could be doing, right, 'cos people *like* cats. But owing to being incredibly, you know, *stupid* and *kind-hearted*, I decided to help a bunch of rod_nts who are, and let's be frank here, not exactly number-one favorites with humans. Now some of you"—and here he cast a yellow eye toward Dangerous Beans—"have some idea of going to some island somewhere and starting up a kind of rat civilization of your very own, which I think is very, you know, *admirable*, but for that you need . . . what did I tell you that you need?"

"Money, Maurice," said Dangerous Beans, "but—"

"Money. That's right, 'cos what can you get with money?" He looked around at the rats. "Begins with a B," he prompted.

"Boats, Maurice, but—"

"And then there's all the tools you'll need, and food, of course—"

"There's coconuts," said the stupid-looking kid, who was polishing his flute.

"Oh, did someone speak?" said Maurice. "What do you know about it, kid?"

"You get coconuts," said the kid. "On desert islands. A man selling them told me."

"How?" said Maurice. He wasn't too sure about coconuts.

"I don't know. You just get them."

"Oh, I suppose they just grow on trees, do they?" said Maurice sarcastically. "Sheesh, I just don't know what you lot would do without . . . anyone?" He glared at the group. "Begins with an M."

"You, Maurice," said Dangerous Beans. "But, you see, what we think is, really—"

"Yes?" said Maurice.

"Ahem," said Peaches. Maurice groaned.

"What Dangerous Beans means," said the female rat, "is that all this stealing grains and cheese and gnawing holes in walls is, well"—she looked up into Maurice's yellow eyes—"is *not morally right*."

"But it's what rats do!" said Maurice.

"But we feel we shouldn't," said Dangerous Beans. "We should be making our own way in the world!"

"Oh dear oh dear oh dear," said Maurice, shaking his head. "Ho for the island, eh? The Kingdom of the Rats! Not that I'm laughing at your dream," he added hastily. "Everyone needs their little dreams." Maurice truly believed that, too. If you knew what it was that people really, *really* wanted, you very nearly controlled them.

Sometimes he wondered what the stupid-looking kid really, really wanted. Nothing, as far as Maurice could tell, but to be allowed to play his music and be left alone. But . . . well, it was like that thing with the coconuts. Every so often the kid would come out with something that suggested he'd been listening all along. People like that are hard to steer.

But cats are *good* at steering people. A miaow here, a purr there, a little gentle pressure with a claw . . . and Maurice had never had to *think* about it before. Cats didn't have to think. They just had to know what they wanted. Humans had to do the thinking. That's what they were for.

Maurice thought about the good old days before his brain had started whizzing like a fire-work. He'd turn up at the door of the university kitchens and look sweet, and then the cooks would *try to work out* what he wanted. It was amazing! They'd say things like "Does oo want a bowl of milk, den? Does oo want a biscuit? Does oo want dese nice scraps, den?" And all Maurice would have to do was wait patiently until they got to a sound he recognized, like "turkey legs" or "minced lamb."

But he was sure he'd never eaten anything magical. There was no such thing as enchanted chicken giblets, was there?

It was the rats who'd eaten the magical stuff. The dump they called "home" and also called "lunch" was round the back of the university, and it was a university for wizards, after all. The old Maurice hadn't paid much attention to people who weren't holding bowls, but he was aware that the big men in pointy hats made strange things happen.

And now he knew what happened to the stuff they used, too. It got tossed over the wall when they'd finished with it. All the old worn-out spell books and the stubs of dribbly candles and the remains of the green bubbly stuff in the cauldrons all ended up on the big dump, along with the tin cans and old boxes and the kitchen waste. Oh, the wizards had put up signs saying DANGEROUS and TOXIC, but the rats hadn't been able to read in those days, and they *liked* dribbly candle ends.

Maurice had *never* eaten anything off the dump. A good motto in life, he'd reckoned, was: Don't eat anything that glows.

But he'd become intelligent, too, at about the same time as the rats. It was a mystery.

Since then he'd done what cats always did. He steered people. Now some of the rats counted as people too, of course. But people were people, even if they had four legs and had called themselves names like Dangerous Beans, which is the kind of name you gave yourself if you learned to read before you understood what all the words actually meant, and reading the warning notices and the labels on the old rusty cans gave you names you liked the sound of.

The trouble with thinking was that, once you started, you went on doing it. And as far as Maurice was concerned, the rats were thinking a good deal too much. It was Peaches who was the worst. Maurice's usual trick of just talking fast until people got confused didn't work on her at all.

"Ahem," she began. "We think that this should be the last time."

Maurice stared. The other rats backed away slightly, but Peaches just stared back.

"This must be the very last time we do the

silly 'plague of rats' trick," said Peaches. "And that's final."

"And what does Hamnpork think about this?" said Maurice. He turned to the head rat, who had been watching them. It was always a good idea appealing to Hamnpork when Peaches was giving trouble, because he didn't like her very much.

"What d'you mean, think?" said Hamnpork.

"I . . . sir,* I think we should stop doing this trick," said Peaches, dipping her head nervously.

"Oh, *you* think too, do you?" said Hamnpork. "Everyone's thinking these days. I think there's a good deal too much of this thinking, that's what *I* think. We never thought about thinking when I was a lad. We'd never get anything done if we thought first."

He gave Maurice a glare too. Hamnpork didn't like Maurice. He didn't like most things that had happened since the Change. In fact, Maurice wondered how long Hamnpork was going to last as leader. He didn't like thinking. He belonged to the days when a rat leader just

---

*It's hard to translate "sir" into Rat. The rat word for "sir" isn't a word, it's a sort of momentary crouch, indicating that, just at the moment, the crouching rat is prepared to accept that the other rat is the boss, but that he or she shouldn't get funny about it.

had to be big and mean. The world was moving far too fast for him now, which made him angry.

He wasn't so much leading now as being pushed.

"I . . . Dangerous Beans, sir, believes that we should be thinking of settling down, sir," said Peaches.

Maurice scowled. Hamnpork wouldn't listen to Peaches, and she knew it, but Dangerous Beans was the nearest thing the rats had to a wizard, and even big rats listened to him.

"I thought we were going to get on a boat and find an island somewhere," said Hamnpork. "Very ratty places, boats," he added approvingly. Then he went on, with a slightly nervous and slightly annoyed look at Dangerous Beans: "And people tell me that we need this money stuff because, now that we can do all this *thinking*, we've got to be eff . . . efit . . ."

"Ethical, sir," said Dangerous Beans.

"Which sounds unratty to me. Not that my opinion counts for anything, it seems," said Hamnpork.

"We've got enough money, sir," said Peaches. "We've already got a *lot* of money. We *have* got a lot of money, haven't we, Maurice." It wasn't a question; it was a kind of accusation.

"Well, when you say a *lot*—" Maurice began.

"And in fact we've got more money than we thought," said Peaches, still in the same tone of voice. It was very polite, but it just kept going and it asked all the wrong questions. A wrong question for Maurice was one that he didn't want anyone to ask.

Peaches gave her little cough again. "The reason I say we've got more money, Maurice, is that you said what were called 'gold coins' were shiny like the moon and 'silver coins' were shiny like the sun, and you'd keep all the silver coins. In fact, Maurice, that's the wrong way around. It's the silver coins that are shiny like the moon."

Maurice thought a rude word in cat language, which has a great many of them. What was the point of education, he thought, if people went out afterward and used it?

"So we think, sir," said Dangerous Beans to Hamnpork, "that after this one last time, we should share out the money and go our separate ways. Besides, it's getting dangerous to keep repeating the same trick. We should stop before it's too late. There's a river here. We should be able to get to the sea."

"An island with no humans or *krllrrt* cats would be a good place," said Hamnpork.

Maurice didn't let his smile fade, even though he knew what *krllrrt* meant.

"And we wouldn't want to keep Maurice from his wonderful new job with the conjurer," said Peaches. Maurice's eyes narrowed. For a moment he came close to breaking his iron rule of not eating anyone who could talk.

"What about you, kid?" he said, looking up at the stupid-looking kid.

"I don't mind," said the kid.

"Don't mind what?" said Maurice.

"Don't mind anything, really," said the kid. "Just so long as no one stops me playing."

"But you've got to think of the future!" said Maurice.

"I am," said the kid. "I want to go on playing my flute in the future. It doesn't cost anything to play. But maybe the rats are right. We've had a couple of narrow squeaks, Maurice."

Maurice gave the kid a sharp look to see if he was making a joke, but the kid had never done that kind of thing before.

He gave up. Well, not *exactly* gave up. Maurice hadn't got where he was by giving up on problems. He just put them to one side. After all, something always turned up.

"Okay, fine," he said. "We'll do it one more

25

time and split the money three ways. Fine. *Not* a problem. But if this is going to be the last time, let's make it one to remember, eh?"

He grinned. The rats, being rats, were not keen on seeing a grinning cat, but they understood that a difficult decision had been made. They breathed tiny sighs of relief.

"Are *you* happy with that, kid?" said Maurice.

"I can go on playing my flute afterward?" said the kid.

"Absolutely."

"Okay," said the kid.

The money, shiny like the sun and shiny like the moon, was solemnly put back in its bag. The rats dragged the bag under the bushes and buried it. No one could bury money like rats, and it didn't pay to take too much into towns.

Then there was the horse. It was a valuable horse, and Maurice was very, very sorry to turn it loose. But as Peaches pointed out, it was a highwayman's horse, with a very ornate saddle and bridle. Trying to sell it here could be dangerous. People would talk. It might attract the attention of the government. This was no time to have the Watch on their tails.

Maurice walked to the edge of the rock and

looked down at the town, which was waking up under the sunrise.

"Let's make this the *big* one, then, eh?" he said, as the rats came back. "I want to see maximum squeaking and making faces at people and widdling on stuff, okay?"

"We think that widdling on stuff is not really—" Dangerous Beans began, but "Ahem" said Peaches, and so Dangerous Beans went on: "Oh, I suppose, if it's the last time . . ."

"I've widdled on everything since I was out of the nest," said Hamnpork. "*Now* they tell me it's not right. If that's what *thinking* means, I'm glad I don't do any."

"Let's leave 'em *amazed*," said Maurice. "Rats? They think they've seen rats in that town? After they've seen *us*, they'll be making up *stories*!"

CHAPTER 2

❦

Mr. Bunnsy had a lot of friends in Furry Bottom. But what Mr. Bunnsy was friendly with more than anything else was food.

—From *Mr. Bunnsy Has an Adventure*

This was the plan:

And it was a good plan. Even the rats, even Peaches, had to admit that it had worked.

Everyone knew about plagues of rats. There were famous stories about the rat pipers, who made their living going from town to town getting rid of plagues of rats. Of course there weren't just rat plagues—sometimes there were plagues of accordion players, bricks tied up with string, or fish—but it was the rats everyone knew about.

And that, really, was it. You didn't need *many* rats for a plague, if they knew their business. One rat, popping up here and there, squeaking loudly, taking a bath in the fresh cream and widdling in the flour, could be a plague all by himself.

After a few days of this, it was amazing how glad people were to see the stupid-looking kid with his magical rat pipe. And they were amazed when rats poured out of every hole to follow him out of town. They were so amazed that they didn't bother much about the fact that there were only a few hundred or so rats.

They'd have been *really* amazed if they'd ever found out that the rats and the piper met up with a cat somewhere in the bushes outside of town, and solemnly counted out the money.

◆ ◆ ◆

Bad Blintz was waking up when Maurice entered with the kid. No one bothered them, although Maurice got a lot of interest. This did not worry him. He knew he was interesting. Cats walked as if they owned the place anyway, and the world was full of stupid-looking kids, and people weren't rushing to see another one.

It looked as though today was a market day, but there weren't many stalls and they were mostly selling, well, junk. Old pans, pots, used shoes . . . the kinds of things people have to sell when they're short of money.

Maurice had seen plenty of markets on their

journey through other towns, and he knew how they should go.

"There should be fat women selling chickens," he said. "And people selling sweets for the kids, and ribbons. Acrobats and clowns. Even weasel jugglers, if you're lucky."

"There's nothing like that. There's hardly anything to buy, by the look of it," said the kid. "I thought you said this was a *rich* town, Maurice."

"Well, it *looked* rich," said Maurice. "All those big fields in the valley, all those boats on the river . . . you'd think the streets'd be paved with gold!"

The kid looked up. "Funny thing," he said.

"What?"

"The people look poor," he said. "It's the buildings that look rich."

And they did. Maurice wasn't an expert on architecture, but the wooden buildings had been carefully carved and painted. He noticed something else, too. There was nothing careful about the sign that had been nailed up on the nearest wall.

It said:

**RATS WANTED DEAD! 50 cents per tail!
Apply to: The Rat Catchers c/o The Rathaus**

The kid was staring at it.

"They must *really* want to get rid of their rats here," said Maurice cheerfully.

"No one has ever offered a reward of half a dollar a tail!" said the kid.

"I *told* you this would be the big one," said Maurice. "We'll be sitting on a pile of gold before the week's out!"

"What's a rat house?" asked the kid doubtfully. "It can't be a house for rats, can it? And why is everyone staring at you?"

"I'm a handsome-looking cat," said Maurice. Even so, it was a little surprising. People were nudging one another and pointing at him.

"You'd think they'd never seen a cat before," he muttered, staring at the big building across the street. It was a big, square building, sur-rounded by people, and the sign said: RATHAUS.

"Oh, Rathaus's just the local word for . . . like the town hall," he said. "It's nothing to do with rats, amusing though it may be."

"You really know a lot of words, Maurice," said the kid admiringly.

"I amaze myself sometimes," said Maurice.

A line of people was standing in front of one huge open door. Other people, who had pre-sumably done whatever it was the line was lining up to do, were emerging from another doorway in ones and twos. They were all carrying loaves of bread.

"Shall we line up too?" asked the kid.

"I shouldn't think so," said Maurice carefully.

"Why not?"

"See those men on the door? They look like the Watch. They've got big truncheons. And everyone's showing them a bit of paper as they go past. I don't like the look of that," said Maurice. "That looks like *government* to me."

"We haven't done anything wrong," said the kid. "Not here, anyway."

"You never know, with governments," said Maurice. "Just stay here, kid. I'll take a look."

People stared at Maurice when he stalked into the building, but it seemed that in a town beset by rats, a cat was quite popular and no one was inclined to turn him out. A man did try to pick him up, but lost interest when Maurice turned and clawed the back of his hand.

The line wound into a big hall and passed in front of a long trestle table. There, each person showed the piece of paper to two women in front of a big tray of bread, and was given some bread. Then they moved on to a man with a vat of sausages, and got considerably less sausage.

Watching over all this, and occasionally saying something to the food servers, was the mayor. Maurice recognized him instantly because he had a gold chain around his neck. He'd run across a lot of mayors since working with the rats. This one was different from the rest. He was smaller, looked far more worried, and had a bald spot that he'd tried to cover with three strands of hair. He was a lot thinner than other mayors Maurice had seen, too.

So . . . food is scarce, Maurice thought. They're having to ration it out. Looks like they'll be needing a piper any day now. Lucky for us we arrived just in time. . . .

He walked out again, but this time a bit faster because he realized that someone was playing a pipe.

It was, as he'd feared, the kid. He did it if you left him alone for any length of time. He'd put his cap on the ground in front of him, and had even accumulated a few coins. The line had bent round so that people could hear him, and one or two small children were dancing.

Maurice was only an expert on cat singing, which consists of standing two inches in front of another cat and screaming at him until he gives in. Human music always sounded thin and watery to him. But people tapped their feet when they heard the kid play. They smiled for a while.

Maurice waited until the kid had finished the tune. While the line was clapping, he sidled up behind the kid, brushed up against him, and hissed, "Well done, fish-for-brains! We're supposed to be *inconspicuous*! Come on, let's go. Oh, grab the money, too."

He led the way across the square until he stopped so suddenly that the kid almost walked into him.

"Whoops, here comes some more government," he said. "And we know what these are, don't we."

The kid did. They were rat catchers, two of them. Even here they wore the long dusty coats and battered black top hats of their profession. They each carried a pole over one shoulder, from which dangled a variety of traps.

From the other shoulder hung a big bag, the kind you really wouldn't want to look inside. And each man had a terrier on a string. They were skinny, argumentative dogs, and they growled at Maurice when they were dragged past.

The line cheered as the men approached, and clapped when they both reached into their bags and held up a couple of handfuls of what looked, to Maurice, like black string.

"Two hundred today!" shouted one of the rat catchers.

One of the terriers lunged at Maurice, tugging frantically on its string. The cat didn't move. Probably only the stupid-looking kid heard him say, in a low voice, "Heel, fleabag! Bad dog!"

The terrier's face screwed up in the horribly worried expression of a dog trying to have two thoughts at the same time. It knew cats shouldn't talk, and this cat had just talked. This posed a terrible problem. The dog sat down awkwardly and whined.

Maurice washed himself. It was a deadly insult.

The rat catcher, annoyed at such a cowardly performance from his dog, jerked it away.

And dropped a few of the black strings.

"Rat tails!" said the kid. "They really *must* have a problem here!"

"A bigger one than you think," said Maurice, staring at the bunch of tails. "Just pick those up when no one's looking, will you?"

The kid waited until people weren't looking toward them, and reached down. Just as his fingers touched the tangle of tails, a large, shiny black boot trod heavily on it.

"Now, you don't want to go touching them, young sir," said a voice above him. "You can get plague, you know, from rats. It makes your legs explode."

It was one of the rat catchers. He gave the kid a big grin, but it was not a humorous one. It smelled of beer.

"That's right, young sir, and then your brains come down your nose," said the other rat catcher, coming up behind the kid. "You wouldn't dare use your hanky, young sir, if you got the plague."

"My associate has as usual put his finger right on it, young sir," said the first rat catcher, breathing more beer into the kid's face.

"Which is more than you'd be able to do, young sir," said Rat Catcher 2, "because when you get the plague your fingers go all—"

"*Your* legs haven't exploded," said the kid. Maurice groaned. It was never a good idea to be rude to a smell of beer. But the rat catchers were at the stage when, against all the odds, they thought they were funny.

"Ah, well said, young sir, but that's because lesson one at the Guild of Rat Catchers' school is not letting your legs explode," said Rat Catcher 1.

"Which is a good thing 'cos the second lesson is upstairs," said Rat Catcher 2. "Oh, I am a one, aren't I, young sir?"

The other rat catcher picked up the bundle of black strings, and his smile faded as he stared at the kid. "Ain't seen you before, kid," he said. "And my advice to you is keep your nose clean and don't say nothing to nobody about nothing. Not a word. Understand?"

The kid opened his mouth and then shut it hurriedly. The rat catcher grinned his awful grin again.

"Ah. You catch on quick, young sir," he said. "Perhaps we'll see you around, eh?"

"I bet you'd like to be a rat catcher when you grow up, eh, young sir?" said Rat Catcher 2, patting the kid too heavily on the back.

The kid nodded. It seemed the best thing to do. Rat Catcher 1 leaned down until his red, pockmarked nose was an inch away from the kid's face.

"*If* you grow up, young sir," he said.

The rat catchers walked away, dragging their dogs with them. One of the terriers kept looking back at Maurice.

"Very unusual rat catchers they have hereabouts," said the cat.

"I haven't seen rat catchers like them before," said the kid. "They looked *nasty*. Like they enjoyed it."

"I haven't seen rat catchers who've been so busy but still have nice clean boots," said Maurice.

"Yes, they *did*, didn't they . . ." said the kid.

"But even that's not as odd as the rats round here," said Maurice in the same quiet voice, as though he was adding up money.

"What's odd about the rats?" said the kid.

"Some of them have very strange tails," said Maurice.

The kid looked around the square. The line for bread was still quite long, and it made him nervous. But so did the steam. Little bursts of it puffed up from gratings and manhole covers all over the place, as if the whole town had been built on a kettle. Also, he had the distinct feeling that someone was watching him.

"I think we ought to find the rats and move on," he said.

"No, this smells like a town with *opportunities*," said Maurice. "Something's going on, and when something's going on, that means someone's getting rich, and when someone's getting rich, I don't see why that shouldn't be m— us."

"Yes, but we don't want those people killing Dangerous Beans and the rest of them!"

"They won't get caught," said Maurice. "Those men wouldn't win any prizes for thinking. Even Hamnpork could run rings round 'em, I'd say. And Dangerous Beans has got brains coming out of his ears."

"I hope not!"

"Nah, nah," said Maurice, who generally told people what they wanted to hear, "I mean our rats can outthink most humans, okay? Remember back in Scrote when Sardines got in that kettle and blew a raspberry at the old woman when she lifted the lid? Hah, even *ordinary* rats can outthink humans. Humans think that just because they're bigger, they're better— Hold on, I'll shut up—someone's watching us. . . ."

A man carrying a basket had stopped on his way out of the Rathaus and was staring at Maurice with a good deal of interest. Then he looked at the kid and said, "Good ratter, is he? I'll bet he is, a big cat like that. Is he yours, boy?"

"Say yes," Maurice whispered.

"Sort of, yes," said the kid. He picked Maurice up.

"I'll give you five dollars for him," said the man.

"Ask for ten," Maurice hissed.

"He's not for sale," said the kid.

"Idiot!" Maurice purred.

"Seven dollars, then," said the man. "Look, I'll tell you what I'll do: four whole loaves of bread, how about that?"

"That's silly. A loaf of bread shouldn't cost more'n twenty cents," said the kid.

The man gave him a strange look.

"New here, are you? Got plenty of money, have you?"

"Enough," said the kid.

"You think so? It won't do you much good, anyway. Look, four loaves of bread and a bun— I can't say fairer than that. I can get a terrier for ten loaves, and they're mad for rats. . . . No? Well, when you're hungry, you'll give it away for half a slice of bread and scrape* and think you've done well, believe me."

He strode off. Maurice wriggled out of the kid's arms and landed lightly on the cobbles.

"Honestly, if only I was good at ventrilo-skwism, we could make a fortune," he grumbled.

"Ventriloskwism?" said the kid, watching the man's retreating back.

"It's where you open and shut your mouth and I do the talking," said Maurice. "Why didn't

*You scrape the butter on. Then you scrape the butter off. Then you eat the bread.

you sell me? I could've been back in ten minutes! I heard of a man who made a fortune selling homing pigeons, and he only had the one!"

"Don't you think there's something wrong with a town where people'd pay more than a dollar for a loaf of bread?" said the kid. "And pay half a dollar for a rat tail?"

"Just so long as they've got enough money left to pay the piper," said Maurice. "Bit of luck there *already* being a plague of rats here, eh? Quick, pat me on the head, there's a girl watching us."

The kid looked up. There *was* a girl watching them. People were passing up and down the street, and some of them walked between the kid and the girl, but she stood stock-still and just stared at him. And at Maurice. She had the same nail-you-to-the-wall expression that he associated with Peaches. She looked like the kind of person who asked *questions*. And her hair was too red and her nose was too long. And she wore a long black dress with black lace fringing. No good comes of that sort of thing.

She marched across the street and confronted the kid.

"You're new, aren't you? Come here looking for work, have you? Probably sacked from your last job, I expect. Probably because you fell asleep, and things got spoiled. That was probably what it was. Or you ran away because he beat you with a big stick, although," she added, as another idea struck her, "you probably deserved it because of being lazy. And then you probably stole the cat, knowing how much people would pay for a cat here. And you must have gone mad with hunger, because you were talking to the cat and everyone knows that cats can't talk."

"Can't say a single word," said Maurice.

"And probably you're a mysterious boy who—" The girl stopped and gave Maurice a puzzled look. He arched his back and said *"Prppt,"* which is Cat language for "Biscuits!"

"Did that cat just say something?" she demanded.

"I thought that everyone knew that cats can't talk," said the kid.

"Ah, but maybe you were apprentice to a wizard," said the girl. "Yes, that sounds about right. That'll do for now. You were an apprentice to a wizard, but you fell asleep and let the cauldron of bubbling green stuff boil over, and he threatened to turn you into a, a, a—"

"Gerbil," said Maurice helpfully.

"—a gerbil, and you stole his magical cat because you hated it so much and—what's a gerbil? Did that *cat* just say 'gerbil'?"

"Don't look at me!" said the kid. "I'm just standing here!"

"All right, and then you brought the cat here because you know there's a terrible famine and that's why you were going to sell it and that man would have given you ten dollars, you know, if you'd held out for it."

"Ten dollars is too much money even for a good ratter," said the kid.

"Ratter? He wasn't interested in catching rats!" said the red-haired girl. "Everyone's hungry here! There's at least two meals on that cat!"

"What? You *eat* cats here?" said Maurice, his tail fluffing like a brush.

The girl leaned down to Maurice with a dreadful grin, just like the one that Peaches always wore when she'd won an argument with him, and prodded him on the nose with a finger.

"*Got* you!" she said. "You fell for a very simple trick! I think you two had better come with me, don't you? Or I'll scream. And people *listen* to me when *I'm* screaming!"

CHAPTER 3

❧

"Never go into the Dark Wood, my friend," said Ratty
Rupert. "There are bad things in there."
—From *Mr. Bunnsy Has an Adventure*

Far below Maurice's paws the rats were creeping
through the undertown of Bad Blintz. Old
towns are like that. People build down as well as
up. Cellars butt against other cellars, and some of
the cellars get forgotten—except by creatures
that want to stay out of sight.

In the thick, warm, damp darkness a voice
said, "All right, who's got the matches?"

"Me, Dangerous Beans. Feedsfour."

"Well done, young rat. And who has the
candle?"

"Me, sir. I'm Bitesize."

"Good. Put it down and Peaches will light it."

There was a lot of scuffling in the darkness.
Not all the rats had got used to the idea of

making fire, and they were getting out of the way.

There was a scratching noise, and then the match flared. Holding the match with both front paws, Peaches lit the candle stub. The flame swelled for a moment and settled down to a steady glow.

"Can you really see it?" asked Hamnpork.

"Yes, sir," said Dangerous Beans. "I am not completely blind. I can tell the difference between light and dark."

"Y'know," said Hamnpork, watching the flame suspiciously, "I don't like it at all, even so. Darkness was good enough for our parents. It'll end in trouble. Besides, setting fire to a candle is a waste of perfectly good food."

"We have to be able to control the fire, sir," said Dangerous Beans calmly. "With the flame we make a statement to the darkness. We say: We are separate. We say: We are not just rats. We say: We are The Clan."

"Hrumph," said Hamnpork, which was his usual response when he didn't understand what had just been said. Just lately he'd been hrumph-ing a lot.

"I've heard the younger rats are saying that the shadows frighten them," said Peaches.

"Why?" said Hamnpork. "They're not frightened

of complete darkness, are they? Darkness is ratty! Being in the dark is what a rat is all about!"

"It's odd," said Peaches, "but we didn't know the shadows were there until we had the light."

One of the younger rats timorously raised a paw.

"Um . . . and even when the light has gone out, we know the shadows are still around," she said.

Dangerous Beans turned toward the young rat.

"You're—?" he said.

"Delicious," said the younger rat.

"Well, Delicious," said Dangerous Beans in a kindly voice, "being afraid of shadows is all part of us becoming more intelligent, I think. Your mind is working out that there's a *you*, and there's also everything *outside you*. So now you're not just frightened of things that you can see and hear and smell, but also of things that you can. . . sort of . . . *see* inside your head. Learning to face the shadows outside helps us to fight the shadows inside. And you can control *all* the darkness. It's a big step forward. Well done."

Delicious looked slightly proud, but mostly nervous.

"I don't see the point, myself," said Hamnpork.

"We used to do all right on the dump. And I was never scared of anything."

"We were prey to every stray cat and hungry dog, sir," said Dangerous Beans.

"Oh, well, if we're going to talk about *cats*," growled Hamnpork.

"I think we can trust Maurice, sir," said Dangerous Beans. "Perhaps not when it comes to money, I admit. But he is very good at not eating people who talk, you know. He checks, every time."

"You can trust a cat to be a cat," said Hamnpork. "Talking or not!"

"Yes, sir. But we are different, and so is he. I believe he is a decent cat at heart."

"Ahem. That remains to be seen," said Peaches. "But now that we are here, let's get organized."

Hamnpork growled.

"Who are you to say, 'Let's get organized'?" he asked sharply. "Are you the leader, young female who refuses to *rllk* with me? No! *I* am the leader. It's *my* job to say, 'Let's get organized'!"

"Yes, sir," said Peaches, crouching low. "How would you like us to be organized, sir?"

Hamnpork stared at her. He looked at the waiting rats, with their packs and bundles, and then around at the ancient cellar, and then back to the still-crouching Peaches.

"Just . . . get organized," he muttered. "Don't bother me with details! *I* am the leader."

And he stalked off into the shadows.

When he'd gone, Peaches and Dangerous Beans looked around the cellar, which was filled with trembling shadows created by the candle-light. A trickle of water ran down one crusted wall. Here and there stones had fallen out, leaving inviting holes. Earth covered the floor, and there were no human footprints in it.

"An ideal base," said Dangerous Beans. "It smells secret and safe. A perfect place for rats."

"Right," said a voice. "And you know what's worrying me about that?"

The rat called Darktan stepped into the candle-light and hitched up one of his belts of tools. A lot of the watching rats suddenly paid attention. People listened to Hamnpork because he was the leader, but they listened to Darktan because he was often telling you things that you really, really needed to know if you wanted to go on living. He was big, and lean, and tough, and spent most of his time taking traps apart to see how they worked.

"What is worrying you, Darktan?" asked Dangerous Beans.

"There *aren't* any rats here. Except us. Rat tunnels, yes. But we've seen no rats. No rats at all. A town like this should be full of them."

"Oh, they're probably scared of us," said Peaches.

Darktan tapped the side of his scarred muzzle. "Maybe," he said. "But things don't smell right. Thinking is a great invention, but we were given noses, and it pays to listen to them. Be extra careful." He turned to the assembled rats and raised his voice.

"Okay, troops! You know the drill!" he shouted. "Plague rats, in front of me, in your platoons, *now!*"

It didn't take long for the rats to form three groups. They'd had plenty of practice.

"Very nice," said Darktan, as the last few shuffled into position. "Right! This is tricky territory, people, so we're going to be careful. . . ."

Darktan was unusual among the rats because he wore things.

When the rats had discovered books—and the whole idea of books was still a difficult one for most of the older rats—they found, in the bookshop they invaded every night, the Book. Up until they were Changed, books had only been useful for eating the glue off the bindings and making nests out of the pages.

They'd never *looked* at one before.

This book was amazing.

Even before Peaches and Donut Enter had learned how to read human words, they'd been amazed by the pictures.

There were animals in there *wearing clothes*. There was a rabbit who walked on its hind legs and wore a blue suit. There was a rat in a hat, and he wore a sword and a big red vest, complete with a watch on a chain. Even the snake had a collar and tie. And all of them talked, and none of them ate any of the others, and—and this was the unbelievable part—*they all talked to humans*, who treated them like, well, smaller humans. There were no traps, no poisons. Admittedly (according to Peaches, who was painstakingly working her way through the book, and sometimes read out parts) Olly the snake was a bit of a rascal, but nothing truly *bad* happened. Even when the rabbit got lost in the Dark Wood, he just had a bit of a scare.

Yes, *Mr. Bunnsy Has an Adventure* was the cause of much discussion amongst the Changelings. What was it for? Was it, as Dangerous Beans believed, a vision of some bright future? Had it been made by humans? The shop had been for humans, true, but surely even humans wouldn't make a book about Ratty Rupert the Rat, who wore a hat, *and* poison rats under the floorboards at the same time. Would they? How mad would anything have to be to think like that?

Some of the younger rats had suggested that perhaps clothes were more important than everyone thought. They'd tried wearing vests, but it had been very difficult to bite out the pattern, they couldn't make the buttons work, and frankly, the things got caught on every splinter and were very hard to run in. Hats just fell off.

Darktan just thought that humans *were* mad, as well as bad. But the pictures in the Book had given him an idea.

What he wore was not so much a vest as a network of wide belts, easy to wriggle into and out of. On them he'd sewn pockets—and that *had* been a good idea, like giving yourself extra hands—to hold all the things he needed, like metal rods and bits of wire. Some of the rest of the squad had taken up the idea, too. You never knew what you were going to need next, on the Trap Disposal Squad. It was a tough, ratty life.

The rods and wires jangled as Darktan walked up and down in front of his teams. He stopped in front of one large group of younger rats.

"All right, Number Three platoon, you're on widdling duty," he said. "Go and have a good drink."

"Oooh, we're *always* on widdling," a rat complained. Darktan pounced on him and faced him nose to nose, until he backed away.

"That's 'cos you're *good* at it, my lad! Your mother *raised* you to be a widdler, so off you go and do what comes naturally! Nothing puts humans off like seeing that rats have been there before, if you catch my meaning! And if you get the opportunity, do some gnawing as well. And run around under the floorboards and squeak! And remember, no one is to move in until they get the all-clear from the Trap Squad. To the water, now, on the double! Hup! Hup! Hup! One two, one two, one two!"

The platoon headed off, at speed.

Darktan turned to Number Two platoon. They were some of the older rats, scarred and bitten and ragged, some of them with stubs of tails or no tails at all, some of them missing a paw or an ear or an eye. In fact, although there were about twenty of them, they had among them only enough bits to make up about seventeen complete rats.

But because they were old, they were cunning,

since a rat who isn't cunning and shifty and suspicious doesn't *become* an old rat. They'd all been
grown-up when the Change came. They were
more set in their old ways. Hamnpork always
said he liked them that way. They still had a lot
of basic rattiness, the kind of raw cunning that
would get you out of the traps that overexcited
intelligence got you into. They thought with
their noses. And you didn't have to tell them
where to widdle.

"All right, people, you know the drill," said
Darktan. "I want to see lots of cheeky stuff.
Stealing the food out of cats' bowls, pies from
under the cooks' noses—"

"—false teeth from out of old men's
mouths—" said a small rat, who seemed to be
dancing on the spot while he stood there. His
feet moved all the time, tippity-tapping on the
cellar floor. He wore a hat, too, a battered, home-
made thing out of straw. He was the only rat
who could make a hat work, by wedging his ears
through it. He said to get ahead, you had to get
a hat.

"That was a fluke, Sardines. I bet you can't do
it again," said Darktan. "And don't keep on
telling the kids how you went for a swim in
someone's bathtub. Yeah, I know you did, but I

don't want to lose anyone who can't scramble out of a slippery tub. Anyway . . . if I don't hear ladies screaming and running out of their kitchens within ten minutes, I'll know you're not the rats I think you are. Well? Why are you all standing around? Get on with it! And . . . Sardines?"

"Yes, boss?"

"Easy on the tap dancing this time, all right?"

"I just got these dancing feets, boss!"

"And do you have to keep wearing that stupid hat?" asked Darktan, grinning.

"Yes, boss!" Sardines was one of the older rats, but most of the time you wouldn't know it. He danced and joked and never got into fights. He'd lived in a theater and once eaten a whole box of greasepaint. It seemed to have gotten into his blood.

"And no going on ahead of the Trap Squad!" said Darktan.

Sardines grinned in turn. "Aw, boss, can't I have *any* fun?"

He danced after the rest of them, toward the holes in the walls.

Darktan moved on, to Number One platoon. It was the smallest. You had to be a certain kind of rat to last a long time in the Trap Disposal Squad. You had to be slow, and patient, and thorough. You had to have a good memory. You had to be careful. You *could* join the squad if you were fast and slapdash and hasty. You just didn't last very long.

He looked them up and down and smiled. He was proud of these rats.

"Okay, people, you know it all by now," he said. "You don't need a long lecture from me. Just remember that this is a new town, so we don't know what we're going to find. There's bound to be plenty of new types of traps, but we learn fast, don't we? Poisons, too. They might be using stuff we've never run across before, so be careful. Never rush, never run. We don't want to be like the first mouse, eh?"

"No, Darktan," the rats chorused dutifully.

"I *said*, what mouse don't we want to be like?" Darktan demanded.

"We don't want to be like the first mouse!" shouted the rats.

"Right! What mouse do we want to be like?"

"The second mouse, Darktan!" said the rats, like people who'd had this lesson dinned into them many times.

"Right! And why do we want to be like the second mouse?"

"Because the second mouse gets the cheese, Darktan!"

"Good!" said Darktan. "Inbrine will take Squad Two. Bestbefore? You're promoted, you take Squad Three, and I hope you're as good as old Farmhouse was right up until the time she forgot how to disengage the trip catch on a Snippet and Polson Ratsnapper Number 5. Overconfidence is our enemy! So if you see anything suspicious, any little trays you don't recognize, anything with wires and springs and stuff, you mark it and send a runner to me—Yes?"

A young rat was holding up her hand.

"Yes? What's your name . . . miss?"

"Er . . . Nourishing, sir," said the rat. "Er . . . can I ask a question, sir?"

"Are you new in this platoon, Nourishing?" said Darktan.

"Yes, sir! Transferred out of the Light Widdlers, sir!"

"Ah, they thought you'd be good at trap disposal, did they?"

Nourishing looked uneasy, but there was no going back now.

"Er . . . not really, sir. They said I couldn't be any worse than I am at widdling, sir."

There was general laughter from the ranks.

"How can a rat not be good at *that*?" asked Darktan.

"It's just so . . . so . . . so *embarrassing*, sir," said Nourishing.

Darktan sighed to himself. All this new thinking was producing some strange things. He personally approved of the idea of the Right Place, but some of the ideas the kids were coming up with were . . . odd.

"All right," he said. "What was your question, Nourishing?"

"Er . . . you said the second mouse gets the cheese, sir?"

"That's right! That is the squad motto, Nourishing. Remember it! It is your friend!"

"Yes, sir. I will, sir. But . . . doesn't the *first* mouse get something, sir?"

Darktan stared at the young rat. He was slightly impressed that she stared back instead of cringing.

"I can see you're going to be a valuable addition to the squad, Nourishing," he said. He raised his voice. "Squad! What does the *first* mouse get?"

The roar of voices made dust fall down from the ceiling. "The Trap!"

"And don't you forget it," said Darktan. "Take 'em out, Specialoffer. I'll be with you in a minute."

A younger rat stepped forward and faced the squads.

"Let's go, rats! Hut, hut, hut . . ."

The Trap Squad trotted away. Darktan walked over to Dangerous Beans and Peaches.

"That's got us started," he said. "If we can't get the humans looking for a good rat catcher by tomorrow, we don't know our business."

"We need to stay longer than that," said Peaches. "Some of the ladies are going to have their babies."

"I said we don't know it's safe here yet," said Darktan.

"Do *you* want to be the one to tell Big Savings?" asked Peaches sweetly. Big Savings was the old head female, widely agreed to have a bite like a pickaxe and muscles like rock. She also had a short temper with males. Even Hamnpork kept out of her way when she was in a bad mood.

"Nature has to take its course, obviously," said Darktan quickly. "But we haven't explored.

There *must* be other rats here."

"The *keekees* all keep out of the way of us," said Peaches.

That was true, Darktan had to agree. Ordinary rats *did* keep out of the way of the Changelings. Oh, there was some trouble sometimes, but the Changelings were big and healthy and could *think* their way through a fight. Dangerous Beans was unhappy about this, but as Hamnpork said, it was either us or them and when you got right down to it, it was a rat-eat-rat world. . . .

"I'm going to go and join my squad," said Darktan, still unnerved at the thought of confronting Big Savings. He moved closer. "What's up with Hamnpork?"

"He's . . . thinking about things," said Peaches.

"Thinking," said Darktan, blankly. "Oh. Right. Well, I've got traps to see to. Smell you later!"

"What *is* the matter with Hamnpork?" asked Dangerous Beans when he and Peaches were alone again.

"He's getting old," said Peaches. "He needs to rest a lot. And I think he's worried that Darktan or one of the others is going to challenge him."

"Will they, do you think?"

"Darktan's more wrapped up in breaking traps

and testing poisons. There's more *interesting* things to do now than bite one another."

"Or do *rllk*, from what I hear," said Dangerous Beans.

Peaches looked down demurely. If rats could blush, she would have done so. It was amazing how pink eyes that could hardly see you could look straight through you at the same time.

"The ladies are a lot more choosy," she said. "They want to find fathers who can think."

"Good," said Dangerous Beans. "We must be careful. We don't *need* to breed like rats. We don't have to rely on numbers. We are the Changelings."

Peaches watched him anxiously. When Dangerous Beans was thinking, he seemed to be staring into a world only he could see.

"What is it this time?" she asked.

"I have been thinking that we shouldn't kill other rats. No rat should kill another rat."

"Even *keekees*?" she asked.

"They are rats too."

Peaches shrugged. "Well, we've tried talking to them, and that didn't work. Anyway, they mostly stay away these days."

Dangerous Beans was still staring at the unseen world.

"Even so," he said quietly, "I should like you to write it down."

Peaches sighed but went off anyway to one of the packs the rats had carried in and pulled out her bag. It was no more than a roll of cloth with a handle made from a scrap of string, but it was big enough to hold a few matches, some pieces of pencil lead, a tiny sliver of a broken knife blade for sharpening the leads, and a grubby piece of paper. All the important things.

She was also the official carrier of *Mr. Bunnsy*. "Carrier" wasn't quite correct; "dragger" would be more accurate. But Dangerous Beans always liked to know where it was and seemed to think better when it was around, and it gave him some comfort, and that was good enough for Peaches.

She smoothed out the paper on an ancient brick, picked up a piece of lead, and looked down the list.

The first Thought had been: In the Clan is Strength.

This had been quite a hard one to translate, but she had made an effort. Most rats couldn't read Human. It was just too hard to make the lines and squiggles turn into any sense. So Peaches had worked very hard on making a language that rats *could* read.

She'd tried to draw a big rat made up of little rats:

The writing had led to trouble with Hamn-pork. New ideas needed a running jump to get into the old rat's head. Dangerous Beans had explained in his strange calm voice that writing things down would mean that a rat's knowledge would go on existing even when the rat had died. He said that all the rats could learn the knowledge of Hamnpork. Hamnpork had said: Not likely! It had taken him *years* to learn some of the tricks he'd learned! Why should he give it all away? That'd mean any young rat would know as much as him!

Dangerous Beans had said: We cooperate, or we die.

That had become the next Thought. "Coop-erate" had been difficult, but even *keekees* would sometimes lead a blind or wounded comrade by using a stick to guide them, and that was cer-tainly cooperation. The thick line, where she'd pressed heavily, had to mean "no." The trap sign could mean "die" or "bad" or "avoid."

Peaches had written down a great many Thoughts.

The last Thought on the paper was: Not to Widdle where you Eat. That one was quite simple.

She grasped the piece of lead in both paws and carefully drew No Rat Shall Kill Another Rat.

She sat back. Yes . . . not bad. "Trap" was a good sign for death, and she'd added the dead rat to make it all more *serious*.

"But supposing you have to?" she said, still staring at the drawings.

"Then you have to," said Dangerous Beans. "But you shouldn't."

Peaches shook her head sadly. She supported Dangerous Beans because there was . . . well, something about him. He wasn't big or fast, and he was almost blind and quite weak and sometimes he forgot to eat, because he came up with thoughts that nobody—at least, nobody who was a rat—had thought before. Most of them had annoyed Hamnpork no end, like the time when Dangerous Beans had said, "What *is* a rat?" and Hamnpork had replied, "Teeth. Claws. Tail. Run. Hide. Eat. That's what a rat is."

Dangerous Beans had said, "But now we can also say 'What is a rat?' And that means we're more than that."

"We're *rats*," Hamnpork had argued. "We run around and squeak and steal and make more rats. That's what we're *made* for!"

"Who by?" Dangerous Beans had asked, and that had led to another argument about the Big

Rat Deep Under the Ground theory.

But even Hamnpork followed Dangerous Beans, and so did rats like Darktan and Donut Enter, and they listened when he talked.

Peaches listened when *they* talked. "We were given noses," Darktan had told the platoons. *Who* had given them noses? The thoughts of Dangerous Beans worked their ways into other people's heads without their noticing.

He came up with new ways of thinking. He came up with new words. He came up with ways of understanding the things that were happening to them. Big rats, rats with scars, listened to the little rat because the Change had led them into dark territory, and he seemed to be the only one with an idea of where they were going.

She left him sitting by the candle and went and looked for Hamnpork. He was sitting by a wall. Like most of the old rats, he always stuck to walls and kept away from open spaces and too much light.

He was shaking.

"Are you all right?" she said.

The shaking stopped.

"Fine, fine, nothing wrong with me!" snapped

Hamnpork. "Just a few twinges, nothing perma-
nent!"

"Only I noticed you didn't go out with any of
the squads," said Peaches.

"There's nothing wrong with me!" shouted
the old rat.

"We've still got some potatoes in the bag-
gage—"

"I *don't* want any *food*! There is *nothing* wrong
with me!"

. . . Which meant that there was. It was the
reason he didn't want to share all the things he
knew. What he knew was all he had left. Peaches
knew what rats traditionally did to leaders who
were too old. She'd watched Hamnpork's face
when Darktan—younger, stronger Darktan—
had been talking to his squads, and knew that
Hamnpork was thinking about it, too. Oh, he
was fine when people were watching him, but
lately he'd been resting more, and skulking in
corners.

Old rats were driven out, to lurk around by
themselves and go rotten and funny in the head.
Soon there would be another leader.

Peaches wished she could make him understand one of the Thoughts of Dangerous Beans,
but the old rat didn't much like talking to females.

He'd grown up thinking females weren't for talking to.

The Thought was:

It meant: We Are the Changelings. We Are Not Like Other Rats.

CHAPTER 4

❦

The important thing about adventures, thought Mr. Bunnsy, was that they should not be so long as to make you miss mealtimes.

—From *Mr. Bunnsy Has an Adventure*

The kid and the girl and Maurice were in a large kitchen. The kid could tell it was a kitchen because of the huge black iron range and the pans hanging on the walls and the long scarred table. What it didn't seem to have was what a kitchen traditionally had, which was food.

The girl went to a metal box in the corner and fumbled round her neck for a string, which, it turned out, held a big key.

"You can't trust anybody," she said. "And the rats steal a hundred times what they eat, the devils."

"I don't think they do," said the kid. "Ten times, at most."

"You know all about rats all of a sudden?" said the girl, unlocking the metal case.

"Not all of a sudden, I learned it when— Ow! That really *hurt!*"

"Sorry about that," said Maurice. "I accidentally scratched you, did I?" He tried to make a face that said *Don't be a complete twerp, okay?*— which is quite hard to do with a cat head.

The girl gave him a suspicious look and then turned back to the metal box.

"There's some milk that's not gone hard yet and a couple of fish heads," she said, peering inside.

"Sounds good to me," said Maurice.

"What about your human?"

"Him? He'll eat any old scraps."

"There's bread and sausage," said the girl, taking a can from the metal cupboard. "We're all very suspicious about the sausages. There's a tiny bit of cheese, too, but it's rather ancestral."

"I don't think we should eat your food if it's so short," said the kid. "We have got money."

"Oh, my father says it'd reflect very badly on the town if we weren't hospitable. He's the mayor, you know."

"He's the government?" said the kid.

The girl stared at him. "I suppose so," she said.

"Funny way of putting it. The town council makes the laws, really. He just runs the place and argues with everyone. And *he* says we shouldn't have any more rations than any other people, to show solidarity in these difficult times. It was bad enough that tourists stopped visiting our hot baths, but the rats have made it a lot worse."

She took a couple of saucers from the big kitchen cupboard.

"My father says that if we're all sensible, there will be enough to go around," she went on. "Which I think is very commendable. I entirely agree. But I think that once you've *shown* solidarity, you should be allowed just a little extra. In fact, I think we get a bit less than everyone else. Can you imagine? Anyway . . . So you really are a magical cat, then?" she finished, pouring the milk into a saucer. It oozed rather than gushed, but Maurice was a street cat and would drink milk so rotten that it would try to crawl away.

"Oh, yes, that's right, magical," he said, with a yellow-white ring around his mouth. For two fish heads he'd be anything for anybody.

"Probably belonged to a witch, I expect, with a name like Griselda or one of those names," said the girl, putting the fish heads on another saucer.

"Yeah, right, Griselda, right," said Maurice, not raising his head.

"Who lived in a gingerbread cottage in the forest, probably."

"Yeah, right," said Maurice. And then, because he wouldn't have been Maurice if he couldn't be a bit inventive, he added: "Only it was a melba toast cottage, 'cos she was slimming. Very healthy witch, Griselda."

The girl looked puzzled for a moment. "That's not how it should go," she said.

"Sorry, my mistake, it was gingerbread really," said Maurice quickly. Someone giving you food was always correct.

"And she had big warts, I'm sure."

"Miss," said Maurice, trying to look sincere, "some of those warts had so much personality, they used to have friends of their own. Er . . . what's your name, miss?"

"Promise not to laugh?"

"All right." After all, there might be more fish heads.

"It's . . . Malicia."

"Oh."

"Are you laughing?" she asked, in a threatening voice.

"No," said Maurice, mystified. "Why should I?"

71

"You don't think it's a funny name?"

Maurice thought about the names he knew: Hamnpork, Dangerous Beans, Darktan, Sardines . . .

"Sounds like an ordinary kind of name to me," he said.

Malicia gave him another suspicious look but turned her attention to the kid, who was sitting with the usual happy, faraway smile he wore when he didn't have anything else to do.

"And have *you* got a name?" she said. "You're not the third and youngest son of a king, are you? If your name starts 'Prince,' that's a definite clue."

The kid said, "I think it's Keith."

"You never said you had a name!" said Maurice.

"No one ever asked before," said the kid.

"Keith is not a promising name start," said Malicia. "It doesn't hint of mystery. It just hints of Keith. Are you sure it's your real name?"

"It's just the one they gave me."

"Ah, that's more like it. A *slight* hint of mystery," said Malicia, suddenly looking interested. "Enough to build up suspense. You were stolen away at birth, I expect. You probably *are* the rightful king of some country, but they found someone who looked like you and did a swap. In that case you'll have a magic sword, only it won't *look* magic, you see, until it's time for you to manifest your destiny. You were probably found on a doorstep."

"I was, yes," said Keith.

"See? I'm always right!"

Maurice was always on the lookout for what people wanted. And what Malicia wanted, he felt, was a gag. But he'd never heard the stupid-looking kid talk about himself before.

"What were you doing on a doorstep?" he asked.

"I don't know. Gurgling, I expect," said Keith.

"You never said," said Maurice accusingly.

"Is it important?" asked Keith.

"There was a magic sword or a crown in the basket with you, probably. And you've got a mysterious tattoo or a strange-shaped birthmark, too," said Malicia.

"I don't think so. No one ever mentioned them," said Keith. "There was just me and a blanket. And a note."

"A note? But that's *important*!"

"It said '19 pints and a strawberry yogurt,'" said Keith.

"Ah. Not helpful, then," said Malicia. "Why nineteen pints of milk?"

"It was the Guild of Musicians," said Keith. "Quite a large place. I don't know about the strawberry yogurt."

"Abandoned orphan is good," said Malicia. "After all, a prince can only grow up to be a king, but a mysterious orphan could be *anybody*. Were you beaten and starved and locked in a cellar?"

"I don't think so," said Keith, giving her a funny look. "Everyone at the Guild was very kind. They were mostly nice people. They taught me a lot."

"We've got Guilds here," said Malicia. "They teach boys to be carpenters and stonemasons and things like that."

"The Guild taught me music," said Keith. "I'm a musician. I'm good at it, too. I've been earning my own living since I was six."

"Aha! Mysterious orphan, strange talent, distressed upbringing . . . it's all shaping up," said Malicia. "The strawberry yogurt is probably not important. Would your life have been different if it had been banana flavored? Who can say? What kinds of music do you play?"

"Kinds? There aren't any kinds. There's just music," said Keith. "There's always music, if you listen."

Malicia looked at Maurice.

"Is he always like this?" she demanded.

"This is the most I've ever heard him say," said the cat.

"I expect you're very keen to know all about me," said Malicia. "I expect you're just too polite to ask."

"Gosh, yes," said Maurice.

"Well, you probably won't be surprised to know that I've got two dreadful stepsisters," said Malicia. "And I have to do all the chores!"

"Gosh, really," said Maurice, wondering if there were any more fish heads and, if there were any more fish heads, whether they were worth all this.

"Well, most of the chores," said Malicia, as if revealing an unfortunate fact. "Some of them, definitely. I have to clean up my own room, you know! And it's *extremely* untidy!"

"Gosh, really."

"*And* it's very nearly the smallest bedroom. There's practically no closets and I'm running out of bookshelf space!"

"Gosh, really."

"And people are incredibly cruel to me. You will note that we're here in a *kitchen*. And I'm the mayor's daughter. Should the daughter of a mayor be expected to wash up at least once a week? I think *not*!"

"Gosh, really."

"And will you just look at these torn and bedraggled clothes I have to wear!"

Maurice looked. He wasn't good on clothes. Fur was enough for him. As far as he could tell, Malicia's dress was pretty much like any other dress. It seemed to be all there. There weren't any holes, except where the arms and head poked through.

"Here, just here," said Malicia, pointing to a place on the hem which, to Maurice, looked no different from the rest of the dress. "I had to sew that back myself, you know?"

"Gosh, re—" Maurice stopped. Sardines was rapelling down from a crack in the ancient ceiling. He had a knapsack on his back.

"And on top of this *I'm* the one who has to line up for the bread and sausages every day—" Malicia continued, but Maurice was listening even less than he had been before.

It *would* have to be Sardines, he thought. Idiot! He always goes ahead of the Trap Squad! Of all the kitchens in all the town he could turn up in, he's turned up in this one. Any minute she's going to turn around and scream.

Sardines would probably treat it as applause, too. He lived life as if it was a performance. Other rats just ran around squeaking and messing up things, and that was quite good enough to convince humans there was a plague. But, oh, no, Sardines always had to go further. Sardines and his *yowoorll* song and dance act!

"—and the rats take everything," Malicia was saying. "What they don't take, they spoil. It's been terrible! We have to buy corn and stuff from the traders who sail up the river. That's why bread is so expensive."

"Expensive, eh?" said Maurice.

"We've tried traps and dogs and cats and poison, and still the rats keep coming," said the girl. "They've learned to be really sneaky, too. They hardly ever end up in our traps anymore. What's the good of the rat catchers offering us fifty cents a tail if the rats are so cunning? The rat catchers have to use all kinds of tricks to get them, they say." Behind her, Sardines looked carefully around the room and then signaled to the rats in the ceiling to pull the rope up.

"Don't you think this would be a good time to *go away*!" said Maurice.

"Why are you making faces like that?" asked Malicia, staring at him.

"Oh . . . well, you know that kind of cat that grins all the time? Heard of that? Well, I'm the kind that makes, you know, weird faces," said Maurice desperately. "And sometimes I just burst out and say things *get away get away* see, I did it again. It is an affliction. I probably need counseling *oh no don't do that this is not the time to do that* whoops, there I go again . . ."

Sardines had pulled his straw hat out of his knapsack and was holding a small walking stick.

It was a *good* routine, even Maurice had to admit. Some towns had advertised for a rat piper the very first time he'd done it. People could tolerate rats in the cream, and rats in the roof, and rats in the teapot, but they drew the line at tap dancing. If you saw tap-dancing rats, you were in big trouble. Maurice had reckoned that if only the rats could play an accordion as well, they could do two towns a day.

He'd stared for too long. Malicia turned and her mouth opened in shock and horror as Sardines went into his routine. The cat saw her hand reach out for a pan that was on the table. She threw it, very accurately.

But Sardines was a good pot dodger. The rats were used to having things thrown at them. He was already running when the pan was halfway across the room, and then he leaped onto the chair and then he jumped onto the floor and then he dodged behind the cupboard and then there was a sharp, final, metallic . . . *snap*.

"Hah!" said Malicia, and Maurice and Keith stared at the cupboard. "That's one rat less, at any rate. I really *hate* them—"

"It was Sardines," said Keith.

"No, it was definitely a rat," said Malicia. "Sardines hardly ever invade a kitchen. I expect you're thinking about the plague of lobsters over in—"

"He just called himself Sardines because he saw the name on a rusty old tin and thought it sounded stylish," said Maurice. He wondered if he dared look behind the cupboard.

"He was a good rat," said Keith. "He used to steal books for me when they were teaching me to read."

"Excuse me, are you mad?" said Malicia. "It was a *rat*. The only good rat is a *dead* rat!"

"Hello?" said a little voice.

It came from behind the cupboard.

"It can't be alive! It's a *huge* trap!" said Malicia. "It's got teeth!"

"Anyone there? Only the stick is bending . . ." said the voice.

The cupboard was massive, the wood so old

that time had turned it black and as solid and heavy as stone.

"That's not a rat talking, is it?" said Malicia. "Please tell me rats can't talk!"

"In fact it's bending quite a bit now," said the voice, which was slightly muffled.

Maurice squinted into the space behind the cupboard.

"I can see him," he said. "He wedged the stick in the jaws as they closed! Wotcha, Sardines, how're you doing?"

"Fine, boss," said Sardines in the gloom. "If it wasn't for this trap, I'd say everything was perfect. Did I mention the stick is bending?"

"Yes, you said."

"It's bent some more since then, boss."

Keith grabbed one end of the cupboard and grunted as he tried to move it.

"It's like a rock!" he said.

"It's full of crockery," said Malicia, now quite bewildered. "But rats don't *really* talk, do they?"

"Get out of the way!" shouted Keith. He grabbed the back edge of the dresser with both hands, braced one foot against the wall, and heaved.

Slowly, like a mighty forest tree, the cupboard

pitched forward. The crockery started to fall out as it tipped, plate slipping off plate like one glorious chaotic deal from a very expensive pack of cards. Even so, some of them survived the fall onto the floor, and so did some of the cups and saucers as the cupboard opened and added to the fun, but that didn't make any difference because then the huge, heavy woodwork thundered down on top of them.

One miraculously whole plate rolled past Keith, spinning round and round and getting lower on the floor with the *groiyoiyoiyoo-ooinnnnggg* sound you always get in these distressing circumstances.

Keith reached down to the trap, grabbing Sardines. As he pulled the rat up, the stick gave way and the trap snapped shut. A bit of the stick spun away through the air.

"Are you all right?" said Keith.

"Well, boss, all I can say is it's a good job rats don't wear underwear . . . thanks, boss," said Sardines.

There was the sound of a tapping foot.

Malicia, with arms folded and an expression like a thunderstorm, looked at Sardines, and then at Maurice, and then at stupid-looking Keith, and then at the wreckage on the floor.

"Er . . . sorry about the mess," said Keith. "But he was—"

She waved this away.

"O-kay," she said, as if she'd been thinking deeply. "It goes like this, I think. The rat is a magical rat. I bet he's not the only one. Something happened to him, or them, and now they're really quite intelligent, despite the tap dancing. And . . . they're friends with the cat. So . . . why would rats and a cat be friends? And it goes . . . there's some kind of an arrangement, right? I know! Don't tell me, don't tell me . . ."

"Huh?" said Keith.

"I shouldn't think anyone ever has to tell you *anything*," said Maurice.

". . . it's something to do with plagues of rats, right? All those towns we've heard about . . . well, you heard about them too, and so you got together with thingy here—"

"Keith," said Keith.

"—yes—and so you go from town to town pretending to be a plague of rats, and thingy—"

"Keith."

"—yes—pretends to be a rat piper and you all follow him out. Right? It's all a big swindle, yes?"

Sardines looked up at Maurice.

"She's got us dead to rights, boss," he said.

"So now you've got to give me a good reason why I don't call the Watch out on you," said Malicia triumphantly.

I don't have to, Maurice thought, because you won't. Gosh, humans are so *easy*.

He rubbed up against Malicia's legs and gave her a smirk.

"If you do, you'll never find out how the story ends," he said.

"Ah, it'll end with you going to *prison*," said Malicia, but Maurice saw her staring at stupid-looking Keith and at Sardines. Sardines still had his little straw hat on. When it comes to attracting attention, that sort of thing counts for a lot.

When he saw her frowning at him, Sardines hastily removed his straw hat and held it in front of him, by the brim.

"There's something *I'd* like to find out, boss," he said, "if we're finding out things."

Malicia raised an eyebrow.

"Well?" she said. "And don't call me boss!"

"I'd like to find out why there's no rats in this city, guv'nor," said Sardines. He tap-danced a few steps nervously. Malicia could glare better than a cat.

"What do you mean, no rats?" she said. "There's a *plague* of rats! And you're a rat, anyway!"

"There's rat runs all over the place and there's

83

a few dead rats, but we haven't found a living rat anywhere, guv'nor."

Malicia leaned down. "But *you* are a *rat*," she said.

"Yes, guv. But *we* only arrived this morning."

Sardines grinned nervously as Malicia gave him another long stare.

"Would you like some cheese?" she said. "I'm afraid it's only mousetrap."

"I don't think so, thanks very much all the same," said Sardines, very carefully and politely.

"It's no use—I think it really is time to tell the truth," said Keith.

"Nonononononono," said Maurice, who *hated* that kind of thing. "It's all because—"

"You were right, miss," said Keith wearily. "We go from town to town with a bunch of rats and fool people into giving us money to leave. That's what we do. I'm sorry we've been doing it. This was going to be the last time. I'm very sorry. You shared your food with us, and you haven't got much, either. We ought to be ashamed."

It seemed to Maurice, while he was watching Malicia make up her mind, that her mind worked in a different way from other people's minds. She understood all the hard things without even thinking. Magical rats? Yeah, yeah.

Talking cats? Been there, done that. It was the simple things that were hard.

Her lips were moving. She was, Maurice realized, *making up a story out of it.*

"So . . ." she said, "you come along with your trained rats—"

"We prefer 'educated rodents,' guv," said Sardines.

"—all right, your educated rodents, and you move into a city, and . . . what happens to the rats that are there already?"

Sardines looked helplessly at Maurice. Maurice nodded at him to keep on. They were all going to be in big trouble if Malicia didn't make up a story she liked.

"They keep out of our way, boss, I mean guv," said Sardines.

"Can they talk too?"

"No, guv."

"I think the Clan thinks of them a bit like monkeys," said Keith.

"I was talking to Sardines," said Malicia.

"Sorry," said Keith.

"And there's no other rats here *at all*?" Malicia went on.

"No, guv. A few old skeletons and some piles of poisons and lots of traps, boss. But no rats, boss."

"But the rat catchers nail up a load of rat tails every day!"

"I speak as I find, boss. Guv. No rats, boss. Guv. No other rats anywhere we've been, boss guv."

"Have you ever *looked* at the rat tails, miss?" asked Maurice.

"What do you mean?" asked Malicia.

"They're fake," said Maurice. "Some of them, anyway. They're just old leather bootlaces. I saw some in the street."

"They weren't real tails?" asked Keith.

"I'm a cat. You think I don't know what rats' tails look like?"

"Surely people would notice!" said Malicia.

"Yeah?" said Maurice. "Do you know what an aglet is?"

"Aglet? Aglet? What's an aglet got to do with anything?" snapped Malicia.

"It's those little metal bits on the ends of shoelaces," said Maurice.

"How come a cat knows a word like that?" asked the girl.

"Everyone's got to know *something*," said Maurice. "Have you ever looked closely at the rat tails?"

"Of course not. You can get the plague from rats!" said Malicia.

"That's right, your legs explode," said Maurice, grinning. "That's why you didn't see the aglets. Your legs exploded lately, Sardines?"

"Not today, boss," said Sardines. "Mind you, it's not even lunchtime yet."

Malicia looked, well, grim.

"Ah-*ha*," she said, and it seemed to Maurice that the "ha" had a very nasty edge to it.

"So . . . you're not going to tell the Watch about us?" he ventured hopefully.

"What, that I've been talking to a rat and a cat?" said Malicia. "Of course not. They'll tell my father I've been telling stories, and I'll get locked out of my room again."

"You get locked *out* of your room as a punishment?" said Maurice.

"Yes. It means I can't get at my books. I'm rather a special person, as you may have guessed," said Malicia proudly. "Haven't you heard of the Sisters Grim? Agonista and Eviscera Grim? They were my grandmother and my great-aunt. They wrote . . . fairy tales."

Ah, so we're temporarily out of trouble here, thought Maurice. Best to keep her talking.

"I'm not a big reader, as cats go," he said. "So what were these, then? Stories about little people with wings going tinkle-tinkle?"

"No," said Malicia. "They were not big on tin-kling little people. They wrote . . . *real* fairy tales. Ones with lots of blood and bones and bats and rats in them. *I've* inherited the storytelling talent," she added.

"I kind of thought you had," said Maurice.

"And if there's no rats under the town, but the rat catchers are nailing up *bootlaces*, I smell a rat," said Malicia.

"Sorry," said Sardines. "I think that was me. I'm a bit nervous—"

There were sounds from upstairs.

"Quick, go out across the backyard!" Malicia commanded. "Get up into the hayloft over the stable! I'll bring you some food! I know exactly how this sort of thing goes!"

CHAPTER 5

Ratty Rupert was the bravest rat that ever was. Everyone in Furry Bottom said so.

—From *Mr. Bunnsy Has an Adventure*

Darktan was in a tunnel several streets away, hanging from four bits of string attached to his harness. These were tied onto a stick, which had been balanced like a seesaw on the back of a very fat rat; two other rats were sitting on the other end, and several other rats were steering it.

Darktan was hanging just above the teeth of the big steel trap that completely filled the tunnel.

He squeaked the signal to stop. The stick vibrated a little under his weight.

"I'm right over the cheese," he said. "Smells like Lancre Blue Vein, Extra Tasty. Not been touched. Pretty old, too. Move me in about two paws."*

The stick bounced up and down as he was pushed forward.

"Careful, sir," said one of the younger rats who crowded the tunnel behind the Trap Disposal Squad.

Darktan grunted and looked down at the teeth, an inch away from his nose. He pulled a short piece of wood out of one of his belts; a tiny sliver of mirror had been glued to one end of it.

"You lot move the candle this way a bit," he commanded. "That's right. That's right. Let's see, now. . . ." He pushed the mirror past the teeth and turned it gently. "Ah, just as I thought— it's a Prattle and Johnson Little Snapper, sure enough. One of the old Mk.3s, but with the extra safety catch. That's come a long way. Okay. We know about these, don't we? Cheese for tea, lads!"

There was nervous laughter from the watchers, but a voice said, "Oh, they're *easy*. . . ."

"Who said that?" asked Darktan sharply.

There was silence. Darktan craned his head back. The young rats had carefully moved aside,

*Rat measurement. About an inch.

90

leaving one looking very, very alone.

"Ah, Nourishing," said Darktan, turning back to the trap's trigger mechanism. "Easy, is it? Glad to hear it. You can show us how it's done, then."

"Er, when I said easy . . ." Nourishing began. "I mean, Inbrine showed me on the practice trap, and he said—"

"No need to be modest," said Darktan, a gleam in his eye. "It's all ready. I'll just watch, shall I? You can get into the harness and do it, can you?"

"—but, but, but, I couldn't see too well when he showed us, now that I come to think about it, and, and, and—"

"I'll tell you what," said Darktan, "*I'll* work on the trap, shall I?"

Nourishing looked very relieved.

"And you can tell me *exactly* what to do," Dartkan added.

"Er . . ." Nourishing began. Now she looked like a rat prepared to rejoin the widdling squad really quickly.

"Jolly good," said Darktan. He carefully put his mirror away and pulled a length of metal out of his harness. He prodded the trap carefully. Nourishing shuddered at the sound of metal on metal. "Now, where was I? Oh, yes, here's a bar and a little spring and a catch. What shall I do now, Miss Nourishing?"

"Er, er, er," Nourishing stuttered.

"Things are *creaking* here, Miss Nourishing," said Darktan from the depths of the trap.

"Er, er, you wedge the thingy . . ."

"Which one *is* the thingy, Miss Nourishing? Take your time, whoops, this bit of metal is wobbling, but don't let me hurry you in any way . . ."

"You wedge the, er, the thingy, er, the thingy . . . er . . ." Nourishing's eyes rolled wildly.

"Maybe it's this big SNAP argh argh argh. . . ."

Nourishing fainted.

Darktan slipped out of the harness and dropped onto the trap.

"All fixed," he said. "I've clipped it firm—it won't go off now. You boys can drag it out of the way." He walked back to the squad and dropped a lump of hairy cheese onto Nourishing's quivering stomach. "It's very important in the trap business to be definite, you see. You're definite or you're dead. The second mouse gets the cheese." Darktan sniffed. "Well, no human coming here would have any difficulty thinking there's rats around *now* . . ."

The other trainees laughed in the nervous, tittering way of people who've seen someone else attract the teacher's attention and are glad it isn't them.

Darktan unrolled a scrap of paper. He was a rat of action, and the idea that the world could be pinned down in little signs worried him a bit. But he could see how useful it was. When he drew pictures of a tunnel layout, the paper *remembered*. It didn't get confused by new smells. Other rats, if they knew how to read, could see in their heads what the writer had seen.

He'd invented maps. It was a drawing of the world.

"Amazing stuff, this new technology," he said. "So . . . there's poison marked here, two tunnels back. Did you see to it, Inbrine?"

"Buried and widdled on," said Inbrine, his deputy. "It was the gray Number Two poison, too."

"Good rat," said Darktan. "That's nasty eating."

"There were dead *keekees* all around it."

"I'll bet there were. No antidote for that stuff."

"We found trays of Number One and Number Three too," said Inbrine. "Lots of them."

"You can survive Number One poison if you're sensible," said Darktan. "Remember that, all of you. And if you ever eat Number Three poison, we've got some stuff that'll sort you out.

I mean, you'll live in the end, but there'll be a day or two when you'd wish you were dead—"

"There's *lots* of poison, Darktan," said Inbrine nervously. "More than I've ever seen before. Rat bones all over the place."

"Important safety tip there, then," said Darktan, setting off along a new tunnel. "Don't eat a dead rat unless you know what they died of. Otherwise you'll die of it, too."

"Dangerous Beans says he thinks we shouldn't eat rats at all," said Inbrine.

"Yeah, well, maybe," said Darktan. "But out in the tunnels you have to be practical. Never let good food go to waste. And someone wake up Nourishing!"

"A *lot* of poison," said Inbrine, as the squad moved on. "They must really *hate* rats here."

Darktan didn't answer. He could see people were already getting nervous. There was a smell of fear in the rat runs. They'd never come across so much poison before. Darktan didn't usually worry about anything, and he hated to feel the worry starting, deep in his bones—

A small rat, out of breath, scurried up the tunnel and crouched in front of him.

"Kidney, sir, Number Three Heavy Widdlers," it burst out. "We've found a trap, sir! Not like the usual sort! Fresh walked right into it! Please come!"

◆　◆　◆

There was a lot of straw in the loft over the stable, and the heat of the horses coming up from below made it quite snug.

Keith was lying on his back, staring at the ceiling and humming to himself. Maurice was watching his lunch, which was twitching its nose.

Right up until the time he pounced, Maurice looked like a sleek killing machine.

It all went wrong just before he jumped. His rear rose, it waggled faster and faster from side to side, his tail slashed at the air like a snake, and then he dived forward, claws out—

"Squeak!"

"Okay, here's the deal," said Maurice to the shivering ball in his claws. "You only have to say something. Anything. 'Let me go,' maybe, or even 'Help!' *Squeak* does not cut the mustard. It's just a noise. Just ask, and I'll let you go. No one can say I'm not highly moral in that respect."

"Squeak!" screamed the mouse.

"Fair enough," said Maurice, and killed it instantly. He carried it back to the corner, where Keith was now sitting up in the straw and eating a pickled beef sandwich.

"It couldn't talk," said Maurice hurriedly.

"I didn't ask you," said Keith.

"I mean, I gave it a chance," said Maurice. "You heard me, right? It only had to say it didn't want to be eaten."

"Good."

"It's all right for you—I mean, it's not as though you have to speak to sandwiches," said Maurice, as if he was still bothered about something.

"I wouldn't know what to say to them," said Keith.

"And I'd like to point out that I didn't play with it, either," said Maurice. "One swipe with the ol' paw and it was 'good-bye, that's all she wrote,' except that obviously the mouse didn't write anything, not being intelligent *in any way*."

"I believe you," said Keith.

"It never felt a thing," Maurice went on.

There was a scream from somewhere in a nearby street, and then the sound of crockery breaking. There had been quite a lot of that in the last half hour.

"Sounds like the lads are still at work," said Maurice, carrying the dead mouse behind a pile of hay. "Nothing gets a good scream like Sardines dancing across the table."

The stable doors opened. A man came in, harnessed two of the horses, and led them out. Shortly afterward, there was the sound of a coach leaving the yard.

A few seconds later there were three loud knocks from below.

They were repeated. And then they were repeated again. Finally, Malicia's voice said, "Are you two up there or not?"

Keith crawled out of the hay and looked down.

"Yes," he said.

"Didn't you hear the secret knock?" asked Malicia, staring up at him in annoyance.

"It didn't sound like a secret knock," said Maurice, his mouth full.

"Is that Maurice's voice?" said Malicia suspiciously.

"Yes," said Keith. "You'll have to excuse him—he's eating someone."

Maurice swallowed quickly. "It's not *someone*!" he hissed. "It's not *someone* unless it can talk! Otherwise it's just food!"

"It *is* a secret knock!" Malicia snapped. "I know about these things! And you're supposed to give the secret knock in return!"

"But if it's just someone knocking on the door

in, you know, general high spirits, and we knock back, what are they going to think is up here?" said Maurice. "An extremely heavy beetle?"

Malicia went uncharacteristically silent for a moment. Then she said, "Good point, good point. I know—I'll shout 'It's me, Malicia!' and *then* give the secret knock, and that way you'll know it's me and you can give the secret knock back. Okay?"

"Why don't we just say, 'Hello, we're up here'?" asked Keith innocently.

Malicia sighed. "Don't you have *any* sense of drama? Look, my father's gone off to the Rathaus to see the other council members. He said the crockery was the last straw!"

"The crockery?" said Maurice. "You told him about Sardines?"

"I had to say I'd been frightened by a huge rat and tried to climb up the cupboard to escape," said Malicia.

"You lied?"

"I just told a story," said Malicia calmly. "It was a good one, too. It was much more true than the truth would sound. A tap-dancing rat? Anyway, he wasn't really interested because there's been a *lot* of complaints today. Your tame rats are really upsetting people. I am gloating."

"They're not *our* rats, they're *their* rats," said Keith.

"And they always work fast," said Maurice proudly. "They don't mess about when it comes to . . . messing about."

"One town we were in last month, the council advertised for a rat piper the very next morning," said Keith. "That was Sardines's big day."

"My father shouted a lot and sent for Blunkett and Spears, too," said Malicia. "They're the rat catchers! And you know what that means, don't you?"

Maurice and Keith looked at one another.

"Let's pretend we don't," said Maurice.

"It means we can break into their shed and solve the mystery of the bootlace tails!" said Malicia. She gave Maurice a critical look. "Of course, it would be more . . . satisfying if we were four children and a dog, which is the right number for an adventure, but we'll make do with what we've got."

"Hey, we don't do breaking and entering—we just steal from governments!" said Maurice.

"Er, only governments who aren't people's fathers, obviously," said Keith.

"So?" said Malicia, giving Keith an odd look.

"That's not the same as being criminals!" said Maurice.

"Ah, but when we've got the evidence, we can take it to the council, and then it won't be criminal at all because we will be saving the day," said Malicia, with weary patience. "Of course, it may be that the council and the Watch are in league with the rat catchers, so we shouldn't trust *anyone*. Really, haven't you people *ever* read a book? It'll be dark soon, and I'll come over and pick you up and we can shimmy the nodger."

"Can we?" said Keith.

"Yes. With a hairpin," said Malicia. "I know it's possible, because I've read about it hundreds of times."

"What kind of nodger is it?" asked Maurice.

"A big one," said Malicia. "That makes it easier, of course." She turned around abruptly and ran out of the stable.

"Maurice?" said Keith.

"Yes?" said the cat.

"What *is* a nodger and how do you shimmy it?"

"I don't know. A lock, maybe?"

"But you said—"

"Yes, but I was just trying to keep her talking in case she turned violent," said Maurice. "She's gone in the head, if you ask me. She's one of those people like . . . actors. You know. Acting all the time. Not living in the real world at all. Like it's all a big story. Dangerous Beans is a bit like that. Highly dangerous person, in my opinion."

"He's a very kind and thoughtful rat!"

"Ah, *yes*, but the trouble is, see, that he thinks everyone else is like him. People like that are bad news, kid. And our lady friend, she thinks life works like a fairy tale."

"Well, that's harmless, isn't it?" asked Keith.

"Yeah, but in fairy tales, when someone dies . . . it's just a word."

◆　◆　◆

The Number Three Heavy Widdlers squad was taking a rest, and they'd run out of ammunition in any case. No one felt like going past the trap to the trickle of water that dripped down the wall. And no one liked looking at what was in the trap.

"Poor old Fresh," said a rat. "He was a good rat."

"Should've paid attention to where he was going, though," said another rat.

"Thought he knew it all," said yet another rat. "A decent rat, though, if a bit smelly."

"So let's get him out of the trap, shall we?" said the first rat. "Doesn't seem right, leaving him in there like that."

"Yes. Especially since we're hungry."

One of the rats said, "Dangerous Beans says we shouldn't eat rat at all. . . ."

Another rat said, "No, it's only if you don't know what they died of, 'cos they might have died of poison."

Another rat said, "And we *know* what *he* died of. He died of squashing. You can't *catch* squashing."

They all looked at the late Fresh.

"What do you think happens to you after you're dead?" said a rat slowly.

"You get eaten. Or you get all dried up, or moldy."

"What, *all* of you?"

"Well, people usually leave the feet."

The rat who'd asked the question asked, "But what about the bit inside?"

And the rat who'd mentioned the feet said, "Oh, the squishy green wobbly bit? No, you ought to leave that, too. Tastes *awful.*"

"No, I meant the bit inside you that's *you.* Where does *that* go?"

"Sorry, you've lost me there."

"Well . . . you know, like . . . dreams?"

The rats nodded. They knew about dreams.

Dreams had come as a *big* shock when they'd started to happen.

"Well, then, in the dreams, when you're being chased by dogs or flying or whatever . . . who *is* it who's doing that? It's not your body, 'cos that's asleep. So it must be an invisible part that lives inside you, yes? And being dead is like being asleep, isn't it?"

"Not exactly like asleep," said a rat uncertainly, glancing at the fairly flat thing formerly known as Fresh. "I mean, you don't get all blood and bits sticking out. And you wake up."

"So," said the rat who'd raised the whole question about the invisible part, "when you wake up, where does the dreaming part *go*? When you die, where does that bit that's inside you go?"

"What, the green wobbly bit?"

"No! The bit that's behind your eyes!"

"You mean the pinky-gray bit?"

"No, not that! The invisible bit!"

"How would I know? I've never seen an invisible bit!"

All the rats stared down at Fresh.

"I don't like this kind of talk," said one of them. "It reminds me of the shadows in the candle-light."

Another one said, "Did you hear about the Bone Rat? It comes and gets you when you're dead, they say."

"They say, they say," muttered a rat. "They *say* there's Big Rat Deep Under the Ground who made everything, they *say*. So it made humans, too? Must be really keen on us, to go and make humans too! Huh?"

"How do I know? Maybe they were made by a Big Human?"

"Oh, now you're just being silly," said the doubting rat, who was called Tomato.

"Okay, okay, but you've got to admit that everything couldn't have just, well, turned up, could it? There's got to be a reason. And when Dangerous Beans says there's things we should do 'cos they're *right*, well, who works out what's right? Where does 'right' and 'wrong' come from? They *say* if you've been a good rat, maybe the Big Rat has got this tunnel full of good eating that the Bone Rat will take you to—"

"But Fresh is still here. And I ain't seen a bony rat!" said doubting Tomato.

"Ah, but they say you only see it if it's coming for *you*."

"Oh? Oh?" said another rat, nervous to the point of mad sarcasm. "So how did *they* see it, eh? Tell me that! Life's bad enough as it is without having to worry about invisible things you can't see!"

"All right, all right, what's been happening?"

The rats turned, suddenly incredibly pleased to see Darktan scurry up the tunnel.

Darktan pushed past. He'd brought Nourishing with him. It was never too soon, he said, for a member of the squad to find out what happened to people who got things wrong.

"I see," he said, looking at the trap. He shook his head sadly. "What do I tell everyone?"

"Not to use tunnels that haven't been marked clear, sir," said Tomato. "But Fresh, well, he's not a . . . he never *was* a good listener. And he was keen to get on with it, sir."

Darktan examined the trap and tried to keep his face fixed in an expression of confident purpose. It was hard to do it, though. He'd never seen a trap like it. It looked like a really nasty one, a squeezer rather than a chopper. It had been put where a rat hurrying to the water would be bound to trip it.

"He's not going to do any more listening now, that's for certain," he said. "The face looks familiar. Apart from the bulging eyes and the tongue hanging out, that is."

"Er, you talked to Fresh in the muster this morning, sir," said a rat. "Told him he was raised to be a widdler and to get on with it, sir."

Darktan's expression remained blank. Then he said, "We've got to go. We're finding a lot of traps all over. We'll work our way back to you. No one is to go any farther along that tunnel, understood? Everyone say, 'Yes, Darktan'!"

"Yes, Darktan," the rats chorused.

"And one of you stand guard," said Darktan. "There could be more traps up that way."

"What shall we do with Fresh, sir?" said Tomato.

"Don't eat the green wobbly bit," said Darktan, and hurried off.

Traps! he thought. There were too many of them. And too much poison. Even the experienced members of the squad were getting nervous now. He didn't like to come across unknown things. You found out what unknown things were when they killed you.

The rats were spreading out under the town, and it was like no other town they'd found. The whole place was a rat trap. They hadn't found a single living *keekee*. Not one. That wasn't normal. Everywhere had rats. Where you got humans, you got rats.

And on top of everything else the young rats were spending too much time worrying about . . . things. Things you couldn't see or smell. Shadow things. Darktan shook his head. There was no room in the tunnels for that sort of thinking. Life was real, life was practical, and life could get taken away *really quickly* if you weren't paying attention. . . .

He noticed Nourishing looking around and sniffing the air as they trotted along a pipe.

"That's right," he said approvingly. "You can't be too careful. Never rush in. Even the rat in front of you might have been lucky and missed the trigger."

"Yes, sir."

"Don't worry too much about Fresh, though."

"He did look awfully . . . flat, sir."

"Fools rush in, Nourishing. Fools rush in. . . ."

Darktan could sense the fear spreading. It worried him. If the Changelings panicked, they'd panic as rats. And the tunnels in this city were no place for a terrified rat to be running. But if one rat broke ranks and ran, then most of them would follow. Smell held sway in the tunnels. When things went well, everyone felt good. When fear arrived, it flowed through the runs like floodwater. Panic in the rat world was a kind of disease that could be caught too easily.

Things did not get any better when they caught up with the rest of his squad. This time they'd found a new poison.

"Not to worry," said Darktan, who was worried. "We've come across new poisons before, right?"

"Not for *ages*," said a rat. "Remember that one in Scrote? With the sparkly blue bits? It burned if you got it on your feet? People ran into it before they knew?"

"They've got that here?"

"You'd better come and see."

In one of the tunnels a rat was lying on its side. Its feet were curled up tight, like fists. It was whimpering.

Darktan took one look and knew that, for this rat, it was all over. It was only a matter of time. For the rats back in Scrote, it had been a matter of *horrible* time.

"I could bite her in the back of the neck," a rat volunteered. "It'd be all over quickly."

"It's a kind thought, but that stuff gets into the blood," said Darktan. "Find a snapper trap that hasn't been made safe. Do it carefully."

"*Put* a rat in a *trap*, sir?" said Nourishing.

"Yes! Better to die fast than slow!"

"Even so, it's—" the rat who had volunteered to do the biting started to protest.

The hairs around Darktan's face stood out. He reared up and showed his teeth.

"Do what you're told or I'll gnaw *you*!" he roared. The other rat crouched back.

"All right, Darktan, all right. . . ."

"And warn all the other squads!" Darktan bellowed. "This isn't rat catching, this is *war*! Everyone's to pull back smartly! No one touch *nothing*! We're going to— *Yes?* What is it *this* time?"

A small rat had crept up to Darktan. As the trap hunter spun around, the rat crouched hurriedly, almost rolling on his back to show how small and harmless he was.

"Please, sir . . ." he mumbled.

"Yes?"

"This time we've found a live one. . . ."

CHAPTER 6

There were big adventures and small adventures, Mr. Bunnsy knew. You didn't get told what size they were going to be before you started. Sometimes you could have a big adventure even when you were standing still.

—From *Mr. Bunnsy Has an Adventure*

"Hello? Hello, it's *me*. And I'm going to give the secret knock *now*!" There were three knocks on the stable door, and then Malicia's voice rose again with "Hello, did you *hear* the secret knock?"

"Perhaps she'll go away if we keep quiet," said Keith, in the straw.

"I shouldn't think so," said Maurice. He raised his voice and called out, "We're up here!"

"You've still got to give the secret knock," shouted Malicia.

"Oh, *prblltttrrrp*," said Maurice under his breath, and fortunately no human knows how bad a swear word that is in Cat. "Look, this is me, okay? A cat? Who talks? How will you recognize me? Shall I wear a red carnation?"

"I don't think you're a *proper* talking cat, anyway," said Malicia, climbing the ladder. She was still wearing black, and she had bundled up her hair under a black scarf. She also had a big bag slung over her shoulder.

"Gosh, she's got that right," said Maurice.

"I mean you don't wear boots and a sword and have a big hat with a feather in it," said the girl, pulling herself into the loft.

Maurice gave her a long stare. "Boots?" he said at last. "On *these* paws?"

"Oh, it was in a picture in a book I read," said Malicia, calmly. "A silly one for children. Full of animals that dressed up as humans."

It crossed Maurice's cat mind, and not for the first time, that if he moved fast, he could be out of the city in five minutes and onto a barge or something.

Once, when he was no more than a kitten, he'd been taken home by a small girl who'd dressed him up in doll's clothes and sat him at a small table with a couple of dolls and three quarters of a teddy bear. He'd managed to escape through an open window, but it had taken him all day to get out of the dress. That girl could have been Malicia. She thought animals were just people who hadn't been paying enough attention.

"I don't do clothes," he said. It wasn't much of a line, but it was probably better than saying "I think you are a loony."

"Could be an improvement," said Malicia. "It's nearly dark. Let's go! We shall move like cats!"

"Oh, right," said Maurice. "I expect I can do *that*."

Although, he thought a few minutes later, no cats ever moved like Malicia. She obviously thought that it was no good looking inconspicuous unless people could *see* that you were being inconspicuous. People in the street actually stopped to watch her as she sidled along walls and scuttled from one doorway to another. Maurice and Keith strolled along after her. No one paid them any attention.

Eventually, in a narrow street, she stopped at a black building with a big wooden sign hanging over the door.

The sign showed a lot of rats: a sort of star made of rats, with all their tails tied together in a big knot.

"Sign of the ancient Guild of Rat Catchers,"

whispered Malicia, swinging her bag off her shoulder.

"I know," said Keith. "It looks horrible."

"Makes an interesting design, though," said Malicia.

One of the most significant things about the door below the sign was the big padlock holding it shut.

Odd, Maurice thought. If rats make your legs explode, why do rat catchers have to have a big lock on their shed?

"Luckily I'm prepared for every eventuality," said Malicia, and reached into her bag. There was a sound as of lumps of metal and bottles being moved around.

"What have you got in there?" said Maurice. "Everything?"

"The grapnel and rope ladder take up a lot of the room," said Malicia, still feeling around. "And then there's the big medicine kit, and the small medicine kit, and the knife, and the other knife, and the sewing kit, and the mirror for sending signals, and . . . these."

She pulled out a small bundle of black cloth. When she unrolled it, Maurice saw the gleam of metal.

"Ah," he said. "Lock picks, right? I've seen

113

burglars at work—"

"Hairpins," said Malicia, selecting one. "Hairpins always work in the books I've read. You just push one into the keyhole and twiddle. I have a selection of prebent ones."

Once again, Maurice felt a little chill at the back of his head. They work in *stories*, he thought. Oh dear me.

"And how come you know so much about picking locks?" he said.

"I told you, they lock me out of my room to punish me," said Malicia, twiddling.

Maurice *had* seen thieves at work. Men breaking into buildings at night hated to see dogs, but they didn't mind cats. Cats never attempted to tear their throats out. And what thieves tended to have, he knew, were complicated little tools that were used with great care and precision. They didn't use stupi—

Click!

"Good," said Malicia in a satisfied voice.

"That was just luck," said Maurice as the padlock swung free. He looked up at Keith. "You think it's just luck too, eh, kid?"

"How would I know?" said Keith. "I've never seen it done before."

"I knew it would work," said Malicia. "It

worked in the fairy story 'The Seventh Wife of Greenbeard,' where she broke out of his Room of Terror and stabbed him in the eye with a frozen herring."

"That was a *fairy* story?" said Keith.

"Yes," said Malicia proudly. "Right out of *Grim Fairy Tales.*"

"You've got some *bad* fairies in these parts," said Maurice, shaking his head.

Malicia pushed the door open.

"Oh, *no*," she moaned. "I didn't expect *this.* . . ."

♦ ♦ ♦

Somewhere below Maurice's paws, and about a street away, the one local rat that the Changelings had found alive was crouched in front of Dangerous Beans. The squads had been called back. This was not turning out to be a good day.

Traps that didn't kill, Darktan thought. You found them sometimes. Sometimes humans wanted to catch rats alive.

Darktan didn't trust humans who wanted to catch rats alive. Honest traps that killed out-right—well, they were bad, but you could usually avoid them, and at least there was something honest about them. Live traps were like poison. They *cheated*.

Dangerous Beans was smelling the newcomer, a young female. It was strange, but the rat who could think the most unratlike thoughts was also the best at talking to *keekees*, except that talking wasn't the right word. No one, not even Hamnpork, had a sense of smell like Dangerous Beans.

The new rat certainly wasn't giving any trouble. For one thing, it was surrounded by rats who were big and well fed and tough, so its body was respectfully saying *sir* as hard as it could. The Changelings had also given it some food, which it was engulfing rather than eating.

"It was in a box trap," said Darktan, who was drawing lines on the floor with a stick. "We found a lot of them."

"I got caught in one of those once," said Hamnpork. "Then a female human came along and tipped me out over the garden wall. Couldn't see the point of it."

"I believe some humans do it to be kind," said Peaches. "They get the rat out of the house without killing it."

"Didn't do her any good, anyway," said Hamnpork with satisfaction. "I went back the next night and widdled on the cheese."

"I don't think anyone is trying to be kind

here," said Darktan. "There was another rat in there with it. At least," he added, "there was *part* of a rat in there with it. I think it's been eating it to stay alive."

"Very sensible." Hamnpork nodded.

"We found something else," Darktan said, still drawing furrows in the dirt. "Can you see these, sir?"

He'd drawn a network of lines on the floor.

"Hrumph. I can *see* them, but I don't have to know what they are," said Hamnpork. He rubbed his nose. "I've never needed any more than this."

Darktan gave a patient sigh. "Then *smell*, sir, that this is a . . . a picture of all the tunnels we've explored today. It's . . . the shape I have in my head. We've explored a lot of the town. There's a lot of the"—he glanced at Peaches—"a lot of the *kind* traps, mostly empty. There's poison all over the place. It's mostly quite old. Lots of empty box traps. Lots of killer traps, still set. And no live rats. None at all, except for our . . . new friend. We know that's very odd. I sniffed around a bit near where I found her, and I smelled rats. Lots of rats. I mean *lots*."

"Alive?" asked Dangerous Beans.

"Yes."

"All in one place?"

"It smells that way," said Darktan. "I think a squad should go and look."

Dangerous Beans padded over to the rat and sniffed it. The rat sniffed at him. They touched paws.

The watching Changelings were astonished. Dangerous Beans was treating the *keekee* as an *equal*.

"Lots of things, lots of things," he murmured. "Many rats . . . humans . . . fear . . . lots of fear . . . lots of rats, crowded . . . food . . . rat . . . you said she's been eating rat?"

"It's a rat-eat-rat world," said Hamnpork. "Always has been, always will be."

Dangerous Beans wrinkled his nose. "There's something else. Something . . . odd. Strange . . . she's really scared."

"It was in a trap," said Peaches. "And then it met us."

"Much . . . worse than that," said Dangerous Beans. "She's . . . she's frightened of us because we're strange rats, but she smells relieved that we're not . . . what she's used to."

"Humans!" Darktan spat.

"I . . . don't . . . think . . . so . . ."

"Other rats?"

"Yes . . . no. I . . . don't . . . It's hard to tell."

"Dogs? Cats?"

"No." Dangerous Beans stepped back. "Something new."

"What shall we do with it?" said Peaches.

"Let her go, I suppose."

"We can't do that!" said Darktan. "We've triggered all the traps we've found, but there are still poisons all over the place. I wouldn't send a *mouse* out into that. It hasn't tried to attack us, after all."

"So?" said Hamnpork. "What's another dead *keekee*?"

"I know what Darktan means," said Peaches. "We can't just send it out to die."

Big Savings stepped forward and put a paw around the young female, cuddling it protectively. She glared at Hamnpork. Although she might nip him sometimes if she was annoyed, she wouldn't argue with him. She was too old to do that. But her look said: All males are stupid, you stupid old rat.

He looked lost.

"We've killed *keekees*, haven't we?" he said. "Why do we want this one hanging around?"

"We can't send it out to die," said Peaches again, looking at Dangerous Beans' expression.

He had that faraway look in his pink eyes.

"You want it trailing around eating our food and messing things up?" said Hamnpork. "It can't talk, it can't think . . ."

"Nor could we, not long ago!" snapped Peaches. "We were all like her!"

"We can think now, young female!" said Hamnpork, his hair rising.

"Yes," said Dangerous Beans quietly. "We can think now. We can think about what we do. We can pity the innocent one who means us no harm. And that's why it can stay."

Hamnpork's head turned sharply. Dangerous Beans was still facing the newcomer.

Hamnpork reared up instinctively, a rat ready to fight. But Dangerous Beans couldn't see him.

Peaches watched the old rat with concern. He'd been challenged by a weedy little rat who would not last a second in a fight. And Dangerous Beans hadn't even realized he'd made the challenge.

He doesn't think like that, Peaches told herself.

The other rats were watching Hamnpork. *They* still thought like that, and were waiting to see what he would do.

But it was dawning even on Hamnpork that

pouncing on the white rat would be unthinkable. It would be like cutting off his own tail.

He very carefully let himself relax.

"It's just a rat," he muttered.

"But you, dear Hamnpork, are not," said Dangerous Beans. "Will you go with Darktan's crew to find out where it came from? It could be dangerous."

This made Hamnpork's hair rise again.

"I'm not afraid of danger!" he roared.

"Of course not. That is why you should go. *It* was terrified," said Dangerous Beans.

"I've never been scared of *anything*!" shouted Hamnpork.

Now Dangerous Beans turned to face him. In the candlelight there was a glow in the pink eyes. Hamnpork was not a rat who spent a lot of time thinking about things he couldn't see or smell or bite, but . . .

He looked up. The candlelight made big rat shadows dance on the wall.

Hamnpork had heard the young rats talking about shadows and dreams and what happened to your shadow after you died. He didn't worry about that stuff. Shadows couldn't bite you. There was nothing to be frightened of in shadows. But now his own voice in his head told him, *I'm frightened of what those eyes can see.*

Hamnpork glared at Darktan, who was scratching something in the mud with one of his sticks.

"I'll go, but I will lead the expedition," he said. "I'm senior rat here!"

"That doesn't worry me," said Darktan. "Mr. Clicky is going to be going in front in any case."

"I thought he got smashed last week?" said Peaches.

"We've got two left," said Darktan. "Then we'll have to raid another pet shop."

"*I'm* the leader," said Hamnpork. "*I'll* say what we do, Darktan."

"Fine, sir. Fine," said Darktan, still drawing in the mud. "And you know how to make all the traps safe, do you?"

"No, but I can tell you to!"

"Good. Good," said Darktan, making more marks with his stick and not looking at the leader. "And you'll tell me which levers to leave alone and which bits to wedge open, will you?"

"I don't have to understand about traps," said Hamnpork.

"But I do, sir," said Darktan, speaking in the same calm voice. "And I'm telling you that there's a couple of things about some of these new traps I don't understand, and until I understand them, I'd very *respectfully* suggest you leave it all to me."

"That is not the way to talk to a superior rat!"

Darktan gave him a look, and Peaches held her breath.

This is the showdown, she thought. This is where we find out who is the leader.

Then Darktan said: "I am sorry. Impertinence was not intended."

Peaches picked up the astonishment amongst the older males who were watching.

Darktan. He'd backed down! He hadn't leaped!

But he hadn't cowered, either.

Hamnpork's fur settled. The old rat was at a loss to know how to deal with this. All the signals were mixed up.

"Well, er . . ."

"Obviously, as the leader you must give the orders," said Darktan.

"Yes, er . . ."

"But my advice, sir, is that we investigate this. Unknown things are dangerous."

"Yes. Certainly," said Hamnpork. "Yes, indeed. We will investigate. Of course. See to it. I am the leader, and that is what I am saying."

Maurice looked around at the inside of the rat catchers' shed.

"It *looks* like a rat catchers' shed," he said. "Benches, chairs, stove, lots of rat skins hanging up, piles of old traps, a couple of dog muzzles, rolls of wire netting, a considerable amount of a lack of any dusting ever being done. It's what *I'd* have expected a rat catchers' hut to look like inside."

"I was expecting something . . . horrible yet interesting," said Malicia. "Some ghastly clue."

"Does there have to be a clue?" said Keith.

"Of course!" said Malicia, looking under a chair. "Look, cat, there's two types of people in the world. There are those who have got the plot, and those who haven't."

"The world hasn't got a *plot*," said Maurice. "Things just . . . happen, one after another."

"Only if you think of it like that," said Malicia, far too smugly in Maurice's opinion. "There's always a plot. You just have to know where to look."

She paused for a moment and then said, "Look! That's the word! There'll be a secret passage, of course! Everyone look for the entrance to the secret passage!"

"Er . . . how will we know it's the entrance to a secret passage?" asked Keith, looking even more bewildered than normally. "What does a secret passage *look* like?"

"It won't *look* like one, of course!"

"Oh, *well*, in that case I can see dozens of secret passages," said Maurice. "Doors, windows, that calendar from the Acme Poison Company, that cupboard over there, that rat hole, that desk, that—"

"You're just being sarcastic," said Malicia, lifting up the calendar and sternly inspecting the wall behind it.

"Actually, I was just being flippant," said Maurice. "But I can do sarcastic if you like."

Keith stared at the long bench, which was in front of a window frosted with ancient cobwebs. Traps were piled up on it. All kinds of traps. And beside them were row upon row of battered old tins and jars with labels like "Danger: Hydrogen Dioxide!" and "RatBane" and "Fire-Gut" and "Polyputaketlon: Extreme Caution" and "RatAway!!!" and "Killerat!" and "Essence of Barbed Wire: Danger!!!" and—he leaned closer to look at this one—"Sugar." There were a couple of mugs, too, and a teapot. White and green and gray powders were scattered on the bench. Some of them had even fallen on the floor.

"You might try to be some help," said Malicia, tapping the walls.

"I don't know how to look for something that doesn't look like the thing I'm looking for," said Keith. "And they keep the poison right next to the sugar! So *many* poisons . . ."

Malicia stood back and brushed her hair out of her eyes.

"This isn't working," she said.

"I suppose there might not *be* a secret passage?" said Maurice. "I know it's a rather daring idea, but perhaps this is just an ordinary shed?"

Even Maurice recoiled a little from the force of the stare Malicia turned on him.

"There *has* to be a secret passage," she said. "Otherwise there's no *point*."

She snapped her fingers. "Of course! We're doing it wrong! *Everyone* knows you never find the secret passage by *looking* for it! It's when you give up and lean against the wall that you inadvertently operate the secret switch!"

Maurice looked at Keith for help. He was a human, after all. He should know how to deal with something like Malicia. But Keith was just wandering around the shed, staring at things.

Malicia leaned against the wall with incredible nonchalance.

There was not a click. A panel in the floor did not slide back.

"Probably the wrong place," she said. "I'll just rest my arm innocently on this coat hook."

A sudden door in the wall completely failed to happen.

"Of course, it'd help if there was an ornate candlestick," said Malicia. "They're always a surefire secret-passage lever. Every adventurer knows that."

"There isn't a candlestick," said Maurice.

"I know. Some people totally fail to have any *idea* of how to design a proper secret passage," said Malicia. She leaned against another piece of wall, which had no effect whatsoever.

"I don't think you'll find it that way," said Keith, who was carefully examining a trap.

"Oh? Won't I?" said Malicia. "Well, at least I'm being *constructive* about things! Where would you look, if you're such an expert?"

"Why is there a rat hole in a rat catcher's shed?" said Keith. "It smells of dead rats and wet dogs and poison. I wouldn't come near this place, if I was a rat."

Malicia glared at him. Then her face wrapped itself in an expression of acute concentration, as if she was trying out several ideas in her head.

"Ye-es," she said. "That usually works, in stories. It's often the stupid person who comes up with the good idea by accident."

She crouched down and peered into the hole.

"There's a sort of little lever," she said. "I'll just give it a little push. . . ."

There was a *clonk* under the floor, part of it swung back, and Keith dropped out of sight.

"Oh, yes," said Malicia. "I thought something like that would probably happen."

♦ ♦ ♦

Mr. Clicky bumped along the tunnel, making a whirring noise.

Young rats had chewed his ears, and his string tail had been chopped off by a trap, and other traps had dented his body, but he had this advantage: Surprise traps couldn't kill Mr. Clicky because he wasn't alive, and he wasn't alive because he was powered by clockwork.

His key whirred around. A stub of candle burned on his back.

The rest of the Number One Trap Squad watched.

"Any minute now . . ." said Darktan.

There was a snap, and a sound best described as *gloink*! The light went out. Then a gear wheel rolled slowly back down the tunnel and fell over in front of Hamnpork.

"I *thought* the soil looked a bit disturbed there," said Darktan in a satisfied voice. He turned around. "Okay, lads! Break out another Mr. Clicky, and I want half a dozen of you with a rope to dig out that trap and drag it out of the way!"

"All this testing the ground is slowing us down, Darktan," said Hamnpork.

"Fine, sir," said Darktan, as the squad hurried past them. "*You* go on ahead. That'd be a good idea, because we've got only one Mr. Clicky left. I hope this town's got a pet shop."*

"I just think we should move faster," said Hamnpork.

"Okay, off you go then, *sir*. Try to shout out where the next trap is before it gets you."

"I *am* the leader, Darktan."

"Yes, sir. I'm sorry. We're all getting a bit tired."

"This is not a good place, Darktan," said Hamnpork wearily. "I've been in some bad *rprptlt* holes, and this is worse than any of them."

---

*The rats had found one in the town of Quir, which is where they'd got the Mr. Clickys. They were on a shelf labeled KITTY TOYS, along with a box of squeaky rubber rats called, with great imagination, Mr. Squeaky. The rats had tried to set off traps by poking them with a rubber rat on the end of a stick, but the squeak when the trap shut upset everyone. No one cared about what happened to a Mr. Clicky.

"That's true, sir. This place is *dead*."

"What's that word Dangerous Beans invented?"

"Evil," said Darktan, watching the squad drag the trap out of the walls of the tunnel.

He could see mangled springs and wheels in the jaws. He added, "I couldn't quite understand what he was going on about, at the time. But now I think I can see what he meant."

He looked back along the tunnel to where a candle flame burned and grabbed a passing rat.

"Peaches and Dangerous Beans are to stay all the way back, understand?" he said. "They're *not* to come any farther."

"Right, sir!" said the rat, and hurried away.

The expedition moved forward cautiously, as the tunnel opened up into a large, old drain. It had a trickle of water in the bottom. There were ancient pipes in the roof of it. Here and there steam hissed from them. Weak light came from a street grating, farther down the drain.

The place smelled of rats. It smelled *freshly* of rats. In fact there was a rat in there, nibbling at a tray of food that had been set on a crumbling brick. It glanced at the Changelings and fled.

"Get after it!" Hamnpork yelled.

"No!" shouted Darktan. A couple of rats,

who'd begun to chase the *keekee*, hesitated.

"That was an *order* I gave!" roared Hamnpork, turning on Darktan. The trap expert made a very brief crouch and said, "Of course. But I think the view of Hamnpork *in possession of all the facts* will be a little different from the view of Hamnpork who just shouted because he saw a rat run away, hmm? Sniff the air!"

Hamnpork's nose wrinkled.

"Poison?"

Darktan nodded.

"Gray Number Two," he said. "Foul stuff. It's best to keep well away."

Hamnpork looked both ways along the pipe. It went on for a long way, and it was just about high enough for a human to crawl along it. Lots of smaller pipes hung near the ceiling.

"It's *warm* here," said Hamnpork.

"Yes, sir. Peaches has been reading the guide-book. Hot springs come up out of the ground here, and they pump the water around to some of the houses."

"Why?"

"To bathe in, sir."

"Hrumph." Hamnpork didn't like that idea. A lot of the young rats were keen on taking baths.

Darktan turned to the squad. "Hamnpork

wants that poison buried and widdled on and a marker on it right *now*!"

Hamnpork heard a metallic sound beside him. He turned and saw that Darktan had drawn, from his web of tools, a long, thin piece of metal.

"What the *krckrck* is that?" he said.

Darktan swished the thing backward and forward.

"I got the stupid-looking kid to make this for me," he said.

And then Hamnpork realized what it was.

"That's a *sword*," he said. "You got the idea out of *Mr. Bunnsy Has an Adventure*?"

"That's right."

"I've never believed that stuff," Hamnpork grumbled. "It's too far-fetched."

"But a spike is a spike," said Darktan calmly. "I think we're close to the other rats. It'd be a good idea if most of us stay here . . . sir."

Hamnpork felt he was being given orders again, but Darktan *was* being polite.

"I suggest that a few of us go on ahead to sniff them out," Darktan went on. "Sardines would be useful, and I'll go, of course—"

"And me," said Hamnpork.

He glared at Darktan, who said, "Of course."

CHAPTER 7

❦

And because of Olly the Snake's trick with the road sign, Mr. Bunnsy did not know that he had lost his way. He wasn't going to Howard the Stoat's tea party. He was heading into the Dark Wood.

—From *Mr. Bunnsy Has an Adventure*

Malicia looked at the open trapdoor as if giving it points out of ten.

"Quite well hidden," she said. "No wonder we didn't see it."

"I'm not hurt much," Keith called up from the darkness.

"Good," said Malicia, still inspecting the trapdoor. "How far down are you?"

"It's some sort of cellar. I'm okay because I landed on some sacks."

"All right, all right, no need to go *on* about it. This wouldn't be an adventure if there weren't some minor hazards," said the girl. "Here's the top of a ladder. Why didn't you use it?"

"I was unable to on account of falling past," said the voice of Keith.

"Shall I carry you down?" said Malicia to Maurice.

"Shall I scratch your eyes out?" said Maurice.

Malicia's brow wrinkled. She always looked annoyed when she didn't understand something.

"Was that sarcasm?" she asked.

"That was a suggestion," said Maurice. "I don't do 'picking up' by strangers. You go down. I'll follow."

"But you haven't got the legs for ladders!"

"Do I make personal remarks about *your* legs?"

Malicia descended into the dark. There was a metallic noise, and then the flare of a match.

"It's full of sacks!" said Malicia.

"I know," came the voice of Keith. "I landed on them. I did say."

"It's grain! And . . . and there's strings and strings of sausages! There's smoked meat! Bins of vegetables! It's full of food! Aargh! Get out of my hair! Get *off*! That *cat* just jumped onto my head!"

Maurice leaped off her and onto some sacks.

"Hah!" said Malicia, rubbing her head. "We were *told* that the rats had got it all. I see it all now. The rat catchers get everywhere, they know all the sewers, all the cellars . . . and to think those thieves get paid out of *our* taxes!"

Maurice looked around the cellar, lit by the flickering lantern in Malicia's hand. There was indeed a lot of food. Nets hanging from the ceiling were indeed stuffed with big, white, heavy cabbages. The aforesaid sausages did indeed loop from beam to beam. There were indeed jars and barrels and sacks and sacks. And indeed they all worried him.

"That's it, then," said Malicia. "What a hiding place! We're going to go right away to the town Watch and report what we've found, and then it's a big bang-up tea with cream buns all around and possibly a medal and then—"

"I'm suspicious," said Maurice.

"Why?"

"Because I'm a suspicious character! I wouldn't trust your rat catchers if they told me the sky was blue. What have they been doing? Pinching the food and then saying, 'It was the rats, honest'? And everyone *believed* them?"

"No, stupid. People have found gnawed bones and empty egg baskets, that sort of thing," said Malicia. "And rat droppings all over the place!"

"I suppose you could scratch the bones, and I

suppose rat catchers could shovel up a lot of rat droppings . . ." Maurice conceded.

"And they're killing all the real rats so that there's more for them!" said Malicia triumphantly. "Very clever!"

"Yeah, and that's a bit puzzling," said Maurice, "because we've met your rat catchers and, frankly, if it was raining meatballs, they wouldn't be able to find a fork."

"I'm thinking about something," said Keith, who had been humming to himself.

"Well, I'm glad *someone* is," Malicia began.

"It's about wire netting," said Keith. "There was wire netting in the shed."

"Is this *important*?"

"Why do rat catchers need rolls of wire netting?"

"How should I know? Cages, maybe? Does it matter?"

"Why would rat catchers put rats in cages? Dead rats don't run away, do they?"

There was silence. Maurice could see that Malicia was not happy about that comment. It was an unnecessary complication. It spoiled the story.

"I may be stupid-looking," Keith added, "but I'm not stupid. I have time to think about things because I don't keep on talking *all the time*. I look at things. I listen. I try to learn. I—"

"I *don't* talk all the time!"

Maurice let them argue and stalked away into the corner of the cellar. Or cellars. They seemed to go on a long way.

He saw something streak across the floor in the shadows and leaped before he could think. His stomach remembered that it had been a long time since the mouse, and it connected itself straight to his legs.

"All right," he said, as the thing squirmed in his paws, "speak up or—"

A small stick hit him very sharply.

"Do you *mind*?" said Sardines, struggling to get up.

"Dere's bno ned to be like dab!" muttered Maurice, trying to lick his smarting nose.

"I've got a *rkrklk* hat on, right?" snapped Sardines. "Do you ever bother to look?"

"All ride, all ride, sorwy. . . . Why're you here?"

Sardines brushed himself off. "Looking for you or the stupid-looking kid," he said. "Hamnpork sent me! We're in trouble now! You just won't believe what we've found!"

"He wants *me*?" said Maurice. "I thought he didn't like me!"

"Well, he said it's nasty and evil so you'd know

what to do, boss," said Sardines, picking up his hat. "Look at that, will you? Your claw went right through it!"

"But I *did* ask you if you could talk, didn't I?" said Maurice.

"Yes, you did, but—"

"I always ask!"

"I know, so—"

"I'm very *definite* about asking, you know!"

"Yes, yes, you've made your point, I believe you," said Sardines. "I only complained about the hat!"

"I'd hate anyone to think I don't ask," said Maurice.

"There's no need to go on and on about it," said Sardines. "Where's the kid?"

"Back there, talking to the girl," said Maurice sulkily.

"What, the mad one?"

"That's her."

"You'd better get them. This is seriously evil. There's a door at the other end of these cellars. I'm amazed you can't smell it from here!"

"I'd just like everyone to be clear that I asked, that's all."

"Boss," said Sardines, "this is *serious*!"

◆ ◆ ◆

Peaches and Dangerous Beans waited for the exploration party. They were with Toxie, another young male rat, who was good at reading and acted as a kind of assistant.

Peaches had also brought *Mr. Bunnsy Has an Adventure*.

"They've been gone a long time," said Toxie.

"Darktan checks every step," said Peaches.

"Something's wrong," said Dangerous Beans. His nose wrinkled.

A rat scurried down the tunnel and pushed frantically past them.

Dangerous Beans sniffed the air.

"Fear," he said.

Three more rats scrambled past, knocking him over.

"What's happening?" asked Peaches, as another rat spun her around in an effort to get past. It squeaked at her and rushed on.

"That was Finest," she said. "Why didn't she say anything?"

"More . . . fear," said Dangerous Beans. "They're . . . scared. Terrified . . ."

Toxie tried to stop the next rat. She bit him and ran on, chittering.

"We must go back," said Peaches urgently.

"What've they found up there? Maybe it's a ferret!"

"Can't be!" said Toxie. "Hamnpork killed a ferret once!"

Three more rats ran past, trailing fear behind them. One of them squealed at Peaches, gibbered madly at Dangerous Beans, and ran on.

"They . . . they've forgotten how to talk," whispered Dangerous Beans.

"Something terrible must have frightened them!" said Peaches, snatching up her notes.

"They've never been that frightened!" said Toxie. "Remember when that dog found us? We were all frightened but we *talked* and we trapped it and Hamnpork saw it off whimpering. . . ."

To her shock, Peaches saw that Dangerous Beans was crying. "They've forgotten how to *talk*."

Half a dozen more rats pushed their way past, screeching. Peaches tried to stop one, but she just squeaked at her and dodged out of the way.

"That was Feedsfour!" she said, turning to Toxie. "I was talking to her only an hour ago! She . . . Toxie?"

Toxie's fur was bristling. His eyes were unfocused. His mouth was open, showing his teeth. He stared at her, or right through her, and then turned and ran.

She turned and put her paws around Danger-ous Beans as the fear swept over them.

◆　◆　◆

There were rats. From wall to wall, floor to ceiling, there were rats. The cages were crammed with them; they clung to the wire in front, and to roofs. The netting strained with the weight. Glistening bodies boiled and tumbled, paws and noses thrusting through the holes. The air was solid with squeaking and rustling and chittering, and it stank.

What was left of Hamnpork's exploration party was clustered in the middle of the room. Most of it had fled by now. If the smells in that room had been sounds, they would have been shouts and screams, thousands of them. They filled the long room with a strange kind of pres-sure. Even Maurice could feel it, as soon as Keith opened the door. It was like a headache outside your head, trying to get in. It banged on the ears.

Maurice was staying a little way behind. You didn't need to be very clever to see that this was a bad situation, and one that might need some running away from at any time.

He saw, between Malicia and Keith's legs, Darktan and Hamnpork and a few other Changelings. They were in the middle of the floor, looking up at the cages.

He was amazed to see that even Hamnpork was trembling. But he was trembling with rage.

"Let them out!" he shouted up to Keith. "Let them all out! Let them all out *now*!"

"*Another* talking rat?" asked Malicia.

"*Let them out!*" Hamnpork screamed.

"All these foul cages . . ." said Malicia, staring.

"I did *say* about the wire netting," said Keith. "Look, you can see where it's been repaired . . . they *gnawed* through *wire* to escape!"

"I said *let them out!*" screamed Hamnpork. "Let them out or I will *kill* you! Evil! Evil! Evil!"

"But they're just rats—" said Malicia.

Hamnpork leaped and landed on the girl's waist. He swarmed up toward her neck. She froze. He hissed: "There are rats *eating one another* in there! I will *gnaw* you, you evil—"

Keith's hand grasped him firmly around the waist and pulled him off her neck.

Screeching, hair bristling, Hamnpork sank his teeth into Keith's finger.

Malicia gasped. Even Maurice winced.

Hamnpork drew his head back, blood dripping from his muzzle, and blinked in horror.

Tears welled up in Keith's eyes. Very carefully he put Hamnpork down on the floor.

"It's the smell," he said quietly. "It upsets them."

"I . . . I thought you said they were tame!" said Malicia, able to speak at last. She picked up a lump of wood that was leaning against the cages.

Keith knocked it out of her hand.

"Never, ever threaten one of us!"

"He *attacked* you!"

"Look around! This is not a story! This is real! Do you understand? They're frightened out of their minds!"

"How dare you talk to me like that!" Malicia shouted.

"I *rrkrkrk* will!"

"One of *us*, eh? Was that a rat swear word? Do you even swear in Rat, rat boy?"

Just like cats, Maurice thought. You stand face to face and scream at each other.

His ears swiveled as he heard another sound, in the distance. Someone was coming down the ladder.

Maurice knew from experience that this was no time to talk to humans. They always said things like "What?" and "That's not right!" or "Where?"

"Get out of here *right now*," he said as he ran past Darktan. "Don't get human about it, just run!"

And that was quite enough heroism, he decided.

It didn't pay to let other people actually slow you down.

There was a rusty old drain set into the wall. He skidded on the slimy floor as he changed direction, and there, *yes*, was a Maurice-sized hole where a bar had rusted clean away.

Paws scrabbling for speed, he darted through the hole just as the rat catchers entered the room of cages.

Then, safe in the darkness, he turned around and peered out.

Time to check: Was Maurice safe? All legs present? Tail? Yes. Good.

He could see Darktan tugging at Hamnpork, who seemed to have frozen on the spot, the others scuttling toward another drain in the opposite wall. They moved unsteadily. That's what happens when you let yourself go, Maurice thought. They think they're educated, but in a tight corner a rat is just a rat.

Now *me*, I'm different. Brain functioning perfectly at all times. Always on the lookout. On the case and sniffing bottom.

The caged rats were making a din. Keith and the storytelling girl were watching the rat catchers in amazement. The rat catchers weren't unamazed either.

On the floor Darktan gave up trying to get Hamnpork to move. He drew his sword, looked up at the humans, hesitated, and then ran for the drain.

Yes, let them sort it out. They're all human, Maurice thought. They've got big brains, they can talk, it should be no problem at all.

Hah! Tell them a story, storytelling girl!

◆ ◆ ◆

Rat Catcher 1 stared at Malicia and Keith.

"What're you doing here, miss?" he said, his voice creaking with suspicion.

"Playing mummies and daddies?" said Rat Catcher 2 cheerfully.

"You broke into our shed," said Rat Catcher 1. "That's called 'breaking in,' that is!"

"You've been stealing, yes, *stealing* food and blaming it on rats!" snapped Malicia. "And why have you got all these rats caged up in here? And what about the aglets, eh? Surprised, eh? Didn't think anyone would notice them, eh?"

"Aglets?" said Rat Catcher 1, his brow wrinkling.

"The little bits on the end of bootlaces," mumbled Keith.

Rat Catcher 1 spun around. "You bloody idiot, Bill! I *said* we had enough real ones! I *told* you someone would notice! Didn't I tell you some-one would notice? Someone *noticed*!"

"Yes, don't think you've got away with any-thing!" said Malicia. Her eyes were gleaming. "I know you're only the humorous thugs. One big fat one, one thin one—it's obvious! So who's the big boss?"

Rat Catcher 1's eyes glazed slightly, as they often did when Malicia talked at people. He waved a fat finger at her.

"You know what your father's been and gone and done just now?" he asked.

"Hah! Humorous thug talk!" said Malicia tri-umphantly. "Do go on!"

"He's been and gone and sent off for the rat piper!" said Rat Catcher 2. "He costs a *fortune*! Three hundred dollars a town, and if you don't pay up, he gets really *mean*!"

Oh dear, thought Maurice. Someone's been and gone and sent for the *real* one . . . three hun-dred *dollars*. *Three* hundred dollars? Three *hundred* dollars? And we only charged thirty!

"It's you, isn't it?" said Rat Catcher 1, waving his finger at Keith. "The stupid-looking kid! You turn up, and suddenly there's all these new rats around! There's something I don't like about you! You and your funny-looking cat! If I see that funny-looking cat again, it's going to have *mittens*!"

In the darkness of the drain Maurice shrank back.

"Hur, hur, hur," said Rat Catcher 2. He probably *studied* to get a thug laugh like that, Maurice thought.

"And we don't have a boss," said Rat Catcher 1.

"Yeah, we're our own bosses," said Rat Catcher 2.

And then the story went wrong.

"And you, miss," said Rat Catcher 1, turning to Malicia, "are too mouthy by half."

He swung his fist, lifting her off her feet and slamming her against the rat cages. The rats went mad, and the cages boiled with frantic activity as she slumped to the ground.

The rat catcher turned to Keith.

"You going to try anything, kid?" he said. "You going to try anything? She was a girl, so I was nice and kind, but *you* I'll put in one of the cages—"

"Yeah, and they ain't been fed today!" said a delighted Rat Catcher 2.

Go on, kid! Maurice thought. Do *something*! But Keith just stood there, staring at the man.

Rat Catcher 1 looked him up and down, scornfully.

"What's that you've got there, boy? A pipe? Give it here!"

The pipe was grabbed from Keith's belt, and he was pushed onto the floor.

"A pennywhistle? Think you're the rat piper, do you?" Rat Catcher 1 snapped the pipe in two and tossed the bits aside. "Y'know, they say that over in Porkrhinz the rat piper led all the kids out of the town. Now *there* was a man with the right idea!"

Keith looked up. His eyes narrowed. He got to his feet.

Here it comes, thought Maurice. He's going to leap forward with superhuman strength because he's so angry and they're going to wish they'd never been born. . . .

Keith leaped forward with ordinary human strength, landed one punch on Rat Catcher 1, and was smacked to the floor again by a big, brutal, sledgehammer blow.

All right, all right, he got knocked down, thought Maurice, as Keith struggled for breath, *but* he's going to get up again.

There was a shrill scream, and Maurice thought: Aha!

But the scream hadn't come from the wheezing Keith. A gray figure had launched itself from the top of the rat cages right at the rat catcher's face. It landed teeth first, and blood spurted on the rat catcher's nose.

Aha! thought Maurice again. It's Hamnpork to the rescue! What? *Mrillp!* I'm thinking like the girl! I keep thinking it's a story!

The rat catcher grabbed at the rat and held him out at arm's length by his tail. Hamnpork twisted and turned, squealing with rage.

His captor dabbed at his nose with his spare hand and stared at Hamnpork as he struggled.

"He's a bit of a fighter," said Rat Catcher 2. "How'd he get out?"

"Not one of ours," said Rat Catcher 1. "He's a red."

"Red? What's red about him?"

"A red rat's a kind of gray rat, as you would very well know if you were an hexperienced Guild member like me," said the rat catcher. "They ain't local. You get 'em down on the plains. Funny to find one up here. Very funny. Greasy old devil, too. But game as anything."

"Your nose is all runny."

"Yeah. I know. I've had more rat bites than you've had hot dinners. Don't feel 'em anymore," said Rat Catcher 1, in a voice that suggested that the spinning, screeching Hamnpork was a lot more interesting than his colleague.

"I only have cold sausage for dinner."

"There you are then. What a little fighter you are, to be sure. Real little devil, aren't you . . . plucky as anything."

"Kind of you to say so."

"I was talking to the *rat*, mister." The rat catcher prodded Keith with his boot. "Go and tie up these two somewhere, okay? We'll put them in one of the other cellars for now. One with a proper door. And a proper lock. And no handy little trapdoors. And you give me the key."

"She's the mayor's daughter," said Rat Catcher 2. "Mayors can get really upset about daughters."

"Then he'll do what he's told, right?"

"You gonna give that rat a good squeezing?"

"What, a fighter like this one? Are you joking? It's thinking like that that'll keep you a rat catcher's assistant your whole life. I've got a much better idea. How many's in the special cage?"

Maurice watched Rat Catcher 2 go and examine one of the other cages on the far wall.

"Only two rats left. They've eaten the other four," he reported. "Just skin left. Very neat."

"Ah, so they'll be full o' vim and vinegar. Well,

we'll see what *they* do to him, shall we?"

Maurice heard a little wire door open and shut.

Hamnpork was seeing red. It filled his vision. He'd been angry for months, down inside, angry at humans, angry at the poisons and the traps, angry at the way younger rats weren't showing respect, angry that the world was changing so fast, angry that he was growing old. . . . And now the smells of terror and hunger and violence met the anger coming the other way and they mingled and flowed through Hamnpork in a great red river of rage. He was a cornered rat. But he was a cornered rat who could think. He'd always been a vicious fighter, long before there was all this thinking, and he was still very strong. A couple of dumb, swanking young keekees with no tactics and no experience of down-and-dirty cellar fighting and no fancy footwork and no thoughts were simply not a contest. A tumble, a twist, and two bites were all it took. . . .

The caged rats across the room leaped back from the netting. Even they could feel the fury.

"Now *there's* a clever boy," said Rat Catcher 1 admiringly when it was all over. "I've got a use for *you*, my lad."

"Not the pit?" said Rat Catcher 2.

"Yes, the pit."

"Tonight?"

"Yeah, 'cos Fancy Arthur is putting in his Jacko on a bet to kill a hundred rats in less than a quarter of an hour."

"I bet he can, too. Jacko's a good terrier. He did ninety a few months ago, and Fancy Arthur's been training him up. Should be a good show."

"You'd bet on Jacko doing it, would you?" said Rat Catcher 1.

"Sure. Everyone will be."

"Even with our little friend here among the rats?" said Rat Catcher 1. "Full of lovely spite and bite and boilin' bile?"

"Well, er . . ."

"Yeah, right." Rat Catcher 1 grinned.

"I don't like leaving those kids here, though."

"It's 'them kids,' not 'those kids.' Get it right. How many times have I told you? Rule Twenty-seven of the Guild: Sound stupid. People get suspicious of rat catchers who talk too good."

"Sorry."

"Talk thick, be clever. That's the way to do it," said Rat Catcher 1.

"Sorry, I forgot."

"You tend to do it the other way around."

"Sorry. Them kids. It's cruel, tying people up. And they're only kids, after all."

"So?"

"So it'd be a lot easier to take 'em down the tunnel to the river and hit 'em on the head and throw 'em in. They'll be miles downriver before anyone fishes 'em out, and they prob'ly won't even be recognizable by the time the fish have finished with 'em."

Maurice heard a pause in the conversation. Then Rat Catcher 1 said: "I didn't know you were such a kindhearted soul, Bill."

"Right, and, sorry, *an'* I've got an idea about gettin' rid of the rat piper when he comes, too—"

The next voice came from everywhere. It sounded like a rushing wind and, in the heart of the wind, the groan of something in agony. It filled the air.

NO! We can use the piper!

"No, we can use the piper," said Rat Catcher 1.

"That's right," said Rat Catcher 2. "I was just thinking the same thing. Er . . . how can we use the piper?"

Once again, Maurice heard a sound like wind blowing through a cave, but it seemed to be in his head rather than in the air.

Isn't it OBVIOUS?

"Isn't it obvious?" said Rat Catcher 1.

"Yeah, obvious," muttered Rat Catcher 2. "Obviously it's obvious. Er . . ."

Maurice watched the rat catcher open several of the cages, grab rats, and drop them into a sack. He saw Hamnpork tipped into one, too.

And then the rat catchers had gone, dragging the other humans with them, and Maurice wondered: Where, in this maze of cellars, is a Maurice-sized hole?

Cats can't see in the dark. What they *can* do is see by very little light.

A tiny scrap of moonlight was filtering into the space behind him. It was coming through a tiny hole in the ceiling, barely big enough for a mouse and certainly not big enough for a Maurice even if he could reach it.

It illuminated another cellar. By the looks of it the rat catchers used this one too; there were a few barrels stacked in one corner, and piles of broken rat cages.

Maurice prowled around it, looking for another way out. There were doors, but they had handles, and even his mighty brain couldn't figure out the mystery of doorknobs.

There was another drain grating in a wall. He squeezed through it.

Another cellar. And more boxes and sacks. At

least it was dry, though.

A voice behind him said, *What kind of thing are you?*

He spun around. All he could make out were boxes and sacks. The air still stank of rats, and there was a continuous rustling and the occasional faint squeak, but the place was a little piece of heaven compared to the hell of the cage room.

The voice *had* come from behind him, hadn't it? He must have *heard* it, mustn't he? Because it seemed to him that he just had something like the memory of hearing a voice, something that had arrived in his head without bothering to go through his ragged ears. It had been the same with the rat catchers. They'd talked as if they'd heard a voice and thought it was their own thoughts. The voice hadn't *really* been there, had it?

I can't see you, said the memory. *I don't know what you are.*

It was not a good voice for a memory to have. It was all hisses, and it slid into the mind like a knife.

Come closer.

Maurice's paws twitched. The muscles in his legs started to push him forward. He extended his claws and got control of himself.

Someone was hiding amongst the boxes, he

thought. And it would probably not be a good idea to say anything. People could get funny about talking cats. You couldn't rely on everyone being as mad as the storytelling girl.

Come CLOSER.

The voice seemed to pull at him. He'd have to say *something*.

"I'm happy where I am, thank you," said Maurice.

Then will you share our PAIN?

The last word hurt. But it did not, and this was surprising, hurt a lot. The voice had sounded sharp and loud and dramatic, as if the owner was keen to see Maurice rolling in agony. Instead, it gave him a very brief headache.

When the voice arrived again, it sounded very suspicious.

What kind of creature are you? Your mind is WRONG.

"I prefer amazing," said Maurice. "Anyway, who are you, asking me questions in the dark?"

All he could smell was rat.

He heard a faint sound off to his left and just made out the shape of a very large rat, creeping toward him.

Another sound made him turn. Another rat was coming from the other direction. He could only just see it in the gloom.

A rustle ahead of him suggested that there was a rat right in front, slipping quietly through the dark.

Here come my eyes . . . WHAT? CAT! CAT! KILL!

CHAPTER 8

❦

M_{r.} Bunnsy realized that he was a fat rabbit in the Dark Wood and wished he wasn't a rabbit or, at least, not a fat one. But Ratty Rupert was on the way. Little did he know what was waiting for *him*.

—From *Mr. Bunnsy Has an Adventure*

When the three rats leaped, they were already too late. There was just a Maurice-shaped hole in the air. Maurice was across the room and scrambling up some boxes.

There was squeaking below him. He jumped onto another box and saw a place in the wall where some of the rotten bricks had fallen out. He aimed for it, scrabbled on thin air as bricks moved under him, and pushed himself into the unknown.

It was another cellar. And it was full of water. In fact, what it was full of was not *exactly* water. It was what water eventually becomes when rat cages drain into it, and gutters up above drain into it, and it has had a chance to sit and bubble gently to itself for a year or so. To call it "mud" would be an insult to perfectly respectable swamps all over the world.

Maurice landed in it. It went *gloop*.

He cat-paddled furiously through the thick stuff, trying not to breathe, and dragged himself out on what felt like a pile of rubble on the other side of the room. A fallen rafter, slimy with mold, led up to more tangled, fire-blackened wood in the ceiling.

He could still hear the dreadful voice in his head, but it was muffled. It was trying to give him orders. Trying to give a *cat* orders? It was easier to nail jelly to a wall. What did it think he was, a dog?

Stinking mud oozed off him. Even his ears were full of mud. He went to lick himself clean, and then stopped. It was a perfectly normal cat reaction, licking yourself clean. But licking *this* off would probably kill him—

There was a movement in the dark. He could just make out some big rat shapes pouring through the hole. There were a couple of splashes. Some of the shapes were creeping along the walls.

Ah, said the voice. ***You see them? Watch them come for you, CAT!***

Maurice stopped himself from running. This was no time to listen to his inner cat. His inner cat had got him out of the room, but his inner cat was stupid. It wanted him to attack things small enough and run away from everything else. But no cat could tackle a bunch of rats this size.

He froze and tried to keep an eye on the advancing rats. They were heading directly for him.

Hold on . . . hold on . . .

The voice had said: ***You can see them. . . .***

How did it *know*?

Maurice tried to think loudly: Can . . . You . . . Read . . . My . . . Mind?

Nothing happened.

Maurice had a burst of inspiration. He shut his eyes.

Open them! came the immediate command, and his eyelids trembled.

Shan't, thought Maurice. You *can't* hear my thoughts! he thought. You only use my eyes and ears! You're just *guessing* what I'm thinking.

There was no reply. Maurice didn't wait. He leaped. The sloping beam was where he remembered it. He clawed his way up and hung on. At

160

least all they could do was follow him up. With any luck he could use his claws. . . .

The rats got closer. Now they were sniffing for him down below, and he imagined quivering noses in the darkness.

One started to climb the beam, still sniffing. It must have been within inches of Maurice's tail when it turned around and went back down again.

He heard them reach the top of the rubble. There was more bewildered sniffing and then, in the dark, the sound of the rats paddling through the mud.

Maurice wrinkled his mud-caked forehead in amazement. Rats who couldn't smell a cat? And then he realized. He didn't smell of cat, he stank of mud, he *felt* like mud, in a room full of stinking mud.

He sat, still as stone, until through mud-caked ears he heard claws head back to the hole in the wall.

Then, without opening his eyes, and with his heart beating hard, he crept carefully back down to the rubble and found that it had piled up against a rotten wooden door. What must have been a piece of plank, soggy as a sponge, fell out as he touched it.

A feeling of openness suggested that there was another cellar beyond. It stank of rot and burned wood.

Would the . . . voice know where he was if he opened his eyes now? Didn't one cellar look like another?

Perhaps *this* room was full of rats, too.

His eyes sprang open. There were no rats, but there *was* another rusted drain cover that opened into a tunnel just big enough for him to walk through. He could see a faint light.

So this is the rat world, he thought, as he tried to scrape the mud off himself. Dark and muddy and stinky and full of weird voices. I'm a cat. Sunlight and fresh air, that's my style. All I need now is a hole into the outside world and they won't see me for dust, or at least for bits of dried mud.

A voice in his head, which wasn't the mysterious voice but a voice just like his own, said: But what about the stupid-looking kid and the rest of them? You ought to help them!

And Maurice thought: Where did *you* come from? I'll tell you what, *you* help them and I'll go somewhere warm, how about that?

The light at the end of the tunnel grew brighter. It still wasn't anything like daylight, or even moonlight, but anything was better than this gloom.

At least, nearly anything.

He pushed his head out of the pipe into a much larger one, made of bricks that were slimy with strange underground nastiness, and into the circle of candlelight.

"It's . . . Maurice?" said Peaches, staring at the mud dripping off his matted fur.

"Smells better than he usually does, then," said Darktan, grinning in what Maurice considered an unfriendly way.

"Oh, ha ha," said Maurice, weakly. He wasn't in the mood for repartee.

"Ah, I knew you wouldn't let us down, old friend," said Dangerous Beans. "I have always said that we can depend on Maurice, at least." He sighed deeply.

"Yes," said Darktan, giving Maurice a much more knowing look. "Depend on him to do what, though?"

"Oh," said Maurice. "Er. Good. I've found you all, then."

"Yes," said Darktan, in what Maurice thought was a nasty tone of voice. "Amazing, isn't it. I expect you've been looking for a long time, too. I saw you rush off to look for us."

"Can you help us?" said Dangerous Beans. "We need a plan."

"Ah, right," said Maurice. "I suggest we go upward at every opportun—"

"To rescue Hamnpork," said Darktan. "We don't leave our people behind."

"*We* don't?" said Maurice.

"We *don't*," said Darktan.

"And then there's the kid," said Peaches. "Sardines says he's tied up with the female kid in one of the cellars."

"Oh, well, you know, *humans*," said Maurice, wrinkling his face. "Humans and humans, you know, it's a human kind of thing. I don't think we should meddle, could be misunderstood. I know about humans, they'll sort it out—"

"I don't care a ferret's *shrlt* for humans!" snapped Darktan. "But those rat catchers took Hamnpork off in a cage! You saw that room, cat! You saw the rats crammed in cages! It's the *rat catchers* who are stealing the food! Sardines says there's sacks and sacks of food! And there's something else . . ."

"A voice," said Maurice before he could stop himself.

Darktan looked up, wild-eyed.

"*You* heard it?" he said. "I thought it was just us!"

"The rat catchers can hear it too," said Maurice. "Only they think it's their own thoughts."

"It frightened the others," mumbled Dangerous Beans. "They just . . . *stopped* thinking."

He looked absolutely dejected. Open beside him, grubby with dirt and paw marks, was *Mr. Bunnsy Has an Adventure*.

"Even Toxie ran off," he went on. "And he knows how to write! How can that happen?"

"It seemed to affect some of us more than others," said Darktan in a more matter-of-fact voice. "I've sent some of the more sensible ones out to try and round up the rest, but it's going to be a long job. They were just running blindly. We've got to get Hamnpork. He's the leader. We're rats, after all. A Clan. Rats will follow the leader."

"But he's a bit old, and you're the tough one, and he's not exactly the brains of the outfit—" Maurice began.

"They took him away!" said Darktan. "They're rat catchers! He's one of us! Are you going to help or not?"

Maurice thought he heard a scrabbling noise at the other end of his pipe. He couldn't turn

165

around to check, and he suddenly felt very exposed.

"Yeah, help you, yeah, yeah," he said hurriedly.

"Ahem. Do you really mean that, Maurice?" said Peaches.

"Yeah, yeah, right," said Maurice. He crawled out of the pipe and looked back along it. There was no sign of any rats.

"Sardines is following the rat catchers," said Darktan, "so we'll find out where they're taking him—"

"I've got a bad feeling that I already know," said Maurice.

"How?" snapped Peaches.

"I'm a cat, right?" said Maurice. "Cats hang around places. We see things. A lot of places don't mind cats wandering in, right, because we keep down the vermi—we keep the, er—"

"All right, all right, we know you don't eat anyone who can talk, you keep *telling* us," said Peaches. "Get on with it!"

"I was in a place once. It was a barn. I was up in the hayloft, where you can always find a, er—"

Peaches rolled her eyes. "Yes, yes, *go on!*"

"Well, anyway, all these men came in, and I couldn't get away because they had lots of dogs, and they shut the barn doors and, er, they put up this kind of, kind of big round wooden wall in the middle of the floor, and there were some men with boxes of rats, and they tipped rats into the ring, and then, and then they put some dogs in, too. Terriers," he added, trying to avoid their expressions.

"The rats fought the dogs?" said Darktan.

"Well, I suppose they *could* have done that," said Maurice. "They mostly ran around and around. It's called rat coursing. Rat catchers bring the rats along, of course. Alive. That's what's happening to Hamnpork."

"Rat coursing . . ." said Darktan. "How is it we've never heard of this?"

Maurice blinked at him. For clever creatures, the rats could be amazingly stupid at times.

"Why would you hear about it?" he said.

"Surely one of the rats who—"

"You don't seem to understand," said Maurice. "The rats that go into the pit don't come out. At least, not breathing."

There was silence.

"Can't they jump out?" asked Peaches in a little voice.

"Too high," said Maurice.

"Why don't they fight the dogs?" asked Darktan.

Really, really stupid, Maurice thought.

"Because they're *rats*, Darktan," said Maurice. "Lots of rats. All stinking of one another's fear and panic. You *know* how it happens."

"I bit a dog on the nose once!" said Darktan.

"Right, right," said Maurice, soothingly. "One rat can think and be brave, right. But a bunch of rats is a mob. A bunch of rats is just a big animal with lots of legs and no brain."

"That's not true!" said Peaches. "Together we are strong!"

"Exactly *how* high?" asked Darktan, who was staring at the candlelight as if seeing pictures in it.

"What?" said Peaches and Maurice together.

"The wall . . . how high, exactly?"

"Huh? I don't know! High! Humans were leaning their elbows on it! Does it matter? It's far too high for a rat to jump, I know that."

"Everything we've done, we've done because we've stuck together—" Peaches began.

"We'll rescue Hamnpork together, then," said Darktan. "We'll—"

He spun around at the sound of a rat coming along the pipe, then wrinkled his nose.

"It's Sardines," he said. "And . . . let's see, smells female, young, nervous . . . Nourishing?"

The youngest member of the Trap Disposal Squad was trailing after Sardines. She was wet and dejected.

"You look like a drowned rat, miss," said Darktan.

"Fell in a broken drain, sir," said Nourishing.

"Good to see you, anyway. What's happening, Sardines?"

The dancing rat did a few nervous steps. "I've been climbing up more drainpipes and along more clotheslines than is good for me," he said. "And don't ask me about *krrkk* cats, boss—I'd like to see every last one of 'em dead. Savin' yer honor's presence, o'course," Sardines added, eyeing Maurice nervously.

"And?" said Peaches.

"They've gone to some kind of stable right on the edge of the town," said Sardines. "Smells *bad*. Lots of dogs around. Men, too."

"Rat pit," said Maurice. "I told you. They've been breeding rats for the rat pit!"

"Right," said Darktan. "We're going to get Hamnpork out of there. Sardines, you will show me the way. We'll try to pick up anyone on the way who looks halfway sensible. The rest of you should try to find the kid."

"Why are *you* giving orders?" said Peaches.

"Because someone has to," said Darktan. "Hamnpork might be a bit scabby and set in his ways, but he's the leader and everyone smells that and we need him. Any questions? Right."

"Can I come, sir?" asked Nourishing.

"She's helping me carry my string, boss," Sardines explained. Both he and the younger rat were carrying bundles of it.

"You need all that?" asked Darktan.

"You should never say no to a piece of string, boss," said Sardines earnestly. "It's amazing, some of the stuff I've been finding—"

"All right, so long as she's useful for *something*," said Darktan. "She'd better be able to keep up. Let's go!"

And then there were just Dangerous Beans, Peaches, and Maurice.

Dangerous Beans sighed.

"One rat can be brave, but a bunch of rats is just a mob?" he said. "Are you right, Maurice?"

"No, I was . . . look, there was *something* back there," said Maurice. "It's in a cellar. I don't know what it is. It's the voice that gets into people's heads!"

"Not everyone's," said Peaches. "It didn't frighten you, did it? Or us. Or Darktan. It made Hamnpork very angry. Why?"

Maurice blinked. He could hear the voice in his head again. It was very faint, and it certainly wasn't his own thoughts, and it said, ***I will find a way in, CAT!***

"Did you hear that?" he said.

"I didn't hear anything," said Peaches.

Perhaps you have to be close, Maurice thought. Perhaps, if you've been close, it knows where your head lives.

He'd never seen a rat so miserable as Dangerous Beans. The little rat was huddled by the candle, staring unseeing at *Mr. Bunnsy Has an Adventure*.

"I hoped it would be better than this," said Dangerous Beans. "But it turns out we're just . . . rats. As soon as there's trouble, we're nothing but . . . rats."

It was very unusual for Maurice to feel sympathetic to anyone who wasn't Maurice. In a cat, such sympathy is a major character flaw. I must be ill, he thought.

"If it's any help, I'm just a cat," he said.

"Oh, but you are not. You are kind, and deep down, I sense that you have a generous nature," said Dangerous Beans.

Maurice tried not to look at Peaches. Oh boy, he thought.

"At least you ask people before you eat them," said Peaches.

You'd better tell them, said Maurice's thoughts. Go on, tell them. You'll feel better.

Maurice tried to tell his thoughts to shut up. What a time to get a conscience! What good was a cat with a conscience? A cat with a conscience was a . . . a hamster, or something.

"Um, I've been meaning to talk to you about that," he muttered.

Go on, tell them, said his shiny new conscience. Get it out in the open.

"Yes?" said Peaches.

Maurice squirmed.

"Well, you know I *do* always check my food these days. . . ."

"Yes, and it does you great credit," said Dangerous Beans.

Now Maurice felt even worse.

"Well, you know how we've always wondered how come I got Changed even though I never ate any of that magical stuff on the dump."

"Yes," said Peaches. "That has always puzzled me."

Maurice shifted uneasily.

"Well, you know . . . er . . . did you ever know a rat, quite big, one ear missing, bit of white fur on one side, couldn't run too fast 'cos of a bad leg?"

"That sounds like Additives," said Peaches.

"Oh, yes," said Dangerous Beans. "He disappeared before we met you, Maurice. A good rat. Had a bit of a speech . . . difficulty."

"Speech difficulty," said Maurice gloomily.

"He stammered," said Peaches, giving Maurice a long, cool stare. "Couldn't get his words out very easily."

"Not very easily," said Maurice, his voice now quite hollow.

"But I'm sure you never met him, Maurice," said Dangerous Beans. "I miss him. He was a wonderful rat once you got him talking."

"Ahem. *Did* you meet him, Maurice?" said Peaches, her stare nailing him to the wall.

Maurice's face moved. It tried various expressions one after another. Then he said, *"All right! I ate him, okay? All of him! Except for the tail and the green wobbly bit and that nasty purple lump, no one knows what it is! I was just a cat! I hadn't learned to think yet! I didn't know! I was hungry! Cats eat rats, that's how it goes! It wasn't my fault! And he'd been eating the magic stuff and I ate him, so then I got Changed too! Know how that feels, seeing the green wobbly bit like that? It doesn't feel good! Sometimes on dark nights I think I can hear him talking down there! All right? Satisfied? I didn't know he was*

173

anyone! I didn't know I was anyone! I ate him! He'd been eating the stuff on the dump and I ate him, so that's how I got Changed! I admit it! I ate him! It wasn't my faauulltt!"

And then there was silence. After a while Peaches said, "Yes, but that was a long time ago, wasn't it?"

"What? You mean have I eaten anyone lately? No!"

"Are you sorry for what you did?" asked Dangerous Beans.

"Sorry? What do *you* think? Sometimes I have nightmares where I burp and he—"

"Then that's probably all right," said the little rat.

"All right?" said Maurice. "How can it be all right? And you know the worst part? I'm a cat! Cats don't go round feeling *sorry*! Or guilty! We never *regret* anything! Do you know what it feels like, saying, 'Hello food, can you talk?' That's not how a cat is supposed to behave!"

"We don't act how rats are supposed to behave," said Dangerous Beans. And then his face fell again. "Up until now." He sighed.

"Everyone was frightened," said Peaches. "Fear spreads."

"I hoped we could be more than rats," said Dangerous Beans. "I thought we could be more than things that squeak and widdle, whatever Hamnpork says. And now . . . where is everyone?"

"Shall I read to you from *Mr. Bunnsy*?" said Peaches, her voice full of concern. "You know that always cheers you up when you're in one of your . . . dark times."

There was a nod from Dangerous Beans.

Peaches pulled the huge Book toward her and began to read.

"'One day Mr. Bunnsy and his friend Ratty Rupert the Rat went to see Old Man Donkey, who lived by the river—'"

"Read the bit when they talk to the humans," said Dangerous Beans.

Peaches obediently turned a page. "'"Hello, Ratty Rupert," said Farmer Fred. "What a lovely day it is, to be sure—"'"

This is mad, thought Maurice as he listened to a story about wild woods and fresh bubbling streams, being read to one rat by another rat while they sat beside a drain along which ran something that certainly wasn't fresh. Anything but fresh. To be fair, though, it was bubbling a bit, or at least glooping.

Everything's going down the drain, and they have this little picture in their heads about how nice things could be. . . .

Look at those little pink sad eyes, said Maurice's own thoughts in Maurice's own head. Look at those little wobbly wrinkly noses. If you ran out on them and left them here, how could you look those little wobbly noses in the face again?

"I wouldn't *have* to," said Maurice, out loud. "That's the point!"

"What?" said Peaches, looking up from the Book.

"Oh, nothing." Maurice paused. There was nothing he could do about it. It went against everything a cat stood for. This is what thinking does for you, he thought. It gets you into trouble. Even when you know other people can think for themselves, you start thinking for them *too*.

Of course, humans were useful. They could open doors and provide fish. He groaned.

"We'd better see what's happened to the kid," he said.

◆ ◆ ◆

It was completely black in this cellar. All there were, apart from the occasional drip of water, were voices.

"So," said the voice of Malicia, "let's go over it again, shall we? You don't have a knife of any kind?"

176

"That's right," said Keith.

"Or some handy matches that could burn through the rope?"

"No."

"And no sharp edge near you that you could rub the rope on?"

"No."

"And you can't sort of pull your legs through your arms so that you can get your hands in front of you?"

"No."

"And you don't have any secret powers?"

"No."

"Are you sure? The moment I saw you, I thought: He's got some amazing power that will probably manifest itself when he's in dire trouble. I thought: No one could really be as useless as that unless it was a disguise."

"No. I'm sure. Look, I'm just a normal person. Yes, all right, I was abandoned as a baby. I don't know why. It was something that happened. They say it happens quite a lot. It doesn't make you special. And I don't have any secret markings as if I was some kind of sheep, and I don't think I'm a hero in disguise, and I don't have some kind of amazing talent that I'm aware of. Okay, I'm good at playing quite a few musical instruments. I practice a lot. But I'm the kind of person heroes aren't. I get by and I get along. I do my best. Understand?"

"Oh."

"You should have found someone else."

"In fact you can't be any help at all?"

"No."

There was silence for a while, and then Malicia said, "You know, in many ways I don't think this adventure has been properly organized."

"Oh, really?" said Keith.

"This is *not* how people should be tied up."

"Malicia, do you understand? This isn't a story," said Keith, as patiently as he could. "That's what I'm trying to *tell* you. Real life isn't a story. There isn't some kind of . . . of magic that keeps you safe and makes crooks look the other way and not hit you too hard and tie you up next to a handy knife and not kill you. Do you understand?"

There was some more dark silence.

"My granny and my great-aunt were very famous storytellers, you know," said Malicia eventually, in a strained little voice. "Agonista and Eviscera Grim."

"You said," said Keith.

"My mother would have been a good story-teller, too, but my father doesn't like stories.

That's why I've changed my name to Grim for professional purposes."

"Really . . ."

"I used to get beaten when I was small for telling stories," Malicia went on.

"Beaten?" said Keith.

"All right, then, smacked," said Malicia. "On the leg. But it *did* hurt. My father says you can't run a city on stories. He says you have to be practical."

"Oh."

"Aren't you interested in *anything* except music? He broke your pipe!"

"I expect I'll buy another one."

The calm voice infuriated Malicia.

"Well, I'll *tell* you something," she said. "If you don't turn your life into a story, you just become a part of someone *else's* story."

"And what if your story doesn't work?"

"You keep changing it until you find one that does."

"Sounds silly."

"Huh, look at you. You're just a face in someone else's background. *You* let a cat make all the decisions."

"That's because Maurice is—"

A voice said, "Would you like us to go away

until you've stopped being human?"

"Maurice?" said Keith. "Is that you? Where *are* you?"

"I'm in a drain, and believe me, this has not been a good night. Do you know how many old cellars there are here? Good job you two kept arguing," said the voice of Maurice, in the blackness. "Peaches is bringing a candle in. It's too dark even for me to see you."

"Who's Peaches?" whispered Malicia.

"She's another Changeling. A thinking rat," said Keith.

"Like Anchovies?"

"Like Sardines, yes."

"Aha. See?" hissed Malicia. "A story. I am smug, I gloat. The plucky rats rescue our heroes, probably by gnawing through the ropes."

"Oh, we're back in *your* story, are we?" said Keith. "And what am I in your story?"

"I *know* it's not going to be the romantic interest," said Malicia. "And you're not funny enough for comic relief. I don't know. Probably just . . . someone. You know, like 'man in street,' something like that."

There were faint sounds in the darkness.

"What are they doing now?" she whispered.

"Trying to light their candle, I think."

"Rats play with fire?" Malicia hissed.

"They don't play. Dangerous Beans thinks lights and shadows are very important. They always have a candle alight somewhere in their tunnels, wherever they—"

"Dangerous Beans? What sort of name is that?"

"Shssh! They just learned words off old food tins and signs and things! They didn't know what the words meant—they just chose them because they liked the sounds!"

"Yes, but . . . Dangerous Beans? It sounds as if he makes you—"

"It's his name. Don't make fun of it!"

"Sorry, I'm sure," said Malicia.

The match flared. The candle flame grew.

Malicia looked down at two rats. One was . . . well, just a small rat, although sleeker than most of the ones she'd seen. In fact most of the ones she'd seen had been dead, but even the living ones had always been . . . twitchy, nervy, sniffing the air all the time. This one just . . . watched. It stared right at her.

The other rat was white, and even smaller. It was also watching her, although peering was a better word. It had pink eyes. Malicia had never been very interested in other people's feelings, since she'd always considered that her own were a lot more interesting, but there was something sad and worrying about that rat.

It was dragging a small book, or at least what would be a small book to a human; it was about half the size of a rat. The cover was quite colorful, but Malicia couldn't make out what it was.

"Peaches and Dangerous Beans," said Keith. "This is Malicia. Her father is the mayor here."

"Hello," said Dangerous Beans.

"Mayor? Isn't that like *government*?" said Peaches. "Maurice says governments are very dangerous criminals and steal money from people."

"How did you teach them to speak?" said Malicia.

"They taught themselves," said Keith. "They're not trained animals, you know."

"Well, my father does *not* steal from *anyone*. Who taught them that governments are very—"

"'Scuse me, 'scuse me," said Maurice's voice hurriedly, from the drain grate. "That's right, I'm down here. Can we get on with things?"

"We'd like you to gnaw at our ropes, please," said Keith.

"I've got a bit of broken knife blade," said

Peaches. "It's for sharpening the pencil. Would that be better?"

"Knife?" said Malicia. "Pencil?"

"I did say they weren't ordinary rats," said Keith.

◆ ◆ ◆

Nourishing had to run to keep up with Darktan. And Darktan was running because he had to run to keep up with Sardines. When it came to moving fast across a town, Sardines was champion of the world.

He danced on ahead. He just couldn't help it. And he liked drainpipes, roofs, and gutters. You got no dogs up there, he said, and not many cats.

No cat could have followed Sardines. The people of Bad Blintz had strung clotheslines between the ancient houses, and he leaped onto them, clinging upside down and moving as fast as he would on a flat surface. He went straight up walls, plunged through thatch, tap-danced around smoking chimneys, slid down tiles. Pigeons erupted from their roosts as he sped past, the other rats trailing behind him.

Clouds rolled across the moon.

Sardines reached the edge of a roof and leaped, landing on a wall just below. He ran along the top and disappeared in the crack between two planks.

Darktan and Nourishing followed him into a kind of loft. Hay was piled in parts of it, but a larger part was simply open to the ground floor below, and supported by several heavy beams that ran right across the building. Bright light shone up from below, and there was the buzz of human voices and—Sardines shuddered—the barking of dogs.

"This is a big stable, boss," he said. "The pit's under the beam over there. Come on."

They crept out on the ancient woodwork and peered over the edge.

Far below was a wooden circle, like half a giant barrel. Nourishing realized that they were *right* over the pit; if she fell now, she'd land in the middle of it. Men were crowded around it. Dogs were tied up around the walls, barking at one another and at the universe in general in the mad, I'm-going-to-do-this-forever way of all dogs. And off to one side was a stack of boxes and sacks.

The sacks were moving.

"*Crtlk!* How the *krrp* will we find Hamnpork in this lot?" Darktan said, his eyes gleaming in the light from below.

"Well, with old Hamnpork, boss, I reckon

we'll know when he turns up," said Sardines.

"Could you drop into the pit on a string?"

"I'm game for anything, guv," said Sardines loyally.

"Into a pit with a dog in it, sir?" said Nourishing. "And won't the string cut you in half?"

"Ah, I've got something that helps there, boss," said Sardines. He dropped his thick coil of string and put it aside. There was another coil under it, glistening and light brown. He pulled at a piece of it, and it snapped back with a faint twang.

"Bands of rubber," he said. "I pinched them off a desk when I was looking for more string. I've used 'em before, boss. Very handy for a long drop, boss."

Darktan looked back at the boards. There was an old candle lantern there, lying on its side, the glass smashed, the candle eaten long ago.

"Good," he said. "Because I'm getting an idea. If you can drop down—"

There was a roar from below. The rats looked over the beam again.

The circle of heads had thickened around the lip of the pit. A man was talking in a loud voice. Occasionally there was a cheer.

The black top hats of the rat catchers moved

through the crowd. Seen from above, they were sin-
ister black blobs among the gray and brown caps.

One of the rat catchers emptied a sack into the
pit, and the watchers saw the dark shapes of rats
scurrying in a panic as they tried to find, in that
circle, a corner to hide in.

The crowd opened slightly, and a man walked
to the edge of the pit holding a terrier. There
was some more shouting, then a ripple of laughter, and the dog was dropped in with the rats.

The Changelings stared down at the circle of
death and the cheering humans.

After a minute or two Nourishing tore her
gaze away. When she looked around, she caught
the expression on Darktan's face.

Maybe it wasn't just the lamplight that made
his eyes look full of fire. She saw him look along
the stable to the big doors at the far end. They
had been barred shut.

Then his head turned to the hay and straw
piled up in the loft, and in the cribs and mangers
below.

Darktan pulled a length of wood out of one of
his belts.

Nourishing smelled the sulfur in the red blob
on the end.

It was a match.

Darktan turned and saw her looking at him. He nodded toward the piles of hay in the loft.

"My plan might not work," he said. "If it doesn't, you'll be in charge of the *other* plan."

"Me?" said Nourishing.

"You. Because I won't be . . . around," said Darktan. He held out the match. "You know what to do," he said, nodding to the nearest rack of hay.

Nourishing swallowed.

"Yes. Yes, I think so. Er . . . when?"

"When the time comes. You'll *know* when," said Darktan, and looked back down at the massacre.

"One way or the other I want them to remember tonight," he said quietly. "They'll remember what they did. And they'll remember what we did. For as long as they . . . live."

◆ ◆ ◆

Hamnpork lay in his sack. He could smell the other rats nearby, and the dogs, and the blood. Especially the blood.

He could hear his own thoughts, but they were like a little chirp of insects against the thunderstorm of his senses. Bits of memory danced in front of his eyes.

Cages. Panic. The white rat. Hamnpork. That

was his own name. Odd. Never had names. Just used to smell other rats. Darkness. Darkness *inside*, behind the eyes. That bit was Hamnpork. Everything outside was everything else.

Hamnpork. Me. Leader.

The red-hot rage still boiled inside him, but now it had a kind of shape, like the shape a canyon gives to a river in flood, narrowing it, forcing it to flow faster, giving it *direction*.

Now he could hear voices.

". . . just slip him in, no one'll notice . . ."

". . . okay, I'll shake it up a bit first to get him angry . . ."

The sack was jerked around. It didn't make Hamnpork any more angry than he was already. There wasn't any *room* for more anger.

The sack swung as it was carried. The roar of humans grew louder, the smells grew stronger. There was a moment of silence, the sack was upturned, and Hamnpork slid out into a roar of noise and a pile of struggling rats.

He snapped and clawed his way to the top as the rats scattered, and he saw a growling dog being lowered into the pit. It snatched up a rat, shook it vigorously, and sent the limp body flying.

The rats stampeded.

"Idiots!" screamed Hamnpork. "Work together! You could strip this fleabag to the bone!"

The crowd stopped shouting.

The dog stopped and stared down its nose at Hamnpork. It was trying to think.

The rat had spoken. Only *humans* spoke. And it didn't smell right. Rats usually stank of panic. This one didn't.

The silence rang like a bell.

Then the terrier Jacko grabbed the rat, shook him, not too hard, and tossed him down. He'd decided to do a sort of test; rats shouldn't be able to talk like humans, but this rat looked like a rat, and killing rats was okay, but it talked like a human, and biting humans got you a serious thrashing. He had to find out for sure. If he got a wallop, this rat was a human.

Hamnpork rolled and managed to get upright, but there was a deep tooth wound in his side.

The other rats were still in a boiling huddle as far away from the dog as possible, every rat trying to be the one on the bottom.

Hamnpork spat blood. "All right, then," he snarled, advancing on the puzzled dog. "Now you find out how a *real* rat dies!"

"Hamnpork!"

He looked up.

String uncoiled behind Sardines as he fell through the smoky air toward the frantic circle. He was right above Hamnpork, getting bigger and bigger . . .

. . . and slower and slower . . .

He came to a stop between the dog and the rat.

For a moment he hung there. He raised his hat politely and said, "Good evening!"

Then he wrapped all four legs around Hamnpork.

And now the rope of elastic bands, stretched to twanging point, finally sprang back. Too late, too late, Jacko snapped at empty air. The rats were accelerated upward, out of the pit—and stopped, bouncing in midair, just out of reach.

The dog was still looking up when Darktan leaped off the other side of the beam. As the crowd stared in astonishment, he plummeted down toward the terrier.

Jacko's eyes narrowed. Rats disappearing into the air was one thing, but rats dropping right toward his mouth was something else. It was rat on a plate, it was rat on a *stick*.

Darktan looked back as he fell. Up above, Nourishing was doing some frantic knotting and biting. *Now* Darktan was on the other end of Sardines's string.

Sardines had explained things very carefully. Darktan's weight alone wasn't heavy enough to pull the weight of two other rats back up to the beam . . .

So when Darktan saw that Sardines and his struggling passenger had disappeared safely into the gloom of the roof—

—he let go of the big old candle lantern he'd been holding for the extra weight and bit through the rope.

The lantern landed heavily on Jacko and Darktan landed on the lantern, rolling down onto the floor.

The crowd was silent. They'd been silent since Hamnpork had been propelled out of the pit. Around the top of the wall—which, yes, was far too high for a rat to jump—Darktan saw faces. They were mostly red. The mouths were mostly open. The silence was the silence of big red faces drawing breath, ready to start shouting at any moment.

Around Darktan the surviving rats were scrambling insanely for a foothold on the wall. Fools, he thought. Four or five of you together could make any dog wish you'd never been born. But you scrabble and duck, and you get picked off one at a time. . . .

The slightly stunned Jacko blinked and stared down at Darktan, a growl rising in his throat.

"Right, you *kkrrkk*," said Darktan, loud enough for the watchers to hear. "Now I'm going to show you how a rat can *live*."

He attacked.

Jacko was not a bad dog, according to the way of dogs. He was a terrier and liked killing rats in any case, and killing lots of rats in the pit meant that he got well fed and called a good boy and wasn't kicked very often. Some rats did fight back, and that wasn't much of a problem, because they were smaller than Jacko and he had a lot more teeth. Jacko wasn't that smart, but he was a lot smarter than a rat, and in any case, his nose and mouth did most of the thinking.

And he was surprised, therefore, when his jaws snapped shut on this new rat and it wasn't there.

Darktan didn't run like a rat should. He ducked like a fighter. He nipped Jacko under the chin and vanished. Jacko spun around. The rat *still* wasn't there. Jacko had spent his show-business career biting rats that tried to run away. Rats that stayed really close were unfair!

There was a roar from the watchers. Someone shouted, "Ten dollars on the rat!" and someone else punched him in the ear. Another man started to climb into the pit. Someone smashed a beer bottle on that man's head.

Dancing back and forth under the spinning, yapping Jacko, Darktan waited for his moment . . .

. . . and saw it, and lunged, and bit hard.

Jacko's eyes crossed. A piece of Jacko that was very private and of interest only to Jacko and any lady dogs he might happen to meet was suddenly a little ball of pain.

He yelped. He snapped at the air. And then, in the uproar, he tried to climb out of the pit, out of the way of the pain.

His claws scraped desperately as he reared up against the greasy, smooth planking.

Darktan jumped onto his tail, ran up his back, scampered to the tip of Jacko's nose, and leaped over the wall.

He landed among legs. Men tried to stamp on him, but that meant other men would have to give them room. By the time they'd elbowed one another out of the way and stamped heavily on one another's boots, Darktan was gone.

But there were other dogs. They were half mad with excitement in any case, and now they pulled away from ropes and chains and set off after a running rat. They knew about chasing rats.

Darktan knew about running. He sped across the floor like a comet, with a tail of snarling, barking dogs, headed for the shadows, spied a hole in the planking, and dived through into the nice, safe, darkness—

Click went the trap.

CHAPTER 9

Farmer Fred opened his door and saw all the animals of Furry Bottom waiting for him. "We can't find Mr. Bunnsy or Ratty Rupert!" they cried.

—From *Mr. Bunnsy Has an Adventure*

"At last!" said Malicia, shaking the ropes off. "Somehow I thought rats would gnaw quicker."

"They used a knife," said Keith. "And you *could* say thank you, couldn't you?"

"Yes, yes, tell them I'm very grateful," said Malicia, pushing herself upright.

"Tell them yourself!"

"I'm sorry, I find it terribly embarrassing to . . . talk to rats."

"I suppose that's understandable," said Keith. "If you've been brought up to hate them because they—"

"Oh, it's not *that*," said Malicia, walking over to the door and looking at the keyhole. "It's just that it's so . . . childish. So . . . tinkly-winkly. So . . . Mr. Bunnsy."

"Mr. Bunnsy?" squeaked Peaches, and it really was a squeak, a word that came out as a sort of little shriek.

"What about Mr. Bunnsy?" said Keith.

Malicia reached into her pocket and pulled out her packet of bent hairpins.

"Oh, some books some silly woman wrote," she said, poking at the lock. "Stupid stuff for ickle kids. There's a rat and a rabbit and a snake and a hen and an owl, and they all go around wearing clothes and talking to humans, and everyone's so nice and cozy it makes you absolutely *sick*. D'you know my father kept them all from when *he* was a kid? *Mr. Bunnsy Has an Adventure*, *Mr. Bunnsy's Busy Day*, *Ratty Rupert Sees It Through* . . . he read them all to me when I was small, and there's not an interesting murder in any of them."

"I think you'd better stop," said Keith. He didn't dare look down at the rats.

"There's no subtext, no social commentary," Malicia went on, still twiddling. "The most interesting thing that happens at all is when Doris the Duck loses a shoe—a *duck* losing a *shoe*, right?—and it turns up under the bed after they've spent the entire story looking for it. Do you call that narrative tension? Because I don't. If people are going to make up stupid stories about animals pretending to be human, at least there could be a bit of interesting violence—"

"Oh, boy," said Maurice, from behind the grating.

This time Keith did look down. Peaches and Dangerous Beans had gone.

"You know, I never had the heart to tell them," he said, not to anyone in particular. "They thought it was all true."

"In the land of Furry Bottom, possibly," said Malicia, and stood up as the lock gave a final click. "But not here. Can you imagine someone actually invented that name and didn't laugh? Let's go."

"You upset them," said Keith.

"Look, shall we get out of here before the rat catchers come back?" said Malicia.

The thing about this girl, Maurice thought, was that she was no good at listening to the *way* people spoke. She wasn't much good at listening at all, if it came to that.

"No," said Keith.

"No what?"

"No, I'm not going with you," said Keith.

"There's something bad going on here, much worse than stupid men stealing food."

Maurice watched them argue again. Humans, eh? Think they're lords of creation. Not like us cats. We *know* we are. Ever see a cat feed a human? Case proven.

How the humans shout, hissed a tiny voice in his head.

Is that my conscience? Maurice thought. His own thoughts said, What, me? No. But I feel a lot better now that you've told them about Additives.

Maurice shifted uneasily from paw to paw.

"Well then," he whispered, looking at his stomach, "is that you, Additives?"

He'd been worried about that. Suppose the . . . the *dream* of Additives wandered around inside him? That sort of thing could seriously interfere with a cat's napping time, it really could.

No, said the voice, like the sound of wind in distant trees, *it is I. I am . . . SPIDER.*

"Oh, you're a *spider*?" whispered Maurice. "I could take on a spider with three paws tied behind my back."

Not a spider. SPIDER.

The word actually hurt. It hadn't before.

Now I'm in your HEAD, cat. Cats, cats,

bad as dogs, worse than rats. I'm in your HEAD, and I will never go AWAY.*

Maurice's paw jerked.

I'll be in your DREAMS.

"Look, I'm just passing through," Maurice whispered desperately. "I'm not looking for trouble. I'm unreliable! I'm a cat! I wouldn't trust me, and I *am* me! Just let me get into the nice fresh air, and I'll be right out of your . . . hair or legs or furry bits or whatever!"

You don't want to run AWAY.

That's right, thought Maurice, I don't want to run— Hold on, I *do* want to run away!

"I'm a cat!" he muttered. "No one is going to control *me*. You've tried!"

Yes, came the voice of Spider, *but then you were STRONG. Now your little mind runs in circles and wants someone else to do the thinking for it. I can think for you.*

I can think for EVERYONE.

I will always be with you.

The voice faded away.

Right, thought Maurice. Time to say farewell, then, Bad Blintz. The party is *over*. The rats have got lots of other rats, and even these two humans have each other, but I've just got me, and I'd like to get me somewhere where strange voices don't talk to me.

"'Scuse me," he said, raising his voice. "Are you going or what?"

The two humans turned to look at the grating.

"What?" said Keith.

"I'd prefer going," said Maurice. "Pull this grating out, will you? It's rusted all the way through—it shouldn't be a problem. Good lad. And then we can make a run for it—"

"They've called in a rat piper, Maurice," said Keith. "And the Clan is all over the place. He'll be here in the morning. A *real* rat piper, Maurice. Not a fake one like me. They have magical pipes, you know. Do you want to see that happen to our rats?"

His new conscience gave Maurice a good kicking.

"Well, not exactly *see*," he said reluctantly. "Not as such, no."

"Right. So we're not going to run away," said Keith.

"Oh? And what are we going to do, then?" asked Malicia.

"We're going to talk to the rat catchers when they come back," said Keith. He had a thoughtful look.

"And what makes you think they'll want to talk to us?"

"Because if they don't talk to us," said Keith, "they're going to die."

◆　◆　◆

It was twenty minutes later that the rat catchers arrived. The door was unlocked, thrown back, then slammed shut. Rat Catcher 2 bolted it as well.

"You know where you said it was going to be such a good evening?" he said, leaning against it and panting. "Tell me about it again, 'cos I think I missed that part."

"Shut up," said Rat Catcher 1.

"Someone punched me in the *eye*."

"Shut up."

"*And* I think I lost my wallet. That's twenty dollars I won't see again in a hurry."

"Shut up."

"And I wasn't able to pick up any of the surviving rats from the last fight!"

"Shut up."

"And we left the dogs behind, too! We could've stopped to untie 'em! Someone'll pinch 'em!"

"Shut up."

"Do rats often whiz through the air like that? Or is that the kind of thing you only get to hear about when you are a *hexperienced* rat catcher?"

"Did I say shut up?"

"Yes."

"Shut up. All right, we'll leave right now. We'll take the money and nick a boat down at the jetty, okay? We'll leave the stuff we haven't sold and just *go*."

"Just like that? Johnny No Hands and his lads are coming upriver tomorrow night to pick up the next load, and—"

"We'll *go*, Bill. I can smell things going bad," said Rat Catcher 1.

"Just like that? He owes us two hundred doll—"

"Yes! Just like that! Time to move on! The jig is up, the bird has flowed, and the cat is out of the bag! The— Did you say that?"

"Say what?" said Rat Catcher 2.

"Did you just say 'I wish I was'?"

"Me? No."

Rat Catcher 1 looked around the shed. There was no one else there.

"All right, then," he said. "It's been a long night. Look, when things start to go bad, then it's time to go away. Nothing fancy. We just go, right? I don't want to be here when people come looking for us. And I *don't* want to meet any of them rat pipers. They are sharp men. They pry around. And they cost a lot of money. People are going to ask questions, and the only question I want them to ask is 'Where did the rat catchers go?' Understand? It's a good man who knows when to quit. What's in the kitty— What did you say?"

"What, me? Nothing. Cup of tea? You always feel better after a cup of tea."

"Didn't you say 'kitty yourself'?" Rat Catcher 1 demanded.

"I just asked if you wanted a cup of tea! Honest! Are you all right?"

Rat Catcher 1 stared at his friend as if trying to see a lie in his face. Then he said, "Yeah, yeah. I'm fine. Three sugars, then."

"That's right," said Rat Catcher 2, spooning it in. "Keep up your strength. You have to look after yourself."

Rat Catcher 1 took the mug, sipped the tea, and stared at the swirling surface.

"How did we get into this?" he asked. "I mean, all *this*? Y'know? Sometimes I wake up in the night and think, It's stupid, this, and then I come to work and it all seems, well, sensible. I mean, stealin' stuff and blamin' it on the rats, *yes*, and breeding big tough rats for the rat pits and bringing back the ones that survive so we can breed even *bigger* rats, *yes*, but . . . I dunno . . . I didn't use to be the kind of bloke who ties up kids . . ."

"We've made a big wad of cash, though."

"Yeah." Rat Catcher 1 swirled the tea in his mug and took another drink. "There's that, I suppose. Is this a new tea?"

"No, it's just Lord Green, like normal."

"Tastes a bit different." Rat Catcher 1 drained the mug and put it on the bench. "Okay, let's get the—"

"That's about enough," said a voice overhead. "Now, stand still and listen to me. If you run away, you'll die. If you talk too much, you'll die. If you wait too long, you'll die. If you think you're smart, you'll die. Any questions?"

A few wisps of dust drifted down from the rafters. The rat catchers looked up and saw a cat face peering down.

"It's that kid's damn mog!" said Rat Catcher 1. "I *told* you it was looking at me in a funny way!"

"If I was you, I wouldn't look at me," said Maurice conversationally. "I'd look at the rat poison."

Rat Catcher 2 turned to look at the bench. A bag was missing.

"Here, who stole the poison?" he asked.

"Oh," said Rat Catcher 1, who was a much faster thinker.

"Steal it?" said the cat on high. "We don't *steal*. That's *thieving*. We just put it somewhere else."

"Oh," said Rat Catcher 1, sitting down suddenly.

"That's dangerous stuff!" said Rat Catcher 2, looking for something to throw. "You had no business touching it! You tell me where it is right now!"

There was a thump as the trapdoor in the floor slammed back. Keith stuck his head up, and then came up the ladder while the rat catchers watched in amazement.

He was holding a crumpled paper bag.

"Oh dear," said Rat Catcher 1.

"What have you done with the poison?" Rat Catcher 2 demanded.

"Well," said Keith, "now that you mention it, I think I put most of it in the sugar. . . ."

◆ ◆ ◆

Darktan woke up. His back was on fire and he couldn't breathe. He could feel the weight of the trap's jaw pressing down on him, and the dreadful bite of the steel teeth on his belly.

I shouldn't be alive, he thought. I wish I wasn't. . . .

He tried to push himself upward, which made it worse. The pain came back a little stronger as he sagged down again.

Caught like a rat in a trap, he thought.

I wonder what type it is.

"Darktan?"

The voice was a little way off. Darktan tried to speak, but every tiny movement pushed him farther into the teeth below him.

"Darktan?"

Darktan managed a faint squeak. Words hurt too much.

Feet scrabbled forward in the dry darkness.

"Darktan!"

It smelled like Nourishing.

"Gnh," Darktan managed, trying to turn his head.

"You're caught in a trap!"

That was too much for Darktan, even if every word was agony.

"Oh . . . really?" he said.

"I'll go and fetch S-sardines, shall I?" stammered Nourishing.

Darktan could smell the rat's panic begin. And there wasn't time for panic.

"No! Tell . . . me . . ." he panted, ". . . what . . . kind . . . of . . . trap?"

"Er . . . er . . . er . . ." said Nourishing.

Darktan took a deep, fiery breath.

"*Think*, you . . . miserable widdler!"

"Er, er . . . it's all rusty. . . . Er . . . Rust everywhere! Looks like . . . er . . . could be a . . . Breakback." There was a scratching noise behind Darktan. "Yes! I gnawed the rust off! It says Nugent Brothers Breakback Mk.1, sir!"

Darktan tried to think as the constant, dreadful pressure squeezed him further. Mk.1? Ancient! Something out of the dawn of time! The oldest he'd ever seen was an Improved Breakback Mk.7! And all he had to help him was Nourishing, a complete *drrtlt* with four left feet.

"Can you . . . see how . . ." he began, but there were purple lights in front of his eyes now, a great tunnel of purple lights. He tried again as he felt himself drift toward the lights. "Can . . . you . . . see . . . how . . . the . . . spring . . ."

"It's all rusted, sir!" came the panicking voice. "It looks like it's a nonreturn action like on the Jenkins and Jenkins Big Snapper, sir, but it hasn't got the hook on the end! What does this bit do, sir? Sir? *Sir?*"

Darktan felt the pain go away. So this is how it happens, he thought dreamily. Too late now. She'll panic, and she'll run. That's what we do.

When we're in trouble, we bolt for the first hole. Even me. But it doesn't matter. It *is* just like a dream, after all. Nothing to worry about. Quite nice, really. Perhaps there really *is* a Big Rat Deep Under the Ground. That'd be nice.

He drifted happily, in the warm silence. There were bad things happening, but they were a long way off and they didn't matter anymore....

He thought he heard a sound behind him, like rat claws moving across a stone floor. Perhaps it's Nourishing running away, part of him thought. But another part thought: Perhaps it is the Bone Rat.

The idea didn't frighten him. Nothing could frighten him here. Anything bad that could happen already had. He felt that if he turned his head, he'd see something. But it was easier just to float in this big, warm space.

The purple light was darkening now, to a deep blue and, in the center of the blue, a circle of black.

It looked like a rat tunnel.

If the youngsters were right and there is a Bone Rat, he thought, then that means maybe there is also the Big Rat.

And that's where he lives, thought Darktan.

That's the tunnel of the Big Rat. How simple it all is.

A shining white dot appeared in the center of the tunnel and got bigger quickly.

And here he comes, thought Darktan. He must know a *lot*, the Big Rat. I wonder what he's going to tell me.

The light grew bigger and did indeed begin to look like a rat.

How strange, thought Darktan, as the blue light faded into the black, to find it's all true. Off we go, then, into the tunn—

There was noise. It filled the world. And the terrible, terrible pain was back. And the Big Rat shouted, in the voice of Nourishing:

"I gnawed through the spring, sir! I gnawed through the spring! It was old and weak, sir! Prob'ly why you weren't cut in half, sir! Can you hear me, sir? Darktan? Sir? I gnawed all the way through the spring, sir! Are you still dead, sir? Sir?"

◆ ◆ ◆

Rat Catcher 1 leaped out of his chair, his hands bunching into fists.

At least, it started out as a leap. About halfway it turned into a stagger. He sat down heavily, clutching at his stomach.

"Oh, no. Oh, no. I *knew* that tea tasted funny," he muttered.

Rat Catcher 2 had gone a pale green.

"You nasty little—" he began.

"And don't even think of attacking us," said Malicia. "Otherwise you'll never walk out of here. And we might get hurt and forget where we left the *antidote*. You haven't got *time* to attack us."

Rat Catcher 1 tried standing up again, but his legs didn't want to play.

"What poison was it?" he muttered.

"By the smell of it, it's the one the rats call Number Three," said Keith. "It was in the bag labeled 'Killalot!!!!'"

"The *rats* call it Number Three?" said Rat Catcher 2.

"They know a lot about poison," said Keith.

"And they told you about this antidote, yeah?" said Rat Catcher 2.

Rat Catcher 1 glared at him. "We *heard* them talk, Bill. In the pit, remember?" He looked back at Keith and shook his head. "Nah," he said. "You don't look like the kind of kid that'd poison a man to his face—"

"How about me?" said Malicia, leaning forward.

"*She* would! She *would*!" said Rat Catcher 2, clutching at his colleague's arm. "She's *weird*, that one. Everyone says so!" He clutched his stomach again and leaned forward, groaning.

"*You* said something about an antidote," said Rat Catcher 1 to Malicia. "But there's no antidote to Killalot!!!!"

"And I told you there is," said Keith. "The rats found one."

Rat Catcher 2 fell to his knees. "Please, young sir! Have mercy! If not for me, please think of my dear wife and my four lovely children who'll be without their daddy!"

"You're not married," said Malicia. "You don't have any children!"

"I might want some one day!"

"What happened to that rat you took away?" said Keith.

"Dunno, sir. A rat in a hat come down out of the roof and grabbed it and flew away!" Rat Catcher 2 burbled. "And then *another* big rat come down into the pit, shouted at everyone, bit Jacko on the—on the unutterables, and jumped right out of the pit and did a runner!"

"Sounds like your rats are all right," said Malicia to Keith.

"I haven't finished," said Keith. "You *stole* from

everyone and blamed it on the rats, didn't you?"

"Yes! That's it! Yes! We did, we did!"

"You killed the rats," said Maurice quietly.

Rat Catcher 1's head turned sharply. There was an edge to that voice that he recognized. He'd heard it at the pit. You got them there sometimes, high-rolling types with fancy vests, who traveled through the mountains making a living by betting and sometimes making a killing by knives. They had a look to their eye and a tone to their voice. They were known as "killing gentlemen." You didn't cross a killing gentleman.

"Yes, yes, that's right, we did!" babbled Rat Catcher 2.

"Just go carefully there, Bill," said Rat Catcher 1, still eyeing Keith.

"*Why* did you do it?" asked Keith.

Rat Catcher 2 looked from his boss to Malicia and then to Keith, as if trying to decide who frightened him the most.

"Well, Ron said the rats ate stuff *anyway*," he said. "So . . . he said if we got rid of *all* the rats and pinched the stuff ourselves, well, it wouldn't exactly be like *stealing*, would it? More like . . . *rearranging* stuff. There's a bloke Ron knows who comes up with a sailing barge in the middle of the night and pays us—"

"That is a diabolical lie!" snapped Rat Catcher 1, and then looked as if he was going to be sick.

"But you caught rats alive and crammed them into cages without food," Keith went on. "They live on rats, those rats. Why did you do that?"

Rat Catcher 1 clutched at his stomach.

"I can feel things happening!" he said.

"That's just your imagination!" snapped Keith.

"It is?"

"Yes. Don't you know *anything* about the poisons you use? Your stomach won't start to melt for at least twenty minutes."

"Wow!" said Malicia, seriously impressed.

"And after that," said Keith, "if you blow your nose, your brain will—well, let's just say you'll need a really *big* handkerchief."

"This is great!" said Malicia, rummaging in her bag. "I'm going to take notes!"

"And then if you. . . . Well, just don't go to the lavatory, that's all. Don't ask why. Just don't. It'll all be over in an hour, except for the oozing."

Malicia was scribbling fast. "Will they go runny?" she said.

"Very," said Keith.

"This is inhuman!" shrieked Rat Catcher 2.

"No, it's very human," said Keith. "It's *extremely* human. There isn't a beast in the world that'd do it to another living thing, but your poisons do it to rats every day. *Now tell me about the rats in the cages.*"

Sweat was pouring down the assistant rat catcher's face. He looked as if he, too, was caught in a trap.

"See, rat catchers have always caught rats alive for the rat pits," he moaned. "It's a perk. Nothing wrong with it! Always done it! So we had to keep up a supply, so we bred 'em. Had to! No harm in feeding 'em dead rats from the rat pits. Everyone knows rats eat rats, if you leave out the green wobbly bit! And then—"

"Oh? There's a *then*?" said Keith, calmly.

"Ron said if we bred rats from the rats that survived in the pit, you know, the ones that dodged the dogs, well, we'd end up with bigger, better rats, see?"

"That's *scientific*, that is," said Rat Catcher 1.

"What would be the point of that?" said Malicia.

"Well, miss, we—Ron said—we thought—I thought—we thought that—well, it's not exactly *cheating* to put really tough rats in amongst the others, see, especially if the dog that's going in is a bit borderline. Where's the harm in that? Give us an edge, see, when it comes to betting. I thought—he thought—"

"You seem a bit confused about whose idea it was," said Keith.

"His," said the rat catchers together.

Mine, said a voice in Maurice's head. He almost fell off his perch. *What does not kill us makes us strong,* said the voice of Spider. *The strongest breed.*

"You mean," said Malicia, "if we didn't have rat catchers here, we'd have *fewer* rats?" She paused, head on one side. "No, that's not right. It doesn't feel right. There's something else. Something you haven't told us. Those rats in those cages are . . . mad, insane . . ."

I'd be too, Maurice thought, with this horrible voice in my head every hour of the day.

"I'm going to throw up," said Rat Catcher 1. "I am, I'm going to—"

"Don't," said Keith, watching Rat Catcher 2. "You won't like it. Well, Mr. Assistant Rat Catcher?"

"Ask them what's in the other cellar," said Maurice. He said it fast; he could feel the voice of Spider try to stop his mouth moving even as the sentence came out.

"What is in the other cellar, then?" said Keith.

"Oh, just more stuff, old cages, stuff like

that . . ." said Rat Catcher 2.

"What else?" said Maurice.

"Only the . . . only the . . . that's where . . ." The rat catcher's mouth opened and shut. His eyes bulged.

"Can't say," he said. "Er. There's nothing. Yeah, that's it. There's nothing in there, just the old cages. Oh, and plague. Don't go in there, 'cos there's plague. That's why you shouldn't go in there, see? 'Cos of the plague."

"He's lying," said Malicia. "No antidote for *him*."

"I had to do it!" Rat Catcher 2 moaned. "You've gotta do one to join the Guild!"

"That's a Guild secret!" Rat Catcher 1 snapped at him. "We *don't* give away Guild secrets—" He stopped and clutched at his rumbling stomach.

"What was it you had to do?" asked Keith.

"Make a rat king!" Rat Catcher 2 burst out.

"A rat *king*?" said Keith sharply. "What's a rat king?"

"I—I—I—" the man stuttered. "Stop it, I—I—I don't want to—" Tears ran down his face. "We—I made a rat king—stop it, stop it—stop it . . . a rat king . . ."

"And it's still alive?" said Malicia.

Keith turned to her in amazement. "*You* know

about these things?" he said.

"Of course. There's a lot of stories about them. Rat kings are deadly evil. They—"

"Antidote, antidote, *please*," moaned Rat Catcher 2. "My stomach feels like there's rats running round in it!"

"You *made* a rat king," said Malicia. "Oh, dear. Well, we left the antidote in that little cellar you locked us up in. I should hurry, if I was you."

Both of the men staggered to their feet. Rat Catcher 1 fell through the trapdoor. The other man landed on him. Swearing, moaning, and, it has to be said, farting enormously, they made their way to the cellar.

Dangerous Beans's candle was still alight. Beside it was a fat twist of paper.

The door was slammed behind the men. There was the sound of a piece of wood being wedged under it.

"Oh, we forgot to mention that there's only enough antidote for one person," said Keith's voice, muffled through the wood. "But I'm sure you can sort it out—in a humane sort of way."

◆　　◆　　◆

Darktan tried to get his breath back, but he thought he'd never get it all, even if he breathed in for a year. There was a ring of pain all around his back and chest.

"It's amazing!" said Nourishing. "You were dead in the trap and now you're alive!"

"Nourishing?" said Darktan carefully.

"Yes, sir?"

"I'm very . . . grateful," said Darktan, still wheezing, "but don't get silly. The spring was stretched and weak and . . . the teeth were rusted and blunt. That's all."

"But there's teeth marks all round you! No one's ever come out of a trap before, except the Mr. Squeakys, and they were made of rubber!"

Darktan licked his stomach. Nourishing was right. He looked perforated.

"I was just lucky," he said.

"No rat has ever come alive out of a trap," Nourishing repeated. "Did you see the Big Rat?"

"The what?"

"The Big Rat!"

"Oh, that," said Darktan. He was going to add, "No, I don't go in for that nonsense," but stopped. He could remember the light, and then the darkness ahead of him. It hadn't seemed *bad*. He'd almost felt sorry that Nourishing had got him out. In the trap all the pain had been a long way off. And there had been no more hard decisions.

He settled for saying, "Is Hamnpork all right?"

"Sort of. I mean, we can't see any wounds that won't heal. He's had worse. But, well, he was pretty old. Nearly three years."

"Was?" said Darktan.

"*Is* pretty old, I mean, sir. Sardines sent me to find you because we'll need you to help us get him back, but—" She gave Darktan a doubtful look.

"It's all right—I'm sure it looks nastier than it is," said Darktan, wincing. "Let's get up there, shall we?"

An old building full of handholds for a rat. No one noticed the two of them as they climbed up from manger to saddle harness to hayrack. Besides, no one was looking for them. Some of the *keekees* had taken the Jacko route to freedom, and the dogs were going mad searching for them and fighting with one another. So were the men. Darktan knew a little bit about beer, since he had gone about his business under pubs and breweries, and the rats had often wondered why humans sometimes liked to switch their brains off. To the rats, living in the center of a web of sound and light and smells, it made no sense at all.

To Darktan, now, it didn't sound quite so bad.

The idea that, for a while, you could forget things and not have a head buzzing with troublesome thoughts . . . well, that seemed quite attractive.

He couldn't remember a lot about life before he'd been Changed, but he was certain that it hadn't been so *complicated*. Oh, bad things had happened, because life on the heap had been pretty hard. But when they were over they were over, and tomorrow was a new day.

Rats didn't think about tomorrow. There was just a faint sensation that more things would happen. It wasn't *thinking*. And there was no "good" and "bad" and "right" and "wrong." They were *new* ideas.

Ideas! That was their world now! Big questions and big answers, about life, and how you had to live it, and what you were for. New ideas spilled into Darktan's weary head.

And among the ideas, in the middle of his head, he saw the little figure of Dangerous Beans.

Darktan had never talked much to the little white rat or the little female who scurried around after him and drew pictures of the things he'd been thinking about. Darktan liked people who were *practical*.

But now he thought: He's a trap hunter, just

like me. He goes ahead of us and finds the dangerous ideas and thinks about them and traps them in words and makes them safe, and then he shows us the way through.

We *need* him ... we need him *now*. Otherwise we're all running around like rats in a barrel. . . .

Much later on, when Nourishing was old and gray around the muzzle, and smelled a bit strange, she dictated the story of the climb and how she heard Darktan muttering to himself. The Darktan she'd pulled out of the trap, she said, was a different rat. It was as though his thoughts had slowed down but got bigger.

The strangest bit, she said, was when they reached the beam. Darktan made sure that Hamnpork was all right and then picked up the match he'd shown to Nourishing.

"He struck it on an old bit of iron," said Nourishing, "and then he walked out along the beam with it flaring, and down below I could see all the crowd and the hay racks and the straw all over the place, and the humans milling around, just like, hah, just like rats . . . and I thought, If you drop that, mister, the place will fill with smoke in a few seconds, and they've locked the doors, and by the time they realize it, they'll be caught like, hah, yeah, like rats in a barrel, and we'll be away along the gutters.

"But he just stood there, looking down, until the match went out. Then he put it down and helped us with Hamnpork and never said a word about it. I asked him about it later on, after all the stuff with the piper and everything, and he said, 'Yes. Rats in a barrel.' And that's all he said about it."

◆　◆　◆

"What was it you really put in the sugar?" asked Keith, as he led the way back to the secret trapdoor.

"Cascara," said Malicia.

"That's not a poison, is it?"

"No, it's a laxative."

"What's that?"

"It makes you . . . go."

"Go where?"

"Not *where*, stupid. You just . . . go. I don't particularly want to draw you a picture."

"Oh. You mean . . . *go*."

"That's right."

"And you just happened to have it on you?"

"Yes. Of course. It was in the big medicine bag."

"You mean you take something like *that* just

for something like this?"

"Of course. It could easily be necessary."

"How?" asked Keith, climbing the ladder.

"Well, supposing we were kidnapped? Suppose we ended up right down near the sea?
Supposing we were captured by pirates? Pirates
have a very monotonous diet, which might be
why they're angry all the time. Or supposing we
escaped and swam ashore and ended up on an
island where's there's nothing but coconuts?
They have a very binding effect."

"Yes, but ... but ... *anything* can happen! If you
think like that, you'll end up taking just about
everything in case of anything!"

"That's why it's such a big bag," said Malicia
calmly, pulling herself through the trapdoor and
dusting herself off.

Keith sighed. "How much did you give them?"

"Lots. But they should be all right if they don't
take too much of the antidote."

"What did you give them for the antidote?"

"Cascara."

"Malicia, you are not a nice person."

"Really? *You* wanted to poison them with the
real poison, and *you* were getting very imagina-
tive—all that stuff about their stomachs melting."

"Yes, but rats are my friends. Some of the poisons really do that. And . . . sort of . . . making the antidote *more* of the poison—"

"It's not a poison. It's a medicine. They'll feel lovely and clean afterward."

"All right, all right. But—giving it to them as the antidote as well, that's a bit . . . a bit . . ."

"Clever? Narratively satisfying?" said Malicia.

"I suppose so."

Malicia looked around.

"Where's your cat? I thought he was following us."

"Sometimes he just wanders off. And he's not my cat."

"Yes, you're his boy. But a young man with a smart cat can go a long way, you know."

"How?"

"There was Puss in Boots, obviously," said Malicia, "and of course everyone knows about Dick Livingstone and his wonderful cat, don't they?"

"I don't," said Keith.

"It's a very famous story!"

"Sorry. I haven't been able to read for very long."

"Really? Well, Dick Livingstone was a penniless

boy who became Lord Mayor of Übergurgl because his cat was so good at catching ... er ... pigeons. The town was overrun with ... pigeons, yes, and in fact later on he even married a sultan's daughter because his cat cleared all the ... pigeons out of her father's royal palace—"

"It was rats really, wasn't it?" asked Keith glumly.

"I'm sorry, yes."

"And it was just a story," said Keith. "Never mind stories about mayors. Are there *really* stories about rat kings? Rats have kings? I've never heard of it. How does it work?"

"Not the way you think. They've been known about for years. They really do exist, you know. Just like on the sign outside."

"What, the rats with their tails all knotted together? How do—"

There was a loud and persistent knocking on the door. Some of it sounded as though it was being done with someone's boot.

Malicia went over to it and pulled back the bolts.

"Yes?" she said coldly, as the night air poured in.

There was a group of angry men outside. The leader, who looked as though he was only the leader because he happened to be the one in front, took a step back when he saw Malicia's angry stare.

"Oh . . . it's you, miss," he said, suddenly embarrassed.

"Yes. My father's the mayor, you know," said Malicia.

"Er . . . yes. We all know."

"Why're you all holding sticks?" asked Malicia.

"Er . . . we want to talk to the rat catchers," said the spokesman. He tried to look past her, and she stood aside.

"There's no one in here but us," she said. "Unless you think there's a trapdoor to a maze of underground cellars where desperate animals are caged up and vast supplies of stolen food are hoarded?"

The man gave her another nervous look. "You and your stories, miss," he said.

"Has there been some trouble?" asked Malicia.

"We think they were a . . . a bit naughty," said the man. He blanched under the look she gave him.

"Yes?" she said.

"They cheated us in the rat pit!" said a man behind him, made bold because there was someone else between him and Malicia. "They must've *trained* those rats! One of them flew around on a string!"

"And one of them bit my Jacko on the—the—on the unmentionables!" said someone farther back. "You can't tell me it wasn't trained to do that!"

"I saw one with a hat on this morning," said Malicia.

"There's been a good deal too many strange rats today," said another man. "My mum said she saw one *dancing* on the kitchen shelves! And when my granddad got up and reached for his false teeth, he said a rat *bit* him with them. Bit him with his own teeth!"

"What, wearing them?" said Malicia.

"No, it just snapped them around in the air! And a lady down our street opened her pantry door, and there were rats swimming in the cream bowl. Not just swimming, either! They'd been *trained*. They were making kind of patterns, and diving and waving their legs in the air and stuff!"

"You mean *synchronized* swimming?" said Malicia. "Who's telling stories now, eh?"

"Are you *sure* you don't know where those men are?" asked the leader suspiciously. "People said they headed this way."

Malicia rolled her eyes. "All right, yes," she

227

said. "They got here, and a talking cat helped us to feed them poison, and now they're locked in a cellar."

The men looked at her.

"Yeah, right," said the leader, turning away. "Well, if you *do* see them, tell them we're looking for them, okay?"

Malicia shut the door.

"It's terrible, not being believed," she said.

"Now tell me about rat kings," Keith said.

CHAPTER 10

A nd as night fell, Mr. Bunnsy remembered: There's
something terrible in the Dark Wood.

—From *Mr. Bunnsy Has an Adventure*

Why am I doing this? Maurice asked himself as
he squirmed along a pipe. Cats are not *built* for
this stuff!

Because we are a kind person at heart, said his
conscience.

No, I'm not, thought Maurice.

Actually, that's true, said his conscience. But we
don't want to tell that to Dangerous Beans, do
we? The little wobbly nose? *He* thinks we're a
hero!

Well, I'm not, thought Maurice.

Then why are we scrabbling around underground trying to find him?

Well, *obviously* it's because he's the one with
the big dream about finding the rat island, and

without him the rats won't cooperate and I won't get paid, said Maurice.

We're a *cat*! What does a cat need money for?

Because I have a Retirement Plan, thought Maurice. I'm four years old already! Once I've made a pile, I'm headed for a nice home with a big fire and a nice old lady giving me cream every day. I've got it all worked out, every detail.

Why should she give us a home? We're smelly, we've got ragged ears, we've got something nasty and itchy on our leg, we look like someone kicked us in the face—why should an old lady take us in instead of a fluffy little kitten?

Aha! But black cats are *lucky*, thought Maurice.

Really? Well, we don't want to be first with the bad news, but we're not black! We're a sort of mucky tabby!

There's such a thing as dyes, thought Maurice. A couple of packets of black dye, hold my breath for a minute, and it's hello, cream and fish for the rest of my life. Good plan, eh?

And what about the luck? asked the conscience.

Ah! That's the clever bit. A black cat who brings in a gold coin every month or so, wouldn't you say that's a lucky cat to have?

His conscience fell silent. Probably amazed at

the cleverness of the plan, Maurice told himself.

He had to admit that he was cleverer at plans than at underground navigation. He wasn't exactly lost, because cats never get lost. He merely didn't know where everything else was. There wasn't a lot of earth under the town, that was certain. Cellars and gratings and pipeways and ancient sewers and crypts and bits of forgotten buildings formed a sort of honeycomb. Even humans could get around down here, Maurice thought. The rat catchers certainly had.

He could smell rats everywhere. He wondered about calling out to Dangerous Beans but decided against it. Calling out might help him find out where the little rat was, but it'd also alert . . . *anyone else* to where Maurice was. Those big rats had been, well, big, and nasty-looking.

Now he was in a small, square tunnel with lead pipes in it. There was even a hiss of escaping steam, and here and there warm water dripped into a gutter that ran along the bottom of the tunnel. Up ahead was a grating leading up to the street. Faint light came through it.

The water in the gutter looked clean. Maurice was thirsty. He leaned down, tongue out—

There was a thin, bright-red streak curling gently in the water. . . .

Hamnpork seemed confused and half asleep, but he knew enough to hold on to Sardines' tail as the rats made their way back from the stable. It was a slow journey. Sardines didn't think the old rat would manage the clotheslines. They skulked along gutters, and along drains, hiding in nothing more than the cloak of night.

A few rats were milling around in the cellar when they finally arrived. By then Darktan and Sardines were walking on either side of Hamnpork, who was barely moving his legs.

There was still a candle burning in the cellar. Darktan was surprised. But a lot of things had happened in the last hour.

They let Hamnpork sink to the floor, where he lay, breathing heavily. His body shook with each breath.

"Poison, guv?" whispered Sardines.

"No, I think it was all just too much for him," said Darktan. "Just too much."

Hamnpork opened one eye.

"Am . . . I . . . still . . . the . . . leader?" he asked.

"Yes, sir," said Darktan.

"Need . . . to . . . sleep . . ."

Darktan looked around the circle. Rats were creeping toward the group. He could see them whispering to one another. They kept staring at him. He tried to spot the pale shape of Dangerous Beans.

"Nourishing . . . tells me . . . you saw the . . . tunnel . . . of the . . . Big Rat," said Hamnpork.

Darktan glared at Nourishing, who looked embarrassed.

"I saw . . . something, yes," he said.

"Then I shall dream my way there and . . . never wake up," said Hamnpork. His head sagged again. "This isn't . . . the way a . . . an old rat should die," he mumbled. "Not . . . like this. Not . . . in the light."

Darktan nodded urgently at Sardines, who snuffed out the candle with his hat. The damp, thick underground darkness closed in.

"Darktan," Hamnpork whispered. "You need to know this."

Sardines strained his ears to hear the old leader's last words to Darktan. Then, a few seconds later, he shivered. He could smell the change in the world.

There was movement in the darkness. A match burst into life, and the candle flame grew again, bringing shadows back into the world.

Hamnpork was lying very still.

"Do we have to eat him now?" asked someone.

"He's . . . gone," said Darktan. Somehow the idea of eating Hamnpork didn't feel right. "Bury him," he said. "And mark the place so we know he's there."

There was a sense of relief in the group. However much anyone might have respected Hamnpork, he was still a bit on the whiffy side, even for a rat.

But a rat at the front of the crowd looked uncertain. "Er . . . when you say 'mark the place,'" he said, "do you mean like we mark other places where we bury things?"

"He means by widdling on it," said the rat beside him.

Darktan looked at Sardines, who shrugged. Darktan had a sinking feeling inside. When you were the leader, everyone waited to see what you said. And there was still no sign of the white rat.

He was on his own.

He thought hard for a moment and then nodded.

"Yes," he said at last. "He'd like that. It's very . . . ratty. But do this, too. Draw it in the dirt above him."

He scraped a sign on the ground:

"'He was a rat from a long line of rats, and he thought about rats,'" said Sardines. "Good one, boss."

"And will he come back like Darktan did?" asked someone else.

"If he does, he'll get really mad if we've eaten him," said a voice. There was some nervous laughter.

"Listen, I didn't—" Darktan began, but Sardines nudged him.

"Word in your ear, guv?" he said, raising his charred hat politely.

"Yes, yes . . ." Darktan was getting nervous.

He'd never had so many rats watching him so closely.

He followed Sardines away from the group.

"You know I used to hang around in the theater an' that," said Sardines quietly. "And you pick up stuff in the theater. And the thing is . . . Look, what I'm saying is, you're the leader, right? So you got to act like you know what you're doing, okay? If the leader doesn't know what he's doing, no one else does, either."

"I only know what I'm doing when I'm dismantling traps," said Darktan.

"All right, think of the future as a great big trap," said Sardines. "With no cheese."

"That is *not* a *lot* of *help*!"

"And you should let them think what they like about you and . . . that scar you've got," said Sardines. "That's my advice, guv."

"But I didn't die, Sardines!"

"Are you sure?"

"Huh?"

"*Something* happened, didn't it? You were going to set fire to the place with all the humans in it. And you decided not to. I watched you. Something happened to you in the trap. Don't ask me what it was, I just do tap dancing. I'm just a little rat. Always will be, boss. But there's big rats like Inbrine and Sellby and a bunch of others, boss, and now that Hamnpork's dead, they might think *they* should be the leader. Get my drift?"

"No."

Sardines sighed. "I reckon you do, boss. Do we want a lot of scrapping amongst ourselves at a time like this?"

"No!"

"Right! Well, thanks to chattery little Nourishing, you're the rat that looked the Bone Rat right in the face and came back, aren't you?"

"Yes, but she—"

"Seems to me, boss, that anyone who could stare down the Bone Rat . . . well, no one is going to want to mess with *him*, am I right? A man who wears the teethmarks of the Bone Rat like a belt? Uh-uh, *no*. People'll *follow* a rat like that. Time like this, people *need* someone to follow. That was a good thing you did back there, with ol' Hamnpork. Burying him and widdling on top *and* putting a sign on him— well, the old rats like that, and so do the young ones. Shows 'em you're thinking for everyone."

Sardines put his head to one side and grinned a worried grin.

"I can see I'm going to have to watch you,

Sardines," said Darktan. "*You* think like Maurice."

"Don't worry about me, boss. I'm small. I gotta dance. I wouldn't be any good at leadering."

Thinking for everyone, Darktan thought. Like the white rat . . .

"Where *is* Dangerous Beans?" he said, looking around. "Isn't he here?"

"Haven't seen him, boss."

"What? We need him! He's got the map in his head."

"Map, boss?" Sardines looked concerned. "I thought you drew maps in the mud—"

"Not a map like a picture of tunnels and traps, Sardines. A map of . . . of what we are and where we're going . . ."

"Oh, you mean like that lovely island? Never really believed in it, boss."

"I don't know about any islands," said Darktan. "But when I was in that . . . place, I . . . saw the shape of an idea. There's been a war between humans and rats forever! It's got to end. And here, now, in this place, with these rats . . . I can see that it can. This might be the only time and the only place where it can. I can see the shape of an idea in my head, but I can't think of the *words* for it, do you understand? So we need the white rat, because he knows the map for thinking.

We've got to think our way out of this. Running around and squeaking won't work anymore."

"You're doing fine so far, boss," said the dancer, patting him on the shoulder.

"It's all going wrong," said Darktan, trying to keep his voice down. "We need him. *I* need him."

"I'll get some squads together, boss, if you show me where to start looking," said Sardines meekly.

"In the drains, not far from the cages," said Darktan. "Maurice was with him," he added.

"Is that a good thing or a bad thing, guv?" said Sardines. "You know what Hamnpork always said: 'You can always trust a cat—'"

"'—to be a cat.' Yes. I know. I wish I knew the answer to that, Sardines."

Sardines stepped closer.

"Can I ask a question, guv?"

"Of course."

"What was it Hamnpork whispered to you just before he died? Special leader wisdom, was it?"

"Good advice," said Darktan. "Good advice."

◆ ◆ ◆

Maurice blinked. Very slowly, his tongue wound itself back in.

He flattened his ears and, legs moving in silent

slow motion, crept along beside the gutter.

Right under the grating there was something pale. The red streak was coming from farther upstream, and divided in two as it flowed around the thing, before becoming one swirling thread again.

Maurice reached it. It was a rolled-up scrap of paper, sodden with water and stained with red.

He extended a claw and fished it out. It flopped on the side of the gutter, and as Maurice gently peeled the paper apart, he saw the smudged pictures drawn in thick pencil. He knew what they were. He'd learned them, one day when he had nothing better to do. They were stupidly simple.

"No Rat Shall . . ." he began. Then there was a damp mess, down to the bit that read: "We Are Not Like Other Rats."

"Oh, no," he said. They wouldn't drop this, would they? Not the Thoughts. Peaches carried it around as though it was a hugely precious thing—

Will I find them first? said an alien voice in Maurice's head. *Or perhaps I have. . . .*

Maurice ran, skidding on the slimy stone as the tunnel turned a corner.

What strange things they are, CAT. Rats that think they are not rats. Shall I be like you? Shall I act like a CAT? Shall I keep one of them alive? FOR A WHILE?

Maurice yowled under his breath. Other, smaller tunnels branched off on either side, but the thin red streak led straight ahead, and there, under another grating, the *shape* lay in the water, the red leaking gently from it.

Maurice sagged.

He'd been expecting—what? But this . . . this was . . . this was *worse*, in a way. Worse than anything.

Soaked in water, leaking the red ink from Ratty Rupert the Rat's red vest, was *Mr. Bunnsy Has an Adventure.*

Maurice hooked it out on claw tip, and the cheap paper pages fell out, one by one, and drifted away in the water.

They'd dropped it. Had they been running? Or . . . had they thrown it away? What was it Dangerous Beans had said? "We're nothing but rats?" And he'd said it in such a sad, hollow voice.

Where are they now, CAT? Can you find them? Which way now?

It can see what I see, he thought. It can't read my mind, but it can see what I see and hear what I hear, and it's good at working out what I must be thinking.

It sees what I see.

Once again, he shut his eyes.

In the dark, CAT? How will you fight my rats? The ones BEHIND YOU?

Maurice spun around, eyes wide. There were rats there, dozens of them, some of them nearly half the size of Maurice. They watched him, all with the same blank expression.

Well done, well done, CAT! You see the squeaky creatures and yet you don't leap! How did a cat learn not to be a cat?

The rats, as one rat, moved forward. They rustled as they moved. Maurice took a step backward.

Imagine it, CAT, said the voice of Spider. *Imagine a million clever rats. Rats that don't run. Rats that fight. Rats that share one mind, one vision. MINE.*

"Where are you?" asked Maurice aloud.

You will see me soon. Keep going, pussycat. You have to keep going. One word from me, one mere flicker of a thought, and the rats you see will take you down. Oh, you might kill one or two, but there are always more rats. Always more rats.

Maurice turned and edged forward. The rats followed. He spun around. They stopped. He turned again, took a couple of steps, looked behind him. The rats followed as if they were on a string.

There was a familiar smell in the air here, of old, stale water. He was somewhere near the flooded cellar. But how close? The stuff stank worse than canned cat food. It could be in any direction. He could probably outrun the rats over a short distance.

Bloodthirsty rats right behind you can give you wings.

Are you planning to run to *help* the white rat? said his conscience. Or are you thinking of making a dash for the daylight?

Maurice had to admit that the daylight had never seemed a better idea. There was no point in lying to himself. After all, rats didn't live very long in any case, even if they had wobbly noses—

They are close, CAT. Shall we play a game? Cats like PLAYING. Did you play with Additives? BEFORE YOU BIT HIS HEAD OFF?

Maurice stopped dead. A rat actually bumped into his back legs.

"You are going to *die*," he said softly.

They are getting closer to me, Maurice. So

close now. Shall I tell you that the stupid-looking kid and the silly-sounding girl are going to die? Do you know that rats can eat a human alive?

◆ ◆ ◆

Malicia bolted the shed door.

"Rat kings are deeply mysterious," she said. "A rat king is a group of rats with their tails tied together—"

"How?"

"Well, the stories say it just . . . happens."

"*How* does it happen?"

"I read somewhere that their tails become stuck together when they're in the nest, because of all the muck, and then get twisted up as—"

"Rats generally have six or seven babies, and they have quite short tails, and the parents keep the nests quite clean," said Keith. "Have the people who tell these stories ever *seen* rats?"

"I don't know. Maybe the rats just get crowded together and their tails get twisted up? There's a preserved rat king in a big jar of alcohol in the town museum."

"A dead one?"

"Or very, very drunk. What do *you* think?" said Malicia. "It's ten rats, like a sort of star, with a big knot of tail in the middle. Lots of others have been found, too. One had thirty-two rats! There's *folklore* about them."

"But that rat catcher said he *made* one," said Keith firmly. "He said he did it to get into the Guild. Do you know what a masterpiece is?"

"Of course, it's anything really good—"

"I mean a *real* masterpiece," said Keith. "I grew up in a big city, with guilds everywhere. That's how I know. A masterpiece is something that an apprentice makes at the end of his training to show the senior members of the guild that he deserves to be a 'master.' A full member. You understand? It might be a great symphony, or a beautiful piece of carving, or a batch of magnif-icent loaves—his 'master piece.'"

"Very interesting. So?"

"So what sort of masterpiece would you have to make to become a master rat catcher? To show that you could *really* control rats? Remem-ber the sign over the door?"

Malicia frowned the frown of someone faced with an inconvenient fact.

"Anyone could tie a bunch of rat tails together if they wanted to," she said. "I'm sure I could."

"While they're alive? You'd have to trap them first, and then you've got slippery bits of string that are moving all the time and the other end keeps on biting you? Eight of them? Twenty of them? Thirty-two? Thirty-two *angry* rats?"

Malicia looked around at the untidy shed, trying out the idea.

"It works," she said. "Yes. It makes . . . almost as good a story. Probably there were one or two *real* rat kings . . . all right, all right, maybe just one—and people heard about this and decided that since there was all this interest, they'd *try* to make one. Yes. It's just like crop circles. No matter how many aliens own up to making them, there are always a few diehards who believe that humans go out with garden mowers in the middle of the night—"

"I just think that some people like to be cruel," said Keith. "How would a rat king hunt? They'd all pull in different directions."

"Ah, well, some of the stories about rat kings say that they can control other rats," said Malicia. "With their minds, sort of. Get them to bring them food and go to different places and so on. You're right, rat kings can't move around easily. So they learn how to see out of the eyes of other rats, and hear what they hear."

"Just other rats?" said Keith.

"Well, one or two do say that they can do it to people," said Malicia.

"How? Has it ever happened, *really*?"

"It couldn't, could it?" said Malicia.

Yes.

"Yes, what?" asked Malicia.

"I didn't say anything. You just said, 'Yes,'" said Keith.

Silly little minds. Sooner or later there is always a way in. The cat is much better at resisting! You will OBEY me. Let the rats GO.

"I think we should let the rats go," said Malicia. "It's just too cruel, having them packed into those cages like that."

"I was just thinking that," said Keith.

And forget about me. I am just a story.

"Personally, I think rat kings really are just a story," said Malicia, walking over to the trapdoor and raising it. "That rat catcher was a stupid little man. He was just babbling."

"I wonder if we *really* should let the rats out," Keith mused. "They looked pretty hungry."

"They can't be worse than the rat catchers, can they?" said Malicia. "Anyway, the piper will be here soon. He'll lead them all into the river, or something—"

"Into the river . . ." muttered Keith.

"That's what he does, yes. Everyone knows that," said Malicia.

"But rats can—" Keith began.

Obey me! Don't THINK! Follow the story!

"Rats can what?"

"Rats can . . . rats can . . ." Keith stammered. "I can't remember. Something about rats and rivers. Probably not important."

◆ ◆ ◆

Thick, deep darkness. And, somewhere in it, a little voice.

"I dropped *Mr. Bunnsy*," said Peaches.

"Good," said Dangerous Beans. "It was just a lie. Lies drag us down."

"You said it was important!"

"It was a *lie!*"

. . . endless, dripping darkness . . .

"And . . . I've lost the Thoughts, too."

"So?" Dangerous Beans's voice was bitter. "No one bothered with them."

"That's not true! People tried to. Mostly. And they were sorry when they didn't!"

"They were just another story, too. A story about rats who thought they weren't rats."

"Why're you talking like this? This isn't like you!"

"You saw them run. They ran and squeaked and forgot how to talk. Underneath, we're just . . . rats."

. . . foul, stinking darkness . . .

"Yes, we are," said Peaches. "But what are we on top? That's what you *used* to say. Come on—please? Let's go back. You're not well."

"It was all so clear to me . . ." Dangerous Beans mumbled.

"Lie down. You're tired. I've got a few matches left. You know you always feel better when you see a light. . . ."

Worried in her heart, and feeling lost and a long way from home, Peaches found a wall that was rough enough and dragged a match from her crude bag.

The red head flared and crackled. She raised the match as high as she could.

There were eyes everywhere.

What's the worst part? she thought, her body rigid with fear. That I can see the eyes? Or that I'm going to know they're still there when the match goes out?

"And I've only got two more matches," she mumbled to herself.

The eyes withdrew into the shadows, noiselessly. How can rats be so still and so silent? she thought.

"There's something wrong," said Dangerous Beans.

"Yes."

"There's something here," he said. "I smelled it on that *keekee* they found in the trap. It's a kind of terror. I can smell it on you."

"Yes," said Peaches.

"Can you see what we should do?" asked Dangerous Beans.

"Yes." The eyes in front were gone, but Peaches could still see them on either side.

"What can we do?" asked Dangerous Beans.

Peaches swallowed. "We could wish we had more matches," she said.

And, in the darkness behind their eyes, a voice said: ***And so, in your despair, you come, at last, to me. . . .***

◆ ◆ ◆

Light has a smell.

In the dank, damp cellars the sharp sulfur stink of the match flew like a yellow bird, rising on drafts, plunging through cracks. It was a clean and bitter smell, and it cut through the dull underground reek like a knife.

It filled the nostrils of Sardines, who turned his head.

"Matches, boss!" he said.

"Head that way!" Darktan commanded.

"It's through the room of cages, boss," Sardines warned.

"So?"

"Remember what happened last time, boss?"

Darktan looked around at his squad. It wasn't everything he could have wished for. Rats were still trailing back from their hiding places, and some rats—good, sensible rats—had run into traps and poisons in the panic. But he'd picked the best he could. There were a few of the experienced older ones, like Inbrine and Sardines, but most of them were young. Maybe that wasn't such a bad thing, he thought. It was the older rats who'd panicked most. They hadn't been so used to thinking.

"O-kay," he said. "Now, we don't know what we're going to—" he began, and caught sight of Sardines. The rat was shaking his head slightly.

Oh, yes. Leaders weren't allowed not to know.

He stared at the young, worried faces, thought for a long moment, took a deep breath, and started again.

"There's something new down here," he said, and suddenly he knew what to say. The words came. "Something that no one's ever seen before. Something tough. Something strong." The squad

251

was almost cowering, except for Nourishing, who was staring at Darktan with shining eyes.

"Something fearful. Something new. Something sudden," said Darktan, leaning forward. "And it's *you*. All of you. Rats with brains. Rats who can think. Rats who don't turn and run. Rats who aren't afraid of dark or fire or noises or traps or poisons. Nothing can stop rats like you, right?"

He remembered something else.

"You heard about the Dark Wood in the Book? Well, we're in the Dark Wood now. Oh, yes. There's something else down there. Something terrible. It hides behind your fear. It thinks it can stop you, and it's *wrong*. We're going to find it and drag it out, and we're gonna make it wish we'd never been *born*! And if we die . . . well"— and he saw them, as one rat, stare at the livid wound across his chest—"death ain't so bad. Shall I tell you about the Bone Rat? Me and the Bone Rat, we've got a little . . . understanding. He waits for those who break and run, who hide, who falter. But if you stare right into his eyes, he'll give you a nod and pass on."

Now he could smell their excitement. In the world behind their eyes they were the bravest rats that there ever were. Now he had to lock that thought there.

Without thinking, he touched the wound. It was healing badly, still leaking blood, and there was going to be a huge scar there forever. He brought his hand up, red with his own blood, and the idea came to him right out of his bones.

He walked along the rows touching each rat just above the eyes, leaving a red mark.

"And afterward," he said quietly, "people will say, 'They went there, and they did it, and they came back out of the Dark Wood, and this is how they know their own.'"

He looked across their heads to Sardines, who raised his hat. That broke a spell. The rats started to breathe again. But something of the spell was still there, lodged in the gleam of an eye and the twitch of a tail.

"Ready to die for the Clan, Sardines?" Darktan shouted.

"No, boss! Ready to kill!"

"Good," said Darktan. "Let's go. We *love* the Dark Wood! It belongs to us!"

◆　◆　◆

The smell of light drifted along the tunnels and reached the face of Maurice, who sniffed it up.

Peaches! She was mad about light. It was more or less all Dangerous Beans could see. She always carried a few matches. Mad! Creatures who lived in darkness, carrying matches! Well, obviously not *mad* when you thought about it, but even so . . .

The rats behind were pushing him in that direction.

I'm being played with, he thought. Batted from paw to paw so Spider can hear me squeak.

He heard in his head the voice of Spider: **And so, in your despair, you come, at last, to me. . . .**

And heard with his ears, far off and faint, the voice of Dangerous Beans.

"Who are you?"

I am the Big Rat Deep Under the Ground.

"You are? Really? I have thought . . . a lot about you."

There was a hole in the wall here and, beyond it, the brilliance of a lighted match. Sensing the press of the rats behind him, Maurice sidled through.

There were *big* rats everywhere, on the floor, on boxes, clinging to the walls. And, in the center, a circle of light from one half-burned match held aloft by a trembling Peaches.

Dangerous Beans was standing a little in front of her, staring up at a stack of boxes and sacks.

Peaches spun around. As she did so, the flame

of the match blew wide and flared. The nearest rats jerked away as it did so, bending like a wave.

"Maurice?" she said.

The cat will not move, said the voice of Spider.

Maurice tried to, and his paws wouldn't obey him.

Be still, CAT. Or I shall command your lungs to stop. See, little rat? Even a cat obeys me!

"Yes. Command, obey . . . yes. I see you have a power," said Dangerous Beans, tiny in the circle of light.

Clever rat. I have heard you talk to the others. You understand the truth. You know that by facing the dark, we become strong. You know about the darkness in front of us and the darkness behind the eyes. You know that we cooperate or die. Will you . . . COOPERATE?

"Cooperate?" said Dangerous Beans. His nose wrinkled. "Like these other rats I smell here? They smell . . . strong and stupid."

But the strong survive, said the voice of Spider. *They dodge the rat catchers and bite their way out of cages. And, like you, they are called to me. As for their minds . . . I can think for everyone.*

"I, alas, am not strong," said Dangerous Beans carefully.

You have an interesting mind. You too look forward to the domination of rats.

"Domination?" said Dangerous Beans. "Do I?"

You will have worked out that there is a race in this world that steals and kills and spreads disease and despoils what it cannot use, said the voice of Spider.

"Yes," said Dangerous Beans. "That's easy. It's called humanity."

Well done. See my fine rats? In a few hours the silly piper will come and play his silly pipe, and, yes, my rats will scamper after him out of the town. Do you know how a piper kills rats?

"No."

He leads them into the river where . . . are you listening? . . . where they all drown!

"But rats are good swimmers," said Dangerous Beans.

Yes! Never trust the rat catchers! They will leave themselves work for tomorrow. But humans like to believe stories! They would prefer to believe stories rather than the truth!

But we, we are RATS! And my rats will swim, believe me. Big rats, different rats, rats who survive, rats with part of my mind in them. And they will spread from town to town, and then there will be destruction such as people cannot imagine! We will pay them back a thousand-fold for every trap! Humans have tortured and poisoned and killed, and all of that is now given form in me and there will be REVENGE.

"Given form in you. Yes, I think I begin to understand," said Dangerous Beans.

There was a crackle and flare behind him. Peaches had lit the second match from the dying, flickering flame of the first one. The ring of rats, which had been creeping closer, swayed back again.

One more match, said Spider. *And then, one way or another, little rat, you belong to me.*

"I want to see who I am talking to," said Dangerous Beans firmly.

You are blind, little white rat. Through your pink eyes I see only mist.

"They see more than you think," said Dangerous Beans. "And if you are, as you say, the Big Rat . . . then show yourself to me. Smelling is believing."

There was a scrabbling, and Spider came out of the shadows.

It looked to Maurice like a bundle of rats, rats scampering across the boxes but flowing, as if all the legs were being operated by one creature.

As it crawled into the light, over the top of a sack, Maurice saw that the tails were twisted together into one huge, ugly knot.

And each rat was blind. As the voice of Spider thundered in his head, the eight rats reared and tugged at the knot.

Then tell me the truth, white rat. Do you see me? Come closer! Yes, you see me, in your mist. You see me. Men made me for sport! Tie the rats' tails together and watch them struggle! But I did not struggle. Together we are strong! One mind is as strong as one mind and two minds are as strong as two minds, but three minds are four minds, and four minds are eight minds, and eight minds . . . are one, one mind stronger than eight. My time is near. The stupid men let rats fight and the strong survive, and then they fight, and the strongest of the strong survive . . . and soon the cages will open, and men shall know the meaning of the word "plague"! See the stupid cat? It wants to

leap, but I hold it so easily. No mind can with-
stand me. Yet you . . . you are interesting. You
have a mind like mine, that thinks for many
rats, not just one rat. We want the same things.
We have plans. We want the triumph of rats.
Join us. Together we will be . . . STRONG.

There was a long pause. It was, Maurice thought, too long. And then:

"Yes, your offer is . . . interesting," said Dangerous Beans.

There was a gasp from Peaches, and Dangerous Beans went on, in a small voice: "The world is big and dangerous, indeed. And we are weak, and I am tired. Together we can be strong."

Indeed!

"But what of those who *aren't* strong, please?"

The weak are food. That is how it has always been!

"Ah," said Dangerous Beans. "How it has always been. Things are becoming clearer."

"Don't listen to it!" Peaches hissed. "It's affecting your mind!"

"No, my mind is working perfectly, thank you," said Dangerous Beans, still in the same calm voice. "Yes, the proposition is beguiling. And we would rule the rat world together, would we?"

We would . . . cooperate.

And Maurice, on the sidelines, thought: yeah, right. *You* cooperate, *they* rule. Surely you can't fall for this!

But Dangerous Beans said: "Cooperate. Yes. And together we would give the humans a war they won't believe. Of course, millions of rats would die—"

They die anyway.

"Mmm, yes. Yes. Yes, that is true. And this rat here," said Dangerous Beans, suddenly waving a paw toward one of the big rats that was hypnotized by the flame, "can you tell me what *she* thinks about this?"

Spider sounded taken aback.

Thinks? Why should it think anything? It is a rat!

"Ah," said Dangerous Beans. "How clear it is now. But it would not work."

Would not work?

Dangerous Beans raised his head.

"Because, you see, you just think for many rats," he said. "But you don't think *of* them. Nor are you, for all that you say, the Big Rat. Every word you utter is a lie. If there is a Big Rat, and I hope there is, it would not talk of war and death. It would be made of the best we could be, not the worst that we are. No, I will not join you, liar in the dark. I prefer our way. We are silly and weak sometimes. But together *we* are strong. You have plans for rats? Well, *I* have dreams for them."

Spider reared up, quivering. The voice raged in Maurice's mind.

Oh, so you think you are a good rat? But a good rat is one that steals most! You think a good rat is a rat in a vest, a little human with fur! Oh yes, I know about the stupid, stupid Book! Traitor! Traitor to rats! Will you feel my . . . PAIN?

Maurice did. It was like a blast of red-hot air, leaving his head full of steam. He recognized the sensation. It was how he used to feel before he was Changed. It was how he used to feel before he was Maurice. He'd been just a cat. A bright cat, but nothing more than a cat.

You defy me? Spider screamed at the bowed form of Dangerous Beans. **When I am everything that truly is RAT? I am filth and darkness! I am the noise under the floor, the rustling in the walls! I am the thing that undermines and despoils! I am the sum of all that you deny! I am your true self! Will you OBEY ME?**

"Never," said Dangerous Beans. "You are nothing but shadows."

Feel my PAIN!

Maurice was more than a cat, he knew. He knew the world was big and complex and involved a lot more than wondering if the next meal was going to be beetles or chicken legs. The world was huge and difficult and full of amazing things and . . .

. . . the red-hot flame of that horrible voice was boiling his mind away. The memories were unwinding and whirling into the darkness. All the other little voices, not the horrible voice but the Maurice voices, the ones that nagged at him and argued amongst themselves and told him he was doing wrong or could be better, were getting fainter—

And still Dangerous Beans stood there, small and wobbly, staring up into the dark.

"Yes," said Dangerous Beans. "I feel the pain."

You *are nothing but a rat. A little rat. And I am the very SOUL of ratdom. Admit it, little blind rat, little blind pet rat.*

Dangerous Beans swayed, and Maurice heard him say: "I am not so blind that I can't see darkness."

Maurice sniffed, and realized that Dangerous

Beans was widdling himself in terror. But the little rat didn't move, even so.

Oh, yes, whispered the voice of Spider. *And you can control the dark, yes? You told a little rat that. You can learn to control the dark.*

"I am a rat," whispered Dangerous Beans. "But I am not vermin."

VERMIN?

"Once we were just another squeaking thing in the forest. And then humans built barns and pantries full of food. Of course we took what we could. And so they called us vermin, and they have trapped us and covered us in poison, and somehow, out of that wretchedness, you have come. But you are no answer. You are just another bad thing humans made. You offer rats nothing except more pain. You just have a power that lets you enter people's minds when they are tired or stupid or upset. And you are in mine now."

Yes. Oh, yes!

"And still I stand here," said Dangerous Beans. "Now that I have smelled you, I know you. You have the smell of the Bone Rat about you. Even though my body is shaking, I can keep a place free from you. I can feel you running round in my head, you see, but all the doors are closed to

263

you now. I can control the shadows inside, which is where all darkness is. I am more than just a rat. If I am *not* more than just a rat, I am nothing at all."

The many heads of Spider turned this way and that. There wasn't much left of Maurice's mind to do any thinking now, but it looked as though the rat king was trying to reach a conclusion.

Its reply came in a roar.

THEN BE NOTHING!

♦ ♦ ♦

Keith blinked. He had his hand on the latch of one of the rat cages.

The rats were watching him. All standing the same way, all watching his fingers. Hundreds of rats.

They looked . . . hungry.

"Did you hear something?" said Malicia.

Keith lowered his hand very carefully and took a couple of steps back.

"Why are we letting these out?" he said. "It was like I'd been . . . dreaming."

"I don't know. You're the rat boy."

"But we *agreed* to let them out."

"I . . . it was . . . I had a feeling that—"

"Rat kings can talk to people, can't they?" said Keith. "Has it been talking to us?"

"But this is real life," said Malicia.

"I thought it was an adventure," said Keith.

"Damn! I forgot," said Malicia. "What're they doing?"

It was almost as if the rats were melting. They were no longer upright, attentive statues. Something like panic was spreading through them again.

Then other rats poured out of the walls, running madly across the floor. They were much bigger than the caged ones. One of them bit Keith on the ankle, and he kicked it away.

"Try to stamp on them, but don't lose your balance, whatever you do!" he said. "These are *not* friendly!"

"*Tread* on them?" said Malicia. "Yuk!"

"You mean you haven't got anything in your bag to fight rats? This is a rat catchers' lair! You've got plenty of stuff for pirates and bandits and robbers!"

"Yes, but there's never been a book about having an adventure in a rat catchers' hut!" Malicia shouted. "Ow! One's on my neck! One's on my neck! And there's another one!" She bent down frantically to shake the rats loose and reared up as one leaped at her face.

Keith grabbed her hand. "*Don't* fall over!

They'll go mad if you do! Try to get to the door!"

"They're so fast!" Malicia panted. "Now there's another one on my *hair*—"

"Hold still, stupid human!" said a voice in her ear. "Hold quite still or I'll *gnaw* you!"

There was a scrabble of claws and a swish, and a rat dropped past her eyes. Then another rat thumped onto her shoulder and slid away.

"Right!" said the voice at the back of her neck. "Now *don't* move, *don't* tread on anyone, and keep out of the way!"

"What was *that*?" Malicia gasped, as she felt something slide down her skirt.

"I think it was the one they call Big Savings," said Keith. "Here comes the Clan!"

More rats were pouring into the room, but these moved differently. They stayed together and spread out into a line that moved forward slowly. When an enemy rat attacked it, the line would close up over it quickly, like a fist, and when it opened again, that rat was dead.

Only when the surviving rats smelled the terror of their fellows and tried to escape from the room did the attacking line break, becoming pairs of rats that, with terrible purpose, hunted down one scurrying enemy after another and brought them down with a bite.

And then, seconds after it started, the war was over. The squeaking of a few lucky refugees faded into the walls.

There was a ragged cheer from the Clan, the cheer that says, "I'm still alive! After all that!"

"Darktan?" said Keith. "What happened to you?"

Darktan reared up and pointed a paw to the door at the other end of the cellar.

"If you want to help, open that door!" he shouted. "Move it!" Then he darted into a drain, with the rest of the squad pouring in after him. One of them tap-danced as he went.

CHAPTER 11

And there he found Mr. Bunnsy, tangled in the brambles and his blue coat all torn.

—From *Mr. Bunnsy Has an Adventure*

The rat king raged.

The watching rats clutched at their heads, Peaches shrieked and stumbled back, the last flaring match flying out of her hand.

But something of Maurice survived that roar, that *storm* of thought. Some tiny part hid behind some brain cell and cowered as the rest of Maurice was blown away. Thoughts peeled back and vanished in the gale. No more talking, no more wondering, no more seeing the world as something *out* there. Layers of his mind streamed past as the blast stripped away everything that he'd thought of as *me*, leaving only the brain of a cat. A bright cat, but still . . . just a cat.

Nothing but a cat. All the way back to the

forest and the cave, the tusk and the claw . . .

Just a cat.

And you can always trust a cat to be a cat.

The cat blinked. It was bewildered and angry. Its ears went flat. Its eyes flashed green.

It couldn't think. It didn't think. It was instinct that moved it now, something that operated right down at the level of its roaring blood.

It was a cat, and there was a twitching squeaky thing, and what cats do to twitching squeaking things is this: They *leap*.

The rat king fought back. Teeth snapped at the cat, it was tangled in fighting rats, and it yowled as it rolled across the floor. More rats poured in, rats that could kill a dog . . . but now, just for a few seconds, this cat could have brought down a wolf.

It didn't notice the crackling flame as the dropped match set fire to some straw. It ignored the other rats breaking ranks and running. It paid no attention to the thickening smoke.

What it wanted to do was *kill things*.

Some dark river deep inside had been dammed up over the months. It had spent too much time helpless and fuming while little squeaky people ran around in front of it. It had longed to leap and bite and kill. It had longed to be a *proper cat*.

And now the cat was out of the bag, and so much ancestral fight and spite and viciousness was flowing through Maurice's veins that it sparked off his claws.

And as the cat rolled and struggled and bit, a weak little voice all the way at the back of his tiny brain, cowering out of the way, the last tiny bit of him that was still Maurice and not a blood-crazed maniac, said, "Now! Bite *here*!"

Teeth and claws closed on a lump made up of eight knotted tails and tore it apart.

The tiny part of what had once been the *me* of Maurice heard a thought shoot past.

Noooo—ooo—oo—o . . .

And then it died away, and the room was full of rats, just rats, nothing more than rats, fighting to get out of the way of a furious, spitting, snarling, bloodthirsty cat, catching up on catness. It clawed and bit and ripped and pounced and turned to see a small white rat that had not moved throughout the whole fight. It brought its claws down—

Dangerous Beans screamed.

"*Maurice!*"

◆　◆　◆

The door rattled, and rattled again as Keith's boot hit the lock for the second time. On the third blow the wood split and burst apart.

There was a wall of fire at the other end of the cellar. The flames were dark and evil, as much thick smoke as fire. The Clan were scrambling in through the grating and spreading out on either side, staring at the flames.

"Oh, no! Come on, there's buckets next door!" said Keith.

"But—" Malicia began.

"*We've* got to do it! Quickly! This is a big-people job!"

The flames hissed and popped. Everywhere, on fire or lying on the floor beyond the flames, were dead rats. Sometimes there were only *bits* of dead rats.

"What happened here?" asked Darktan.

"Looks like a war, guv," said Sardines, sniffing the bodies.

"Can we get round it?"

"Too hot, boss. Sorry, but we— Isn't that Peaches?"

She was sprawled close to the flames, mumbling to herself and covered in mud.

Darktan crouched down. She opened her eyes blearily.

"Are you all right, Peaches? What's happened to Dangerous Beans?"

Sardines wordlessly tapped him on the shoulder and pointed.

Coming through the fire, a shadow . . .

It padded slowly between walls of flame.

For a moment the waving air made it look huge, like some monster emerging from a cave, and then it became . . . just a cat.

Smoke poured off its fur. What wasn't smoking was caked with mud. One eye was shut. The cat was leaving a trail of blood, and every few footsteps it sagged a little.

It had a small bundle of white fur in its mouth.

It reached Darktan and continued past without a glance. It was growling all the time, under its breath.

"Is that *Maurice*?" said Sardines.

"That's Dangerous Beans he's carrying!" shouted Darktan. "Stop that cat!" But Maurice had stopped by himself, turned, lain down with his paws in front of him, and looked blearily at the rats.

Then he gently dropped the bundle to the floor. He prodded it once or twice, to see if it would move.

He blinked slowly when it didn't move. He looked puzzled, in a kind of slow-motion way. He opened his mouth to yawn, and smoke came out. Then he put his head down and died.

♦   ♦   ♦

The world seemed to Maurice to be full of the ghost light you get before dawn, when it's just bright enough to see things but not bright enough to see colors.

He sat up and washed himself.

There were rats and humans running around, very, very slowly. Somehow they didn't concern him much. Whatever it was they thought they had to be doing, they were doing it. Other people were rushing about, in a silent, ghostly way, and Maurice was not. This seemed a pretty good arrangement.

And his eye didn't hurt and his skin wasn't painful and his paws weren't torn, which was a big improvement on matters as they had stood recently.

Now that he came to think about it, he wasn't quite sure *what* had happened recently. Something wretchedly bad, obviously.

There was something Maurice-shaped lying beside him, like a three-dimensional shadow. He stared at it, then turned when in this soundless ghost world he heard a noise.

There was movement near the wall. A small figure was striding across the floor toward the small lump that was Dangerous Beans. It was rat sized, but it was much more solid than the rest of the rats, and unlike any rat he'd seen before, it wore a black robe.

A rat in clothes, he thought. But this one did not belong in a *Mr. Bunnsy* book. Just poking out from the hood of the robe was the bony nose of a rat skull. And it was carrying a tiny scythe over its shoulder.

The other rats and the humans, who were drifting back and forth with buckets, paid it no attention. Some of them walked right through it. The rat and Maurice seemed to be in a separate world of their own.

It's the Bone Rat, thought Maurice. It's the Grim Squeaker. He's come for Dangerous Beans.

After all I've been through? That is not *happening*!

He sprang into the air and landed on the Bone Rat. The little scythe skidded across the floor.

"Okay, mister, let's hear you talk—" Maurice began.

SQUEAK!

"Er . . ." said Maurice, as the horrible awareness of what he'd done caught up with him.

A hand grabbed him by the back of the neck and lifted him up, higher and higher, and then turned him around. Maurice stopped struggling immediately.

He was being held by another figure, much taller, human size, but with the same style of black robe, a much bigger scythe, and a definite lack of skin around the face. Strictly speaking, there was a considerable lack of face about the face, too. It was just bone.

DESIST FROM ATTACKING MY ASSOCIATE, MAURICE, said Death.

"Yessir, Mr. Death, sir! Atoncesir!" said Maurice quickly. "Noproblemsir!"

I HAVEN'T SEEN YOU LATELY, MAURICE.

"Nosir," said Maurice, relaxing slightly. "Been very careful, sir. Looking both ways when I cross the street and everything, sir."

AND HOW MANY DO YOU HAVE LEFT NOW?

"Six, sir. Six. Six out of nine. Very definitely. Very definitely six lives, sir."

Death looked surprised.

BUT YOU WERE RUN OVER BY A CART ONLY LAST MONTH, WEREN'T YOU?

"That, sir? Barely grazed me, sir. Got away with hardly a scratch, sir."

EXACTLY!

"Oh."

THAT MAKES FIVE LIVES, MAURICE. UP UNTIL

275

"Fair enough, sir. Fair enough." Maurice swallowed. Oh, well, might as well try. "So let's say I'm left with three, right?"

THREE? I WAS ONLY GOING TO TAKE ONE. YOU CAN'T LOSE MORE THAN ONE LIFE AT A TIME, EVEN IF YOU'RE A CAT. THAT LEAVES YOU FOUR, MAURICE.

"And I say take two, sir," said Maurice urgently. "Two, and call it quits?"

Death and Maurice looked down at the faint, shadowy outline of Dangerous Beans. Some other rats were standing around him now, picking him up.

ARE YOU SURE? asked Death. AFTER ALL, HE IS A RAT.

"Yessir. That's where it all gets complicated, sir."

YOU CAN'T EXPLAIN?

"Yessir. Don't know why, sir. Everything's been a bit odd lately, sir."

THAT IS VERY UNCATLIKE OF YOU, MAURICE. I'M AMAZED.

"I'm pretty shocked too, sir. I just hope no one finds out, sir."

Death lowered Maurice to the floor, next to his body.

You leave me little choice. The sum is correct, even though it is amazing. We came for two, and two we will take. The balance is preserved.

"Can I ask a question, sir?" said Maurice, as Death turned to go.

You may not get an answer.

"I suppose there isn't a Big Cat in the Sky, is there?"

I'm surprised at you, Maurice. Of course there are no cat gods. That would be too much like . . . work.

Maurice nodded. One good thing about being a cat, apart from the extra lives, was that the theology was a lot simpler.

"I won't remember all this, will I, sir?" he said. "It'd be just too embarrassing."

Of course not, Maurice. . . . "Maurice?"

Colors returned to the world, and Keith was stroking him. Every bit of Maurice stung or ached. How could fur ache? And his paws screamed at him, and one eye felt like a lump of ice, and his lungs were full of fire.

"We thought you were dead!" said Keith. "Malicia was going to bury you in her backyard! She says she's already got a black veil."

277

"What, in her adventuring bag?"

"Certainly," said Malicia. "Supposing we'd ended up on a raft in a river full of flesh-eating—"

"Yeah, right, thanks," growled Maurice. The air stank of burned wood and dirty steam.

"Are you all right?" asked Keith, still looking worried. "You're a lucky black cat now!"

"Ha ha, yes, ha ha," said Maurice gloomily. He pushed himself up painfully.

"The little rat okay?" he asked, trying to look around.

"He was out just like you, but when they tried to move him, he coughed up a lot of muck. He's not well, but he's getting better."

"All's well that ends—" Maurice began, and then winced. "I can't turn my head very well," he said.

"You're covered in rat bites, that's why."

"What's my tail like?" asked Maurice.

"Oh, fine. It's nearly all there."

"Oh, well. All's well that ends well, then. Adventure over, time for tea and buns, just like the girl says."

"No," said Keith. "There's still the piper."

"Can't they just give him a dollar for his trouble and tell him to go away?"

"Not the rat piper," said Keith. "You don't say

that sort of thing to the rat piper."

"Nasty piece of work, is he?"

"I don't know. He sounds like it. But we've got a plan."

Maurice growled. "*You've* got a plan?" he said. "You made it up?"

"Me and Darktan and Malicia."

"Tell me your wonderful plan," said Maurice with a sigh.

"We're going to keep the *keekees* caged up, and no rats will come out to follow the piper. That way he'll look pretty silly, eh?" said Malicia.

"That's *it*? That's your plan?"

"You don't think it'll work?" asked Keith. "Malicia says he'll be so embarrassed, he'll leave."

"You don't know anything about people, do you?" Maurice sighed again.

"What? I'm a person!" said Malicia.

"So? *Cats* know about people. We have to. No one else can open cupboards. Look, even the rat king had a better plan than that. A good plan isn't one where someone wins, it's where nobody thinks they've *lost*. Understand? *This* is what you have to do. . . . No, it wouldn't work—we'd need a lot of cotton . . ."

Malicia swung her bag around with a look of triumph.

"As a matter of fact," she said, "I'd worked that out for if I was ever taken prisoner in a giant underwater mechanical squid and needed to block up—"

"You're going to say you've got a lot of cotton, aren't you?" said Maurice flatly.

"Yes!"

"It was silly of me to worry, wasn't it," said Maurice.

◆   ◆   ◆

Darktan stuck his sword in the mud. The senior rats gathered round him, but seniority had changed. Among the older rats were younger ones, each one with a dark-red mark on his or her head, and they were pushing to the front.

All of them were chattering. He could smell the relief that had come when the Bone Rat had gone past and had not turned aside. . . .

"Silence!" he yelled.

It struck like a gong. Every eye turned to him. He felt tired, he couldn't breathe properly, and he was streaked with soot and blood. Some of the blood wasn't his.

"It's not over," he said.

"But we just—"

"It's not over!"

Darktan looked around the circle.

"We didn't get all those big rats, the real fighters," he panted. "Inbrine, take twenty rats and go back and help guard the nests. Big Savings and the old females are back there, and they'll tear any attacker in half, but I want to be *certain*."

For a moment Inbrine glared at Darktan.

"I don't see why you—" he began.

"Do it!"

Inbrine crouched hurriedly, waved at the rats behind him, and scurried away.

Darktan looked at the others. As his gaze passed across them, some of them leaned back as if it was a flame.

"We'll form into squads," he said. "All of the Clan that we can spare from guarding will form into squads. At least one trap disposal rat in each squad! Take fire with you! And some of the young rats'll be runners, so you can keep in touch! *Don't* go near the cages—those poor creatures can wait! But you'll work through all these tunnels, *all* these tunnels and these holes and these corners! And if you meet a strange rat and it cowers, then take it prisoner! Drag it to the cages! But if it tries to fight—and the big ones *will* try to fight, because that's all they know—then you will *kill* it! Burn it or bite it! Kill it *dead*! Do you *hear me*?"

There was a murmur of agreement.

"I said, *Do you hear me!*"

This time there was a roar.

"Good! And we'll go on and on until these tunnels are safe, from end to end! Then we'll do it again! Until these tunnels are *ours*! Because . . ." Darktan grasped his sword but leaned on it for a moment to catch his breath, and when he spoke next, it was almost in a whisper, "because we're in the heart of the Dark Wood now, and we've found the Dark Wood in our hearts, and . . . for tonight . . . we are something . . . terrible." He took another breath, and his next words were heard only by the rats closest to him:

"And we have nowhere else to go."

♦ ♦ ♦

It was dawn. Sergeant Doppelpunkt, who was one half of the city's official Watch (and the larger half), awoke with a snort in the tiny office by the main gates.

He got dressed, a little unsteadily, and washed his face in the stone sink, peering at himself in the scrap of mirror hanging on the wall.

He stopped. There was a faint but desperate squeaking sound, and then the little strainer over the drain hole was pushed aside and a rat plunged out. It was big and gray, and it ran up his arm before leaping onto the floor.

Water dripping from his face, Sergeant Doppelpunkt watched as three smaller rats erupted from the pipe and chased after it.

It turned to fight in the middle of the floor, but the small rats hit it together, from three sides at once. There was a brief struggle, a screech, and then the big rat was dead.

There was an old rat hole in the wall. Two of the rats grabbed the tail and dragged the body into the hole and out of sight. But the third rat stopped at the hole and turned, standing up on its hind legs.

The sergeant felt that it was *staring* at him. It didn't look like an animal watching a human to see if it was dangerous. The rat didn't look scared, merely curious. It had some kind of red blob on its head, the sergeant noticed.

Then it saluted him. It was definitely a salute, even though it took only a second. Then all the rats had gone.

The sergeant stared at the hole for some time.

And then he heard the singing. It was drifting up from the sink's drain hole and it echoed a lot, as if it was coming from a long way away:

"We fight dogs and we kill cats ..."

   "... ain't no trap can stop the rats!"

"Got no plague and got no fleas ..."

 "... we drink poison, we steal cheese!"

"Mess with us and you will see ..."

      "... we'll put poison in your tea!"

"Here we'll fight and here we'll stay ..."

 "...WE WILL NEVER GO AWAY!"

The sound faded. Sergeant Doppelpunkt blinked and looked at the bottle of beer he'd drunk the night before.

He thought it'd probably be a good idea not to mention this to *anyone*. It probably hadn't happened.

The guardhouse door opened and Corporal Knopf stepped in.

"Morning, sergeant," he began. "It's that— What's up with you?"

"Nothing, corporal!" said Doppelpunkt quickly, wiping his face. "I certainly haven't seen anything strange at all! Why're you standing around? Time to get those gates open, corporal!"

The Watch stepped out and swung open the city gates, and the sunlight streamed through.

It brought with it a long, long shadow.

Oh dear, thought Sergeant Doppelpunkt. This

is not going to be a nice day. . . .

The man on horseback rode past them without a glance, and on into the town square. The Watch hurried after him. People aren't supposed to ignore people with weapons.

"Halt, what is your business here?" demanded Corporal Knopf, but he had to run crabwise to keep up with the horse.

The rider was dressed in white and black, like a magpie. He didn't answer but just smiled faintly to himself, staring straight ahead.

"All right, maybe you haven't any actual business, but it won't cost you anything just to say who you are, will it?" said Corporal Knopf, who was not interested in any trouble.

The rider looked down at him and then stared ahead again.

Sergeant Doppelpunkt spotted a small covered wagon coming through the gates, drawn by a donkey that was accompanied by an old man. He was a sergeant, he told himself, which meant that he was paid more than the corporal, which meant that he thought more expensive thoughts. And this one was: They didn't have to check *everyone* who came through the gate, did they? Especially if they were busy. They had to pick people at random. And if you were going to pick people at random, it was a good idea to randomly pick a little old man who looked small enough and old enough to be frightened of a rather grubby uniform with rusty chain mail.

"Halt!"

"Heh, heh! Not gonna," said the old man. "Mind the donkey—he can give you a nasty bite when he's roused. Not that I care."

"Are you trying to show contempt of the Law?" demanded Sergeant Doppelpunkt.

"Well, I'm not trying to conceal it, mister. You want to make something of it, you talk to my boss. That's him on the horse. The *big* horse."

The black-and-white stranger had dismounted by the fountain in the center of the square, and was opening his saddlebags.

"I'll just go and talk to him, shall I?" said the sergeant.

By the time he'd reached the stranger, walking as slowly as he dared, the man had propped a small mirror against the fountain and was having a shave. Corporal Knopf was watching him. He'd been given the horse to hold.

"Why haven't you arrested him?" the sergeant hissed.

"What, for illegal shaving? Tell you what, sarge, *you* do it."

Sergeant Doppelpunkt cleared his throat. A few early risers among the population were already watching him.

"Er . . . now, listen, friend, I'm sure you didn't mean—" he began.

The man straightened up and gave the guards a look that made both men take a step backward. He reached out and undid the thong holding a thick roll of leather behind the saddle.

It unrolled. Corporal Knopf whistled. All down the length of leather, held in place by straps, were dozens of pipes. They glistened in the rising sun.

"Oh, you're the *pipe*—" the sergeant began, but the other man turned back to the mirror and said, as if talking to his reflection, "Where can a man get breakfast around here?"

"Oh, if it's breakfast you want, then Mrs. Shover at the Blue Cabbage will—"

"Sausages," said the piper, still shaving. "Burned on one side. Three. Here. Ten minutes. Where is the mayor?"

"If you go down that street and take the first left—"

"Fetch him."

"Here, you can't—" the sergeant began, but Corporal Knopf grabbed his arm and pulled him away.

"He's *the piper*!" he whispered. "You don't mess with the piper! Don't you know about him? If he blows the right note on his pipes, your legs will fall off!"

"What, like the plague?"

"They say that in Porkrhinz the council didn't pay him, and he played his special pipe and led all the kids up into the mountains, and they were never seen again!"

"Good, do you think he'll do that here? The place'd be a lot quieter."

"Hah! Did you ever hear about that place in Klatch? They hired him to get rid of a plague of mime artists, and when they didn't pay up, he made all the town's Watch dance into the river and drown!"

"No! Did he? The devil!" said Sergeant Doppelpunkt.

"Three hundred dollars he charges, did you know that?"

"Three hundred dollars!"

"We'd better get going, sarge," said Corporal Knopf. "You get the sausages, and I'll get the mayor."

"No, Knopf. *You* get the sausages and *I'll* get the mayor, 'cos the mayor's free and Mrs. Shover will want paying."

The mayor was already up when the sergeant arrived, and wandering around the house with a worried expression.

He looked more worried when the sergeant arrived.

"What's she done this time?" he asked.

"Sir?" said the Watch. "Sir" said like that meant "What are you talking about?"

"Malicia hasn't been home all night," said the mayor.

"You think something might have happened to her, sir?"

"No, I think she might have happened to someone, man! Remember last month? When she tracked down the Mysterious Headless Horseman?"

"Well, you must admit he *was* a horseman, sir."

"That is true. But he was also a short man with a very high collar. *And* he was the chief tax gatherer from Mintz. I'm still getting official letters about it! Tax gatherers do not as a rule like young ladies dropping on them out of trees! And then in September there was that business about the—the—"

"The Mystery of Smuggler's Windmill, sir," said the Sergeant, rolling his eyes.

"Which turned out to be Mr. Vogel, the town

289

clerk, and Mrs. Schuman, the shoemaker's wife, who happened to be there merely because of their shared interest in studying the habits of barn owls . . ."

". . . and Mr. Vogel had his trousers off because he'd torn them on a nail . . ." said the sergeant, not looking at the mayor.

". . . which Mrs. Schuman was very kindly repairing for him," said the mayor, not looking at the sergeant.

"By moonlight," said the sergeant.

"She happens to have very good eyesight!" snapped the mayor. "And she didn't deserve to be bound and gagged along with Mr. Vogel, who caught quite a chill as a result! I had complaints from him and from her, *and* from Mrs. Vogel *and* from Mr. Schuman, *and* from Mr. Vogel after Mr. Schuman went around to his house and hit him with a last, *and* from Mrs. Schuman after Mrs. Vogel called her a—"

"A last what, sir?" said the sergeant.

"What?"

"Hit him with a last what?"

The mayor stared at the sergeant's honest but puzzled expression.

"A last, man!" he said. "It's a kind of wooden foot shoemakers use when they're making shoes!

290

Heaven knows what Malicia's doing this time!"

"I expect we'll find out when we hear the bang, sir."

"And what *was* it you wanted me for, sergeant?"

"The rat piper's here, sir."

The mayor went pale.

"Already?" he said.

"Yessir. He's having a shave in the fountain."

"Where's my official chain?" asked the mayor, staring around wildly. "My official robe? My official hat? Quick, man, help me!"

"He looks like quite a slow shaver, sir," said the sergeant, following the mayor out of the room at a run.

"Over in Klotz the mayor kept the piper waiting too long, and he played his pipe and turned him into a *badger*!" said the mayor, flinging open a cupboard. "Ah, here they are. Help me on with them, will you?"

When they arrived in the town square, out of breath, the piper was sitting on a bench, surrounded at a safe distance by a very large crowd. He was examining half a sausage on the end of a fork. Corporal Knopf was standing next to him like a schoolboy who has just turned in a nasty piece of work and is waiting to be told *exactly* how bad it is.

"And this is called a—?" the piper was saying.

"A sausage, sir," Corporal Knopf muttered.

"This is what you think is a sausage here, is it?" There was a gasp from the crowd. Bad Blintz was very proud of its traditional vole-and-pork sausages.

"Yessir," said Corporal Knopf.

"Amazing," said the piper. He looked up at the mayor. "And you are—?"

"I am the mayor of this town, and—"

The piper held up a hand and then nodded toward the old man, who was sitting on his cart, grinning broadly.

"My agent will deal with you," he said. He threw away the sausage, put his feet up on the other end of the bench, pulled his hat down over his eyes, and lay back.

The mayor went red in the face. Sergeant Doppelpunkt leaned toward him. "Remember the badger, sir!" he whispered.

"Ah . . . yes . . ."

The mayor, with what little dignity he had left, walked over to the cart.

"I believe the fee for ridding the town of rats will be three hundred dollars?" he said.

"Then I expect you'll believe anything," said the old man. He glanced at a notebook on his knee. "Let's see . . . call-out fee . . . plus special charge because it's St. Prodnitz's Day . . . plus pipe tax . . . looks like a medium-sized town, so that's extra . . . wear and tear on cart . . . traveling costs at a dollar a mile . . . miscellaneous expenses, taxes, charges . . ." He looked up. "Tell you what, let's say one thousand dollars, okay?"

"One thousand dollars! We haven't *got* one thousand dollars! That's outrag—"

"Badger, sir!" hissed Sergeant Dopplepunkt.

"You can't pay?" asked the old man.

"We don't have that kind of money! We've had to spend a lot of money bringing in food!"

"You don't have *any* money?" said the old man.

"Nothing like that amount, no!"

The old man scratched his chin. "Hmm," he said. "I can see where that's going to be a bit difficult, because . . . let's see . . ." He scribbled in his notebook for a moment and then looked up. "You already owe us four hundred sixty-seven dollars and nineteen cents for call-out, travel, and miscellaneous sundries."

"What? He hasn't blown a note!"

"Ah, but he's *ready* to," said the old man. "We've come all this way. You can't pay? What they call a bit of a problem, then. He's got to lead *something* out of the town, you see. Otherwise the news'll get around, and no one'll show him any respect, and if you haven't got respect, what have you got? If a piper doesn't have respect, he's—"

"—rubbish," said a voice. "I think he's rubbish."

The piper raised the brim of his hat.

The crowd in front of Keith parted in a hurry.

"Yeah?" said the piper.

"I don't think he can pipe up even one rat," said Keith. "He's just a fraud and a bully. Huh, I bet I can pipe up more rats than him."

Some of the people in the crowd began to creep away. No one wanted to be around when the rat piper lost his temper.

The piper swung his boots down onto the ground and pushed his hat back on his head.

"You a rat piper, kid?" he said softly.

Keith stuck out his chin defiantly.

"Yes. And don't call me kid . . . old man."

The piper grinned.

"Ah," he said. "I *knew* I was going to like this place. And you can make a rat dance, can you, kid?"

"More than you can, piper."

"Sounds like a challenge to me," said the piper.

"The piper doesn't accept challenges from—" the old man on the cart began, but the rat piper waved him into silence.

"Y'know, kid," he said, "this isn't the first time some kid has tried this. I'm walking down the street and someone yells, 'Go for your piccolo, mister!' and I turn around, and it's always a kid like you with a stupid-looking face. Now, I don't want anyone to say I'm an unfair man, kid, so if you'd just care to apologize, you might walk away from here with the same number of legs you started with—"

"You're *frightened*." Malicia stepped out of the crowd.

The piper grinned at her and then stopped grinning. Malicia could do that to people. "Yeah?" he said.

"Yes, because everyone knows what happens at a time like this. Let me ask this stupid-looking kid, who I've never seen before: Are you an orphan?"

"Yes," said Keith.

"You know nothing about your background at all?"

"No."

"Aha!" said Malicia. "That proves it! We *all* know what happens when a mysterious orphan turns up and challenges someone big and power-ful, don't we? It's like being the third and youngest son of a king. He can't *help* but win!"

She looked triumphantly at the crowd. But the crowd looked doubtful. They hadn't read as many stories as Malicia, and were rather more attached to the experience of real life, which is that when someone small and righteous takes on someone big and nasty, he is grilled bread product, very quickly.

However, someone at the back shouted, "Give the stupid-looking kid a chance! At least he'll be cheaper!" and someone else shouted, "Yes, that's right!" and someone else shouted, "I agree with the other two!" and *no one* seemed to notice that all the voices came from near ground level and were associated with the progress around the crowd of a scruffy-looking cat with half its fur missing. Instead, there was a general murmuring, no real words, nothing that would get anyone into trouble if the piper turned nasty, but a muttering indicating, in a general sense, without wishing to cause umbrage, and seeing everyone's point of view, and taking one thing with another, and all things being equal, that people would like to see the boy given a chance, if it's all right with you, no offense meant.

The piper shrugged.

"Fine," he said. "It'll be something to talk

about. And when I win, what will I get?"

The mayor coughed.

"Is a daughter's hand in marriage usual in these circumstances?" he said. "She has very good teeth and would make a goo— a wife for anyone with plenty of free wall space—"

"Father!" said Malicia.

"Later on, later on, obviously. He's unpleasant, but he *is* rich."

"No, I'll just take my payment," said the piper. "One way or another."

"And I said we can't afford it!" said the mayor.

"And I said one way or the other," said the piper. "And you, kid?"

"Your rat pipe," said Keith.

"No. It's magic, kid."

"Then why are you scared to bet it?"

The piper narrowed his eyes.

"Scared? No. Okay, kid . . . the rat pipe," he said.

"And the town must let me solve its rat problem," said Keith.

"And how much will *you* charge?" asked the mayor.

"Thirty gold pieces! Thirty gold pieces. Go on, say it!" shouted a voice at the back of the crowd.

"It won't cost you a thing," said Keith.

"Idiot!" shouted the voice in the crowd. People looked around, puzzled.

"Nothing at all?" said the mayor.

"No, nothing."

"Er . . . the hand-in-marriage thing is still on offer, if you—"

"Father!"

"No, that only happens in stories," said Keith. "And I shall also bring back a lot of the food that the rats stole."

"They *ate* it!" said the mayor. "What're you going to do, stick your fingers down their throats?"

"I said that I'll solve your rat problem," said Keith. "Agreed, Mr. Mayor?"

"Well, if you're not charging—"

"But first I shall need to borrow a pipe," Keith went on.

"You haven't got one?" asked the mayor.

"It got broken."

Corporal Knopf nudged the mayor. "I've got a trombone from when I was in the army," he said. "It won't take a moment to get it."

The rat piper burst out laughing.

"Doesn't that count?" asked the mayor, as Corporal Knopf hurried off.

"What? A trombone for charming rats? No, no, let him try. Can't blame a kid for trying.

Good with a trombone, are you?"

"I don't know," said Keith.

"What do you mean, you don't know?"

"I meant I've never played one. I'd be a lot happier with a flute, trumpet, piccolo, cornet, or Lancre bagpipe, but I've seen people playing the trombone, and it doesn't look too difficult. It's only an overgrown trumpet, really."

"Hah!" said the piper. "This I'd like to see— but not hear."

The Watch came running back, rubbing a battered trombone with his sleeve and therefore making it just a bit more grimy. Keith took it, wiped the mouthpiece, put it to his mouth, moved the slide a few times, and then blew one long note.

"Seems to work," he said. "I expect I can learn as I go along." He gave the rat piper a brief smile. "Do you want to go first?"

"You won't charm one rat with that mess, kid," said the piper, "but I'm glad I'm here to see you try."

Keith gave him a smile again, took a breath, and played.

There was a tune there. The instrument squeaked and wheezed, because Corporal Knopf had occasionally used the thing as a hammer, but there was a tune, quite fast, almost jaunty. You could tap your feet to it.

Someone tapped his feet to it.

Sardines emerged from a crack in a nearby wall, going "hwun*twothree*four" under his breath. The crowd watched him dance ferociously across the cobbles until he disappeared into a drain. Then they broke into applause.

The piper looked at Keith.

"Did that one have a *hat* on?" he asked.

"I didn't notice," said Keith. "Your go."

The piper pulled a short length of pipe from inside his jacket. He took another length from his pocket and slotted it into place on the first piece. It went *click* in a military kind of way.

Still watching Keith, and still grinning, the piper took a mouthpiece from his top pocket and screwed it into the rest of the pipe with another, very final, *click*.

Then he put it to his mouth and played.

From her lookout on a roof Big Savings shouted down a drainpipe, "Now!" Then she pushed two lumps of cotton into her ears.

At the bottom of the pipe, Inbrine shouted into a drain: "Now!" and then he too snatched up his earplugs.

. . . *ow, ow, ow* echoed through the pipes . . .

. . . "Now!" shouted Darktan, in the room of cages. He rammed some straw onto the end of the pipe. "Everyone block your ears!"

They'd done their best with the cages. Malicia had brought blankets, and the rats had spent a feverish hour blocking up holes with mud. They'd done their best to feed the prisoners properly, too, and even though they were only *keekees*, it was heartbreaking to see them cower so desperately.

Darktan turned to Nourishing. "Got your ears blocked?" he said.

"Pardon?"

"Good!" Darktan picked up two lumps of cotton. "The silly-sounding girl better be right about this stuff," he said. "I don't think many of us have got any strength left to dance."

◆ ◆ ◆

The piper blew again, and then stared at his pipe.

"Just one rat," said Keith helpfully. "Any rat you like. No rush."

The piper glared at him and blew again.

"I can't hear anything," said the mayor.

"Humans can't," muttered the piper.

"Perhaps it's broken," said Keith innocently.

The piper tried again. There was murmuring from the crowd.

"You've done something," he hissed.

"Oh yes?" said Malicia, loudly. "What could he have done? Told the rats to stay underground with their ears blocked up?"

The murmuring turned into muffled laughter.

The piper tried one more time. Keith felt the hairs stand up on the back of his neck.

A rat emerged. It moved slowly across the cobbles, bouncing from side to side, until it reached the piper's feet, where it fell over and started making a whirring noise.

People's mouths fell open.

It was Mr. Clicky.

The piper nudged it with his foot. The clock-work rat rolled over a few times, and then its spring, as a result of months of being punished in traps, gave up. There was a *poiyonngggg*, and a brief shower of cogwheels.

The crowd burst out laughing.

"Hmm," said the piper, and this time the look he gave Keith was shaded with grudging admiration.

"Okay, kid," he said. "Shall you and I have a little talk? Piper to piper? Over by the fountain?"

"Provided people can see us," said Keith.

"You don't trust me, kid?"

"Of course not."

The piper grinned. "Good. You've got the makings of a piper, I can see that."

Over by the fountain he sat down with his booted legs in front of him and held out the pipe. It was bronze, with a raised pattern of brass rats on it, and it glinted in the sunlight.

"Here," said the piper. "Take it. It's a good one. I've got plenty of others. Go on, take it. I'd like to hear you play it."

Keith looked at it uncertainly, turning it over and over in his hands.

"It's *all* trickery, kid," said the piper, as the pipe shone like a sunbeam. "See the little slider there? Move it down and the pipe plays a special note humans can't hear. Rats can. Sends 'em nuts. They come rushing out of the ground and you drive 'em into the river, just like a sheep dog."

"That's all there is to it?" said Keith.

"You were expecting something more?"

"Well, yes. They say you turn people into badgers and lead children into magic caves and——"

The piper leaned forward conspiratorially. "It always pays to advertise, kid. Sometimes these little towns can be pretty slow when it comes to parting with the cash. 'Cos the thing about turning people into badgers and all the rest of that stuff is this: It never happens *round here*. Most of the people in these mountains never go more than ten miles away in their lives. They'll believe just about anything could happen fifty miles away. Once the story gets around, it does your work for you. Half the things people say I've done even *I* didn't make up."

"Tell me," said Keith, "have you ever met someone called Maurice?"

"Maurice? Maurice? I don't think so."

"Amazing," said Keith. He took the pipe and gave the piper a long, slow stare.

"And now, piper," he said, "I think you're going to lead the rats out of town. It's going to be the most impressive job you've ever done."

"Hey? What? You won, kid."

"You'll lead out the rats because that's how it should go," said Keith, polishing the pipe on his sleeve. "Why do you charge such a lot?"

"Because I give 'em a show," said the piper. "The fancy clothes, the bullying . . . charging a lot is part of the whole thing. You've got to give 'em magic, kid. Let 'em think you're just a fancy rat catcher, and you'll be lucky to get a cheese lunch and a warm handshake."

"We'll do it together, and the rats will *follow* us, really follow us into the river. Don't bother about the trick note—this will be even better. It'll be . . . it'll be a great . . . story," said Keith. "And you'll get your money. Three hundred dollars, wasn't it? But you'll settle for half, because I'm helping you."

"What are you playing at, kid? I told you, you won."

"Everyone wins. Trust me. They called you in. They should pay the piper. Besides . . ." Keith smiled. "I don't want people to think pipers shouldn't get paid, do I?"

"And I thought you were just a stupid-looking kid," said the piper. "What kind of a *deal* have you got with the rats?"

"You wouldn't believe it, piper. You wouldn't believe it."

◆ ◆ ◆

Inbrine scurried through the tunnels, scrabbled through the mud and straw that had been used to block the last one, and jumped into the cage room. The Clan rats unblocked their ears when they saw him.

"He's doing it?" said Darktan.

"Yessir! Right now!"

Darktan looked up at the cages. The *keekees*

were more subdued, now that the rat king was dead and they'd been fed. But by the smell of it they were desperate to leave this place. And rats in a panic will follow other rats. . . .

"Okay," he said. "Runners, get ready! Open the cages! Make sure they're following you! Go! Go! Go!"

And that was almost the end of the story.

How the crowd yelled when rats erupted from every hole and drain! How they cheered when both pipers danced out of the town, with the rats racing along behind them! How they whistled when the rats plunged off the bridge into the river!

They didn't notice that some rats stayed on the bridge, urging the others over with shouts of "Remember, strong regular strokes!" and "There's a nice beach just downstream!" and "Hit the water feet first—it won't hurt so much!"

Even if they had noticed, they probably wouldn't have said anything. Details like that don't fit in.

And the big piper danced off over the hills and never, ever came back.

◆ ◆ ◆

There was general applause. It had been a good show, everyone agreed, even if it had been expensive. It was definitely something to tell their children.

The stupid-looking kid, the one who had dueled with the piper, strolled back into the square. He got a round of applause too. It was turning out to be a good day all round. People wondered if they'd have to have extra children to make room for all the stories.

But they realized they'd have enough to save for the grandchildren when the *other* rats arrived.

They were suddenly there, pouring up out of drains and gutters and cracks. They didn't squeak, and they weren't running. They sat there, watching everyone.

"Here, piper!" shouted the mayor. "You missed some!"

"No. We're not the rats who follow pipers," said a voice. "We're the rats you have to *deal with*."

The mayor looked down. A rat was standing by his boots, looking up at him.

It appeared to be holding a sword.

"Father," said Malicia, suddenly behind him, "it would be a good idea to listen to this rat."

"But it's a rat!"

"He knows, Father. And he knows how to get your money back and a lot of the food and

307

where to find some of the people who've been stealing food from us."

"But he's a rat!"

"*Yes*, Father. But if you talk to him properly, he can help us."

The mayor stared at the assembled ranks of the Clan. "We should talk to *rats*?" he said.

"It would be a very good idea, Father."

"But they're rats!" The mayor seemed to be trying to hold on to this thought as if it was a life preserver on a stormy sea, and he'd drown if he let go of it.

"'Scuse me, 'scuse me," said a voice from beside him. He looked down this time at a dirty, half-scorched cat, who grinned at him.

"Did that *cat* just *speak*?" asked the mayor.

Maurice looked around. "Which one?" he said.

"You! Did you just talk?"

"Would you feel better if I said no?" said Maurice.

"But cats can't talk!"

"Well, I can't promise that I could give a, you know, full-length after-dinner speech, and don't ask me to do a comic monologue," said Maurice. "And I can't pronounce difficult words like 'marmalade' and 'lumbago.' But I'm pretty happy

with basic repartee and simple wholesome conversation. Speaking as a cat, I'd like to hear what
the rat says."

"Mr. Mayor?" said Keith, strolling up and
twirling the new rat pipe in his fingers. "Don't
you think it's time I sorted out your rat problem
once and for all?"

"Sorted it out? But—"

"All you have to do is talk to them. Get your
town council together and *talk to them*. It's up to
you, Mr. Mayor. You can yell and shout and call
out the dogs, and people can run around and flail
at the rats with brooms, and yes, they'll run away.
But they won't run far. And they'll come back."
When he was standing next to the bewildered
man, he leaned toward him and whispered:
"And they live under your floorboards, sir. They
know how to use fire. They know *all* about
poison. Oh, yes. So . . . listen to this rat."

"Is it *threatening* us?" asked the mayor, looking
down at Darktan.

"No, Mr. Mayor," said Darktan. "I'm offering
you"—he glanced at Maurice, who nodded—"a
wonderful opportunity."

"You really *can* talk? You can think?" asked the
mayor.

Darktan looked up at him. It had been a long

night. He didn't want to remember any of it. And now it was going to be a longer, harder day. He took a deep breath.

"Here's what I suggest," he said. "You pretend that rats can think, and I'll promise to pretend that humans can think, too."

CHAPTER 12

W ell done, Ratty Rupert!" cried the animals of Furry Bottom.

—From *Mr. Bunnsy Has an Adventure*

The crowd clustered into the council hall in the Rathaus. Most of it had to stay outside, craning over other people's heads to see what was going on.

The town council was crammed around one end of the long table. A dozen or so of the senior rats were crouched at the other end.

And in the middle was Maurice. He was suddenly there, leaping up from the floor.

Hopwick the clockmaker glared at the other members of the council.

"We're *talking* to rats!" he snapped, trying to make himself heard above the hubbub. "We'll be a laughingstock if this gets out! 'The Town That Talked to Its Rats.' Can't you just see it?"

311

"Rats aren't there to be spoken to," said Raufman the bootmaker, prodding the mayor with a finger. "A mayor who knew his business would send for the rat catchers!"

"According to my daughter, they are locked in a cellar," said the mayor. He stared at the finger.

"Locked in by your talking rats?" asked Raufman.

"Locked in by my daughter," said the mayor calmly. "Take your finger away, Mr. Raufman. She's taken the Watch down there. She's making very serious allegations, Mr. Raufman. She says there's a lot of food stored under their shed. She says they've been stealing it and selling it to the river traders. The head rat catcher is your brother-in-law, isn't he, Mr. Raufman? I remember you were very keen to see him appointed, weren't you?"

There was a commotion outside. Sergeant Doppelpunkt pushed his way through, grinning broadly, and laid a big sausage on the table.

"One sausage is hardly *theft*," said Raufman.

There was rather more commotion in the crowd, which parted to reveal what was, strictly speaking, a very slowly moving Corporal Knopf. This fact became clear, though, only when he'd been stripped of three bags of grain, eight strings of sausages, a barrel of pickled beets, and fifteen cabbages.

Sergeant Doppelpunkt saluted smartly, to the sound of muffled swearing and falling cabbages.

"Requesting permission to take six men to help us bring up the rest of the stuff, sir!" he said, beaming happily.

"Where are the rat catchers?" asked the mayor.

"In deep . . . trouble, sir," said the sergeant. "I arsked them if they wanted to come out, but they said they'd like to stay in there a bit longer, thanks all the same, although they'd like a drink of water and some fresh trousers."

"Was that *all* they said?"

Sergeant Doppelpunkt pulled out his notebook. "No, sir, they said quite a lot. They were crying, acktually. They said they'd confess to everything in exchange for the fresh trousers. Also, sir, there was this."

A newly deputized Watchman came in carrying a heavy box, which he thumped down onto the polished table.

"Acting on information received from a rat, sir, we took a look under one of the floorboards in their shed. There must be more'n four hundred dollars in it. Ill-gotten gains, sir."

"You got information from a *rat*?"

The sergeant pulled Sardines out of his pocket. The rat was eating a biscuit, but he raised his hat politely.

"Isn't that a bit . . . unhygienic?" asked the mayor.

"No, guv, he's washed his hands," said Sardines.

"I was talking to the sergeant!"

"He's a nice little chap, sir. Very clean," said Sergeant Doppelpunkt. "Reminds me of a hamster I used to have when I was a lad, sir."

"Well, thank you, sergeant, well done, please go and—"

"His name was Horace," added the sergeant helpfully.

"Thank you, sergeant, and now—"

"Does me good to see little cheeks bulging with grub again, sir."

"*Thank* you, sergeant!"

When the sergeant had left, the mayor turned and stared at Mr. Raufman. The bootmaker had the grace to look embarrassed.

"I hardly know the man," he said hurriedly. "He's just somebody my sister married, that's all! I hardly ever see him!"

"I quite understand," said the mayor. "And I've no intention of asking the sergeant to go and search your larder." He gave another little smile, and a sniff, and added, "Yet. Now, where were we?"

"I was about to tell you a story," said Maurice. The town council stared at him.

"And your name is—?" asked the mayor, who was feeling in quite a good mood now.

"Maurice," said Maurice. "I'm a freelance negotiator, you could say. I can see it's difficult for you to talk to rats, but humans like talking to cats, right?"

"Like in Dick Livingstone?" asked Hopwick the clockmaker.

"Yeah, right, him, yeah, and—" Maurice began.

"And Puss in Boots?" asked Corporal Knopf.

"Yeah, right, just like in books," said Maurice, scowling. "*Anyway* . . . cats can talk to rats, okay? And I'm going to tell you a story. But first I'm going to tell you that my clients, the rats, will all leave this town if you want them to, and they won't come back. Ever."

The humans stared at him. So did the rats.

"Will we?" asked Darktan.

"Will they?" asked the mayor.

"Yes," said Maurice. "And now I'm going to tell you a story about the lucky town. I don't know its name yet. Let's suppose my clients leave here and move downriver, shall we? There are lots of towns on this river, I'll be bound. And

315

somewhere there's a town that'll say, Why, we *can* do a deal with the rats. And that will be a very lucky town, because then there'll be *rules*, see?"

"Not exactly, no," said the mayor.

"Well, in this lucky town, right, a lady making, as it might be, a tray of cakes, well, all she'll need to do is shout down the nearest rat hole and say, 'Good morning, rats, there's one cake for you; I'd be much obliged if'n you didn't touch the rest of them,' and the rats will say, 'Right you are, missus, no problem at all.' And then—"

"Are you saying we should *bribe* the rats?" asked the mayor.

"Cheaper than pipers. Cheaper than rat catchers," said Maurice. "Anyway, it'll be wages. Wages for what, I hear you cry?"

"Did I cry that?" said the mayor.

"You were going to," said Maurice. "And I was going to tell you that it'd be wages for . . . for vermin control."

"What? But rats *are* ver—"

"Don't say it!" said Darktan.

"Vermin like cockroaches," said Maurice, smoothly. "I can see you've got a lot of them here."

"Can *they* talk?" asked the mayor. Now he had the slightly hunted expression of anyone who'd been talked at by Maurice for any length of time. It said, "I'm going where I don't want to go, but I don't know how to get off."

"No," said Maurice. "Nor can the mice, and nor can norma— nor can other rats. Well, vermin'll be a thing of the past in that lucky town, because its new rats will be like a police force. Why, the Clan'll *guard* your larders—sorry, I mean the larders in that town. No rat catchers required. Think of the savings. But that'll only be the start. The woodcarvers will be getting richer, too, in the lucky town."

"How?" asked Hauptmann the woodcarver, sharply.

"Because rats will be working for them," said Maurice. "They have to gnaw all the time to wear their teeth down, so they might as well be making cuckoo clocks. And the clockmakers will be doing well too."

"Why?" asked Hopwick the clockmaker.

"Tiny little paws, very good with little springs and things," said Maurice. "And then—"

"Would they just do cuckoo clocks, or could they do other stuff?" asked Hauptmann.

"—and then there's the whole tourism aspect," said Maurice. "For example, the Rat Clock. You know that clock they've got in Bonk? In the town square? Little figures come out every quarter of an hour and bang the bells? Cling bong bang, bing clong *bong*? Very popular—you can get postcards and everything. Big attraction. People come a long way just to stand there waiting for it."

"So what you're saying," said the clockmaker, "is that if we—that is, if the lucky town had a special big clock, and rats, people might come to see it?"

"And stand around waiting for up to a quarter of an hour," said someone.

"A perfect time to buy tooth-crafted models of the clock," said the clockmaker. "At very reasonable prices."

People began to think about this.

"Mugs with rats on them," said a potter.

"Hand-gnawed souvenir wooden plates," said Hauptmann.

"Cuddly toy rats!"

"Rats-on-a-stick!"

Darktan took a deep breath. Maurice said, quickly, "Good idea. Made of *toffee*, naturally." He glanced toward Keith. "And I expect the town would want to employ its very own rat piper, even. You know. For ceremonial purposes. 'Have your picture drawn with the Official Rat

Piper and his Rats' sort of thing."

"Any chance of a small theater?" said a little voice.

Darktan spun around.

"Sardines!" he said.

"Well, guv, I thought if everyone was getting in on the act—" Sardines protested.

"Maurice, we ought to talk about this," said Dangerous Beans, tugging at the cat's leg.

"Excuse me a moment," said Maurice, giving the mayor a quick grin. "I need to consult with my clients. Of course," he added, "I'm talking about the *lucky* town. Which won't be this one because, of course, when my clients move out, some new rats will move in. There are always more rats. And *they* won't talk, and *they* won't have rules, and they'll widdle in the cream, and you'll have to find some new rat catchers, ones you can trust, and you won't have as much money because the tourists will be going to the other town. Just a thought."

He marched down the table and turned to the rats.

"I was doing so well!" he said. "You could be on ten percent, you know? Your faces on mugs, everything!"

"And is this what we fought for all night?"

spat Darktan. "To be *pets*?"

"Maurice, this isn't right," said Dangerous Beans. "Surely it is better to appeal to the common bond between intelligent species than—"

"I don't know about intelligent species. We're dealing with humans here," said Maurice. "Do you know about wars? Very popular with humans. They fight other humans. Not hugely big on common bonding."

"Yes, but we are not—"

"Now listen," said Maurice. "Ten minutes ago these people thought you were pests. Now they think you're . . . useful. Who knows what I can make them think if you give me a half hour?"

"You want us to *work* for them?" said Darktan. "We've *won* our place here!"

"You'll be working for *yourselves*," said Maurice. "Look, these people aren't philosophers. They're just . . . everyday. They don't understand about the tunnels. This is a market town. You've got to approach them the right way. Anyway, you *will* keep other rats away, and you won't go around widdling in the jam, so you might as well get thanked for it." He tried again. "There's going to be a lot of shouting, right, yeah. And then sooner or later you have to talk." He saw the bewilderment still glazing their eyes and turned to Sardines in desperation.

"Help me," he said.

"He's right, boss. You've got to give a 'em a show," said Sardines, dancing a few steps nervously.

"They'll laugh at us!" said Darktan.

"Better laugh than scream, boss. It's a start. You gotta dance, boss. You can think and you can fight, but the world's always movin', and if you wanna stay ahead, you gotta dance."

He raised his hat and twirled his cane. On the other side of the room a couple of humans saw him and chuckled.

"See?" he said.

"I'd hoped there was an island somewhere," said Dangerous Beans. "A place where rats could really be rats."

"And we've seen where that leads," said Darktan. "And, you know, I don't think there's any wonderful islands in the distance for people like us. Not for us." He sighed. "If there's a wonderful island anywhere, it's here. But I'm not intending to dance."

"Figure of speech, boss, figure of speech," said Sardines, hopping from one foot to the other.

There was a thump from the other end of the table. The mayor, who had been arguing with some of the councilors, had hit it with his fist.

"We've got to be *practical*!" he shouted. "How much worse off can we be? They can *talk*. I'm not going to go through all this again, understand? We've got food, we've got a lot of money back, we survived the piper. . . . These are *lucky* rats."

The figures of Keith and Malicia loomed over Maurice and the rats.

"It sounds as if my father's coming round to the idea," said Malicia. "What about you?"

"Discussions are continuing," said Maurice.

"I . . . er . . . I'm sorr . . . er . . . look, Maurice told me where to look, and I found this in the tunnel," said Malicia.

She put something down on the table. The pages were torn and stained, but it was still recognizable as *Mr. Bunnsy Has an Adventure*. It had been inexpertly stitched back together.

"I had to lift up a lot of drain gratings," she said.

The rats looked at it. Then they looked at Dangerous Beans.

"It's *Mr. Bunn*—" Peaches began.

"I know. I can smell it," said Dangerous Beans.

The rats all looked again at the remains of the Book.

"It's a lie," said Peaches.

"Maybe it's just a pretty story," said Sardines.

"Yes," said Dangerous Beans. "Yes." He turned his misty pink eyes to Darktan, who had to stop himself from stepping back, and added: "Perhaps it's a map."

◆　◆　◆

If it was a story, and not real life, then humans and rats would have shaken hands and gone on into a bright new future.

But since it was real life, there had to be a contract. A war that had been going on since people first lived in houses could not end with just a happy smile. And there had to be a committee. There was much detail to be discussed. The town council was on it, and most of the senior rats, and Maurice marched up and down the table, joining in.

Darktan sat at one end. He wanted to sleep. His wound ached, his teeth ached, and he hadn't eaten for ages. For hours the argument flowed backward and forward over his drooping head. He didn't pay attention to who was doing the talking. Most of the time it seemed to be everyone.

"Next item: Compulsory bells on all cats. Agreed?"

"Can we just get back to clause thirty, Mr., er, Maurice? You saying killing a rat would be murder?" said Raufman.

"Yes. Of course."

"But it's just—"

"Talk to the paw, mister, 'cos the whiskers don't want to know!"

"The cat is right," said the mayor. "You're out of order, Mr. Raufman! We've *been* though this."

"Then what about if a rat steals from me?"

"Ahem. Then that'll be theft, and the rat will have to go before the justices," said a little voice.

"Oh, young—?" said Raufman.

"Peaches. I'm a rat, sir."

"And ... er ... and the Watch officers will be able to get down the rat tunnels, will they?" asked Hauptmann.

"Yes! Because there will be rat officers in the Watch. There'll have to be," said Maurice. "No problem!"

"Really? And what does Sergeant Doppelpunkt think about that?" snapped Raufman. "Sergeant Doppelpunkt?"

"Er ... dunno, sir. Could be all right, I suppose. I know *I* couldn't get down a rat hole. We'd have to make the badges smaller, of course."

"I take it that the rat Watch would only arrest rats, yes?"

The sergeant scratched his head. "No, sir. The way I see it, they'd arrest anyone who needed arresting."

"What? Surely you wouldn't suggest a rat officer could be allowed to arrest a *human*?"

"Oh, yes, sir," said the sergeant.

"What?"

"Well, if your rat's a proper sworn-in Watchman . . . I mean, a Watchrat . . . then you can't go around saying you're not allowed to arrest anyone bigger than you, can you? Could be useful, a rat Watchman. I understand they have this trick where they run up your trouser leg—"

"Gentlemen, we should move on. I suggest this one goes to the subcommittee," said the mayor.

"Which one, sir? We've already got seventeen!"

There was a snort from one of the councilors. This was Mr. Schlummer, who was ninety-five and had been peacefully asleep all morning. The snort meant that he was waking up.

He stared at the other side of the table. His whiskers moved.

"There's a *rat* there!" he said, pointing. "Look,

mm, bold as brass! A rat! In a *hat!*"

"Yes, sir. This is a meeting to talk to the rats, sir," said the person beside him.

He looked down and fumbled for his glasses.

"Wassat?" he said. He looked closer. "Here," he said, "aren't, mm, *you* a rat, too?"

"Yes, sir. Name of Nourishing, sir. We're here to talk to humans. To stop all the trouble."

Mr. Schlummer stared at the rat. Then he looked across the table at Sardines, who raised his hat. Then he looked at the mayor, who nodded. He looked at everyone again, his lips moving as he tried to sort this out.

"You're *all* talking?" he said at last.

"Yes, sir," said Nourishing.

"So . . . who's doing the listening?" he asked.

"I expect that'll happen later on," said Maurice.

Mr. Schlummer glared at him.

"Are you a cat?" he demanded.

"Yes, sir," said Maurice.

Mr. Schlummer digested this point too.

"I thought we used to kill rats?" he said, as if he wasn't quite certain anymore.

"Yes, but you see, sir, this is the future," said Maurice.

"Is it?" said Mr. Schlummer. "Really? I always wondered when the future was going to happen. Oh, well. Cats talk now, too? Well done! Got to move with the, mm, the ... things that move, obviously. Wake me up when they bring the tea in."

He settled happily back in his chair and after a while began to snore.

Around him the arguments started again, and kept going. A lot of people talked. Some people listened. Occasionally, they agreed ... and moved on ... and argued again. But the piles of paper on the table grew bigger, and looked more and more official.

Darktan realized that someone was watching him. At the other end of the table the mayor was giving him a long, thoughtful stare.

As he watched, the man leaned back and said something to a clerk, who nodded and walked around the table, past the arguing people, until he reached Darktan.

He leaned down.

"Can ... you ... un-der-stand ... me?" he said, pronouncing each word very carefully.

"Yes ... be-cause ... I'm ... not ... stu-pid," said Darktan.

"Oh, er ... the mayor wonders if he can see

you in his private office," said the clerk. "The door over there. I could help you down, if you like."

"I could bite your finger, if you like," said Darktan. The mayor was already walking away from the table. Darktan slid down and followed him. No one paid any attention to either of them.

The mayor waited until Darktan's tail was out of the way and carefully shut the door.

The room was small and untidy. Paper occupied most flat surfaces. Bookcases filled several of the walls; extra books and more papers were stuffed in between the tops of the books and the bottoms of the next shelves.

The mayor, moving with exaggerated delicacy, went and sat in a big, rather tatty swivel chair, then looked down at Darktan.

"I'm going to get this wrong," he said. "I thought we should have a . . . a little talk. Can I pick you up? I mean, it'd be easier to talk to you if you were on my desk."

"Really?" said Darktan. "I might say it'd be easier to talk to *you* if you lay flat on the floor." He sighed. He was too tired for these games. "Look, if you put your hand flat on the floor, I'll stand on it and you can raise it up to the height of the desk," he said, "but if you try any tricks, I'll bite your thumb off."

The mayor lifted him up with extreme caution. Darktan hopped off into the mass of papers, empty teacups, and old pens that covered the battered leather top, and stood looking up at the embarrassed man.

"Er . . . do you have to do much paperwork in your job?" asked the mayor.

"Peaches writes things down," said Darktan bluntly.

"That's the little female rat who coughs before she speaks, isn't it?" said the mayor.

"That's right."

"She's very . . . definite, isn't she," said the mayor, and now Darktan could see that he was sweating. "She's rather frightening some of the councilors, ha ha."

"Ha ha," said Darktan.

The mayor looked miserable. He seemed to be searching for something to say.

"You are, er, settling in well?" he said.

"I spent part of last night fighting a dog in a rat pit, and then I think I was stuck in a rat trap for a while," said Darktan, in a voice like ice. "And then there was a bit of a war. Apart from that, I can't complain."

The mayor gave him a long, worried stare. For the first time he could remember, Darktan felt sorry for a human. The mayor seemed to be as tired as Darktan felt.

"Look," he said, "I think it might work, if that's what you want to ask me."

The mayor brightened up. "You do?" he said. "There's a lot of arguing."

"That's why I think it might work," said Darktan. "Men and rats arguing. You're not poisoning our cheese, and we're not widdling in your jam. It's not going to be easy, but it's a start."

"But there's something I have to know," said the mayor.

"Yes?"

"You *could* have poisoned our wells. You *could* have set fire to our houses. My daughter tells me you are very . . . advanced. You don't owe us anything. Why didn't you?"

"I asked myself that, too," said Darktan. "And I told myself: What good would it do? What would we have done afterward? Gone to another town? Gone through all this again? Would killing you have made anything *better* for us? Sooner or later we'd have to talk to humans. It might as well be you."

"I'm glad you like us!" said the mayor.

Darktan opened his mouth to say: Like you? No, we just don't hate you enough. We're not *friends*.

But . . .

There would be no more rat pits. No more traps, no more poisons. True, he was going to have to explain to the Clan what a Watch was, and why rat policemen might chase rats who broke the new Rules. They weren't going to like that. They weren't going to like that *at all*. Even a rat with the marks of the Bone Rat's teeth on him was going to have difficulty with that. But Maurice had said: They'll do this, you'll do that. No one will lose very much, and everyone will gain a lot. The town will prosper, *everyone's* children will grow up, and suddenly it'll all be *normal*.

And everyone likes things to be *normal*. They don't like to see normal things changed. It must be worth a try, thought Darktan.

"Now I want to ask you a question," he said. "You've been the leader for . . . how long?"

"Ten years," said the mayor.

"Isn't it hard?"

"Oh, yes. Oh, yes. Everyone argues with me all the time," said the mayor. "Although I must say I'm expecting a little less arguing if all this works

331

out. But it's not an easy job."

"It's ridiculous to have to shout all the time just to get things done," said Darktan.

"That's right," said the mayor.

"And everyone expects you to decide things," said Darktan.

"True."

"The last leader gave me some advice just before he died, and do you know what it was? 'Don't eat the green wobbly bit'!"

"Good advice?" asked the mayor.

"In his world, yes," said Darktan. "But all *he* had to do was be big and tough and fight all the other rats that wanted to be leader."

"It's a bit like that with the council," said the mayor.

"What?" said Darktan. "You *bite* them in the *neck*?"

"Not yet," said the mayor. "But it's a tempting thought, I must say."

"It's just all a lot more complicated than I ever thought it would be!" said Darktan, bewildered. "To be a leader you have to learn to shout! But after you've learned to shout, you have to learn not to!"

"Right again," said the mayor. "That's how it works." He put his hand down on the desk, palm up. "May I?" he said. "I want to show you something."

Darktan stepped aboard and kept his balance as the mayor carried him over to the window and set him down on the sill.

"See the river?" said the mayor. "See the houses? See the people in the streets? I have to make it all work. Well, not the river, obviously, that works by itself. And every year it turns out that I haven't upset enough people for them to choose anyone else as mayor. So I have to do it again. It's a lot more complicated than I ever thought it would be."

"What, for you, too? But you're a human!" said Darktan in astonishment.

"Hah! You think that makes it easier? *I* thought rats were wild and free!"

"Hah!" said Darktan.

They both stared out the window. Down in the square below, Keith and Malicia were walking along, deep in conversation.

"If you like," said the mayor after a while, "you could have a little desk here in my office—"

"I'll live underground, thank you all the same," said Darktan, pulling himself together. "Little desks are a bit too Mr. Bunnsy."

The mayor sighed. "I suppose so. Er . . ." He

looked as if he was about to share some guilty secret and, in a way, he was. "I did like those books when I was a boy, though. Of course I knew it was all nonsense, but all the same, it was nice to think that—"

"Yeah, yeah," said Darktan. "But the rabbit was stupid. Who ever heard of a rabbit talking?"

"Oh, yes. I never liked the rabbit," said the mayor.

"No one likes the rabbit," said Darktan.

"It was the minor characters everyone liked," said the mayor. "Ratty Rupert and Phil the Pheasant and Olly the Snake—"

"Oh, come *on*," said Darktan. "Olly the Snake had a collar and tie!"

"Well?"

"Well, how did it stay on? A snake is tube-shaped!"

"Do you know, I never thought of it like that," said the mayor. "Silly, really. He'd wriggle out of it, wouldn't he?"

"And vests on rats don't work."

"No?"

"No," said Darktan. "I tried it. Tool belts are fine, but not vests. Dangerous Beans got quite upset about that. But I told him, you've got to be *practical*."

"It's just like I always tell my daughter," said the man. "Stories are just stories. Life is complicated enough as it is. We have to plan for the real world. There's no room for the fantastic."

"Exactly," said the rat.

And man and rat talked as the long light faded into the evening.

◆ ◆ ◆

A man was painting, very carefully, a little picture underneath the street sign that said RIVER STREET. It was a long way underneath, only just higher than the pavement, and he had to kneel down. He kept referring to a small piece of paper in his hand.

The picture looked like:

Keith laughed.

"What's funny?" asked Malicia.

"It's in the Rat alphabet," said Keith. "It says 'Water+Fast+Stones.' The streets have got cobbles on, right? So rats see them as stones. It means River Street."

"Both languages on the street signs. Clause One Ninety-Three," said Malicia. "That's fast. They only agreed on that two hours ago. I suppose that means there will be tiny signs in human language in the rat tunnels?"

"I hope not," said Keith.

"Why not?"

"Because rats mostly mark their tunnels by widdling on them."

He was impressed at the way Malicia's expression didn't change a bit.

"I can see we're all going to have to make some important mental adjustments," she said thoughtfully. "It was odd about Maurice, though, after my father told him there were plenty of kind old ladies in the town who'd be happy to give him a home."

"You mean when he said that wouldn't be any fun, getting it that way?" said Keith.

"Yes. Do you know what he meant?"

"Sort of. He meant he's Maurice," said Keith.

"I think he had the time of his life, strutting up and down the table ordering everyone around. He even said me and the rats could keep the money we buried! He said a little voice in his head told him it was really ours!"

Malicia appeared to think about things for a while, and then she said, as if it wasn't very important really:

"And, er . . . you're staying, yes?"

"Clause Nine, Resident Rat Piper," said Keith. "I get an official suit that I don't have to share with anyone, a hat with a feather, and a pipe allowance."

"That will be . . . quite satisfactory," said Malicia. "Er . . ."

"Yes?"

"When I told you that I had two sisters, er, that wasn't entirely true," she said. "Er . . . it wasn't a lie, of course, but it was just . . . enhanced a bit."

"Yes."

"I mean it would be more *literally* true to say that I have, in fact, no sisters at all."

"Ah," said Keith.

"But I have millions of friends, of course," Malicia went on. She looked, Keith thought, absolutely miserable.

"That's amazing," he said. "Most people just

have a few dozen."

"Millions," said Malicia. "Obviously, there's always room for another one."

"Good," said Keith.

"And, er, there's Clause Five," said Malicia, still looking a bit nervous.

"Oh, yes," said Keith. "That one puzzled everyone. 'A bang-up tea with cream buns and a medal,' right?"

"Yes," said Malicia. "It wouldn't be properly over, otherwise. Would you, er, join me?"

Keith nodded. He stared around at the town. It seemed a nice place. Just the right size. A man could find a future here. . . .

"Yes," he said. "Yes, I think I'll stay. It'll make a good story."

◆　◆　◆

There's a town where, every time the clock shows a quarter of an hour, the rats come out and strike the bells.

And people watch, and cheer, and buy the souvenir hand-gnawed mugs and plates and spoons and clocks and other things that have no use whatsoever other than to be bought and taken home. And they go to the Rat Museum, and they eat Rat Burgers (Guaranteed No Rat) and buy Rat Ears that you can wear and buy the books of

Rat poetry in Rat language and say "how odd" when they see the street signs in Rat and marvel at how the whole place seems so clean. . . .

And once a day the town's rat piper, who is rather young, plays his pipes, and the rats dance to the music, usually in a conga line. It's very popular (on special days a little tap-dancing rat organizes vast dancing spectaculars, with hundreds of rats in sequins, and water ballet in the fountains, and elaborate sets).

And there are lectures about the Rat Tax and how the whole system works, and how the rats have a town of their own under the human town, and get free use of the library, and even sometimes send their young rats to the school. And everyone says: How perfect, how well organized, how *amazing*!

And then most of them go back to their own towns and set their traps and put down their poisons, because some minds you couldn't change with a hatchet. But a few see the world as a different place.

It's not perfect, but it works. The thing about stories is that you have to pick the ones that last.

◆ ◆ ◆

And far downstream a handsome cat, with only a few bare patches still in his fur, jumped off a barge, sauntered along the dock, and entered a large and prosperous town. He spent a few days beating up the local cats and getting the feel of the place and, most of all, sitting and watching.

Finally he saw what he wanted. He followed a young lad out of the city. The boy was carrying a stick over his back, on the end of which was a knotted handkerchief of the kind used by people in story circumstances to carry all their worldly goods. The cat grinned to himself. If you knew their dreams, you could handle people.

The cat followed the boy all the way to the first milestone along the road, where the boy sat down for a rest. And heard:

"Hey, stupid-looking kid? Wanna be Lord Mayor? Nah, down here, kid. . . ."

Because some stories end, but old stories go on, and you gotta dance if you want to stay ahead.

AUTHOR'S NOTE

I think I have read, in the past few months, more about rats than is good for me. Most of the true stuff—or, at least, the stuff that people say is true—is so unbelievable that I didn't include it in case readers thought I'd made it up.

Rats have been known to escape from a rat pit using the same method Darktan used on poor Jacko. If you don't believe it, this was witnessed by Old Alf, Jimma, and Uncle Bob. I have it on the best authority.

Rat kings really exist. *How* they come into existence is a mystery; in this book Malicia mentions a couple of the theories. I am indebted to Dr. Jack Cohen for a more modern and depressing one, which is that down the ages some cruel and inventive people have had altogether too much time on their hands.

FROM

The Wee Free Men

Some things start before other things.

It was a summer shower but didn't appear to know it, and it was pouring rain as fast as a winter storm.

Miss Perspicacia Tick sat in what little shelter a raggedy hedge could give her and explored the universe. She didn't notice the rain. Witches dried out quickly.

The exploring of the universe was being done with a couple of twigs tied together with string, a stone with a hole in it, an egg, one of Miss Tick's stockings (which also had a hole in it), a pin, a piece of paper, and a tiny stub of pencil. Unlike wizards, witches learn to make do with a little.

The items had been tied and twisted together to make a . . . device. It moved oddly when she prodded it. One of the sticks seemed to pass right through the egg, for example, and came out the other side without leaving a mark.

"Yes," she said quietly, as rain poured off the

rim of her hat. "There it *is*. A definite ripple in the walls of the world. Very worrying. There's probably another world making contact. That's never good. I ought to go there. But . . . according to my left elbow, there's a witch there already."

"She'll sort it out, then," said a small and, for now, mysterious voice from somewhere near her feet.

"No, it can't be right. That's chalk country over that way," said Miss Tick. "You can't grow a good witch on chalk. The stuff's barely harder than clay. You need good hard rock to grow a witch, believe me." Miss Tick shook her head, sending raindrops flying. "But my elbows are generally very reliable."*

"Why talk about it? Let's go and see," said the voice. "We're not doing very well around here, are we?"

That was true. The lowlands weren't good to witches. Miss Tick was making pennies by doing bits of medicine and misfortune-telling**, and slept in barns most nights. She'd twice

---

*People say things like "listen to your heart," but witches learn to listen to other things too. It's amazing what your kidneys can tell you.

**Ordinary fortune-tellers tell you what you *want* to happen; witches tell you what's going to happen whether you want it to or not. Strangely enough, witches tend to be more accurate but less popular.

2

been thrown into ponds.

"I can't barge in," she said. "Not on another witch's territory. That never, ever works. But . . ." She paused. "Witches don't just turn up out of nowhere. Let's have a look. . . ."

She pulled a cracked saucer out of her pocket and tipped into it the rainwater that had collected on her hat. Then she took a bottle of ink out of another pocket and poured in just enough to turn the water black.

She cupped it in her hands to keep the raindrops out and listened to her eyes.

◆　◆　◆

Tiffany Aching was lying on her stomach by the river, tickling trout. She liked to hear them laugh. It came up in bubbles.

A little way away, where the riverbank became a sort of pebble beach, her brother, Wentworth, was messing around with a stick, and almost certainly making himself sticky.

Anything could make Wentworth sticky. Washed and dried and left in the middle of a clean floor for five minutes, Wentworth would be sticky. It didn't seem to come from anywhere. He just got sticky. But he was an easy child to mind, provided you stopped him from eating frogs.

There was a small part of Tiffany's brain that wasn't too certain about the name Tiffany. She was nine years old and felt that Tiffany was going to be a hard name to live up to. Besides, she'd decided only last week that she wanted to be a witch when she grew up, and she was certain Tiffany just wouldn't work. People would laugh.

Another and larger part of Tiffany's brain was thinking of the word *susurrus*. It was a word that not many people have thought about, ever. As her fingers rubbed the trout under its chin, she rolled the word round and round in her head.

Susurrus . . . according to her grandmother's dictionary, it meant "a low soft sound, as of whispering or muttering." Tiffany liked the *taste* of the word. It made her think of mysterious people in long cloaks whispering important secrets behind a door: *susurruss-susurrusss* . . .

She'd read the dictionary all the way through. No one told her you weren't supposed to.

As she thought this, she realized that the happy trout had swum away. But something else was in the water, only a few inches from her face.

It was a round basket, no bigger than half a coconut shell, coated with something to block up the holes and make it float. A little man, only

4

six inches high, was standing up in it. He had a mass of untidy red hair into which a few feathers, beads, and bits of cloth had been woven. He had a red beard, which was pretty much as bad as the hair. The rest of him that wasn't covered with blue tattoos was covered with a tiny kilt. And he was waving a fist at her and shouting:

"Crivens! Gang awa' oot o' here, ye daft wee hinny! 'Ware the green *heid*!"

With that he pulled at a piece of string that was hanging over the side of his boat, and a second red-headed man surfaced, gulping air.

"Nae time for fishin'!" said the first man, hauling him aboard. "The green heid's coming!"

"Crivens!" said the swimmer, water pouring off him. "Let's offski!"

And with that he grabbed one very small oar and, with rapid back and forth movements, made the basket speed away.

"Excuse me!" Tiffany shouted. "Are you fairies?"

But there was no answer. The little round boat had disappeared in the reeds.

Probably not, Tiffany decided.

Then, to her dark delight, there was a susurrus. There was no wind, but the leaves on the alder bushes by the riverbank began to shake

5

and rustle. So did the reeds. They didn't bend, they just blurred. *Everything* blurred, as if something had picked up the world and was shaking it. The air fizzed. People whispered behind closed doors. . . .

The water began to bubble, just under the bank. It wasn't very deep here—it would only have reached Tiffany's knees if she'd waded—but it was suddenly darker and greener and, somehow, much deeper. . . .

She stood and took a couple of steps backward just before long skinny arms fountained out of the water and clawed madly at the bank where she had been. For a moment she saw a thin face with long sharp teeth, *huge* round eyes, and dripping green hair like waterweed, and then the thing plunged back into the depths.

By the time the water closed over it, Tiffany was already running along the bank to the little beach where Wentworth was making frog pies. She snatched up the child just as a stream of bubbles came around the curve in the bank. Once again the water boiled, the green-haired creature shot up, and the long arms clawed at the mud. Then it screamed and dropped back into the water.

"I wanna go-a *toy-lut*!" screamed Wentworth.

Tiffany ignored him. She was watching the river with a thoughtful expression.

I'm not scared at all, she thought. How strange. I ought to be scared, but I'm just angry. I mean, I can *feel* the scared, like a red-hot ball, but the angry isn't letting it out. . . .

"Wenny wanna wanna *wanna* go-a *toy-lut*!" Wentworth shrieked.

"Go on, then," said Tiffany absentmindedly. The ripples were still sloshing against the bank.

There was no point in telling anyone about this. Everyone would just say, "What an imagination the child has," if they were feeling in a good mood, or, "Don't tell stories!" if they weren't.

She was still very angry. How dare a monster turn up in the river? Especially one so . . . so . . . ridiculous! Who did it think she was?

This is Tiffany, walking back home. Start with the boots. They are big and heavy boots, much repaired by her father, and they belonged to various sisters before her; she wears several pairs of socks to keep them on. They are *big*. Tiffany sometimes feels she is nothing more than a way of moving boots around.

Then there is the dress. It has been owned by many sisters as well and has been taken up, taken

7

out, taken down, and taken in by her mother so many times that it really ought to have been taken away. But Tiffany rather likes it. It comes down to her ankles and, whatever color it had been to start with, is now a milky blue that is, incidentally, exactly the same color as the butterflies skittering beside the path.

Then there is Tiffany's face. Light pink, with brown eyes, and brown hair. Nothing special. Her head might strike anyone watching—in a saucer of black water, for example—as being just slightly too big for the rest of her, but perhaps she'll grow into it.

And then go farther up, and farther, until the track becomes a ribbon and Tiffany and her brother two little dots, and there is her country.

They call it the Chalk. Green downlands roll under the hot midsummer sun. From up here the flocks of sheep, moving slowly, drift over the short turf like clouds on a green sky. Here and there sheepdogs speed over the grass like shooting stars.

And then, as the eyes pull back, it is a long green mound, lying like a great whale on the world . . .

. . . surrounded by the inky rainwater in the saucer.

Miss Tick looked up.

"That little creature in the boat was a Nac Mac Feegle!" she said. "The most feared of all the fairy races! Even trolls run away from the Wee Free Men! And one of them *warned* her!"

"She's the witch, then, is she?" said the voice.

"At that age? Impossible!" said Miss Tick. "There's been no one to teach her! There're no witches on the Chalk! It's too *soft*. And yet . . . she wasn't scared. . . ."

The rain had stopped. Miss Tick looked up at the Chalk, rising above the low, wrung-out clouds. It was about five miles away.

"This child needs watching," she said. "But chalk's too soft to grow a witch on. . . ."

◆ ◆ ◆

Only the mountains were higher than the Chalk. They stood sharp and purple and gray, streaming long trails of snow from their tops even in summer. "Brides o' the sky," Granny Aching had called them once, and it was so rare that she ever said anything at all, let alone anything that didn't have to do with sheep, that Tiffany had remembered it. Besides, it was exactly right. That's what the mountains looked like in the winter, when they were all in white

9

and the snow streams blew like veils.

Granny used old words and came out with odd, old sayings. She didn't call the downland the Chalk, she called it "the wold." Up on the wold the wind blows cold, Tiffany had thought, and the word had stuck that way.

She arrived at the farm.

People tended to leave Tiffany alone. There was nothing particularly cruel or unpleasant about this, but the farm was big and everyone had their jobs to do, and she did hers very well and so she became, in a way, invisible. She was the dairymaid, and good at it. She made better butter than her mother did, and people commented about how good she was with cheese. It was a talent. Sometimes, when the wandering teachers came to the village, she went and got a bit of education. But mostly she worked in the dairy, which was dark and cool. She enjoyed it. It meant she was doing something for the farm.

It was actually *called* the Home Farm. Her father rented it from the Baron, who owned the land, but there had been Achings farming it for hundreds of years and so, her father said (quietly, sometimes, after he'd had a beer in the evenings), as far as the *land* knew, it was owned by the Achings. Tiffany's mother used to tell him not to speak like that, although the Baron was always very respectful to Mr. Aching since Granny had died two years ago, calling him the finest shepherd in these hills, and was generally held by the people in the village to be not too bad these days. It paid to be respectful, said Tiffany's mother, and the poor man had sorrows of his own.

But sometimes her father insisted that there had been Achings (or Akins, or Archens, or Akens, or Akenns—spelling had been optional) mentioned in old documents about the area for hundreds and hundreds of years. They had these hills in their bones, he said, and they'd always been shepherds.

Tiffany felt quite proud of this, in an odd way, because it might also be nice to be proud of the fact that your ancestors moved around a bit, too, or occasionally tried new things. But you've got to be proud of *something*. And for as long as she could remember, she'd heard her father, an otherwise quiet, slow man, make the Joke, the one that must have been handed down from Aching to Aching for hundreds of years.

He'd say, "Another day of work and I'm still Aching," or "I get up Aching and I go to bed Aching," or even "I'm Aching all over." They weren't particularly funny after about the third

11

time, but she'd miss it if he didn't say at least one of them every week. They didn't have to be funny—they were *father* jokes. Anyway, however they were spelled, all her ancestors had been Aching to stay, not Aching to leave.

There was no one around in the kitchen. Her mother had probably gone up to the shearing pens with a bite of lunch for the men, who were shearing this week. Her sisters Hannah and Fastidia were up there too, rolling fleeces and paying attention to some of the younger men. They were always quite eager to work during shearing.

Near the big black stove was the shelf that was still called Granny Aching's Library by her mother, who liked the idea of having a library. Everyone else called it Granny's Shelf.

It was a small shelf, since the books were wedged between a jar of crystallized ginger and the china shepherdess that Tiffany had won at a fair when she was six.

There were only five books if you didn't include the big farm diary, which in Tiffany's view didn't count as a real book because you had to write it yourself. There was the dictionary. There was the Almanack, which got changed every year. And next to that was *Diseases of the*

Sheep, which was fat with the bookmarks that her grandmother had put there.

Granny Aching had been an expert on sheep, even though she called them "just bags of bones, eyeballs, and teeth, lookin' for new ways to die." Other shepherds would walk miles to get her to come and cure their beasts of ailments. *They* said she had the Touch, although she just said that the best medicine for sheep or man was a dose of turpentine, a good cussin', and a kick. Bits of paper with Granny's own recipes for sheep cures stuck out all over the book. Mostly they involved turpentine, but some included cussin'.

Next to the book on sheep was a thin little volume called *Flowers of the Chalk*. The turf of the downs was full of tiny, intricate flowers, like cowslips and harebells, and even smaller ones that somehow survived the grazing. On the Chalk flowers had to be tough and cunning to survive the sheep and the winter blizzards.

Someone had colored in the flowers a long time ago. On the flyleaf of the book was written in neat handwriting *Sarah Grizzel*, which had been Granny's name before she was married. She had probably thought that Aching was at least better than Grizzel.

And finally there was *The Goode Childe's*

Booke of Faerie Tales, so old that it belonged to an age when there were far more *e*'s around.

Tiffany stood on a chair and took it down. She turned the pages until she found the one she was looking for and stared at it for a while. Then she put the book back, replaced the chair, and opened the crockery cupboard.

She found a soup plate, went over to a drawer, took out the tape measure her mother used for dressmaking, and measured the plate.

"Hmm," she said. "Eight inches. Why didn't they just *say*?"

She unhooked the largest frying pan, the one that could cook breakfast for half a dozen people all at once, and took some candies from the jar on the dresser and put them in an old paper bag. Then, to Wentworth's sullen bewilderment, she took him by a sticky hand and headed back down toward the stream.

Things still looked very normal down there, but she was not going to let *that* fool her. All the trout had fled, and the birds weren't singing.

She found a place on the riverbank with the right-sized bush. Then she found a stone and hammered a piece of wood into the ground as hard as she could, close to the edge of the water, and tied the bag of sweets to it. Tiffany was the kind of child who always carried a piece of string.

"Candy, Wentworth," she shouted.

She gripped the frying pan and stepped smartly behind the bush.

Wentworth trotted over to the sweets and tried to pick up the bag. It wouldn't move.

"I wanna go-a *toy-lut*!" he yelled, because it was a threat that usually worked. His fat fingers scrabbled at the knots.

Tiffany watched the water carefully. Was it getting darker? Was it getting greener? Was that just waterweed down there? Were those bubbles just a trout, laughing?

No.

She ran out of her hiding place with the frying pan swinging like a bat. The screaming monster, leaping out of the water, met the frying pan coming the other way with a clang.

It was a good clang, with the *oiyoiyoioioioioi-oinnnnnggggggg* that is the mark of a clang well done.

The creature hung there for a moment, a few teeth and bits of green weed splashing into the water, then slid down slowly and sank with some massive bubbles.

The water cleared and was once again the

15

same old river, shallow and icy cold and floored with pebbles.

"Wanna wanna *sweeties!*" screamed Wentworth, who never noticed anything else in the presence of sweets.

Tiffany undid the string and gave them to him. He ate them far too quickly, as he always did with sweets. She waited until he was sick, then went back home in a thoughtful state of mind.

In the reeds, quite low down, small voices whispered:

"Crivens, Wee Bobby, did yer no' see that?"

"Aye. We'd better offski an' tell the Big Man we've found the hag."